My Country Heart

Sierra Creek Series Book 4

Reggi Allder

ISBN 978-1-989665-04-6

Praise the Sierra Creek Series

"The book is so good I didn't want it to end. Great Characters! Five stars!"

"I'm hooked, can't wait to read the other books in the Sierra Creek Series!"

"I couldn't stop reading to find out what happened next!"

"If you love small towns, second chances, and convincing characters, this is for you!"

ABOUT THE AUTHOR

Reggi Allder writes contemporary and suspense novels. In both genres, as in real life, her characters must overcome difficulties. If you like feel-good books with cowboys, small towns, and second chances, please check out her Sierra Creek Series starting with **Her Country Heart**. If suspense is your thing, try the **Dangerous Series** beginning with **Dangerous Web.**

Reggi enjoys hearing from readers. Check out her website. **Follow her on** Amazon, Bookbub.com, Facebook.com, allauthor.com, Goodreads.com

DEDICATION

To Lee Lee, forever.

Thank you to all the first responders who run toward danger when the rest of us flee.

ACKNOWLEDGMENTS

Thank you to my wonderful critique partners.

Books by Reggi Allder

Sierra Creek Series:
Her Country Heart
His Country Heart
Our Country Heart
My Country Heart

Suspense:
Dangerous Web
Dangerous Denial
Dangerous Money
Dangerous Moves
Shattered Rules

Coming Next:
Dangerous Sisters

Historical:
With Glowing Hearts

Chapter 1

A chill ran through Lauren Walsh. She had made a drastic move and changed her whole life.

A mistake?

She stared at the California town of Sierra Creek, population five thousand, spreading out in the vista before her. She'd never lived in a city with a population of less than a million. Small towns, big outdoors, farmers, and most of all, chickens, no way—she didn't belong.

The sun glistened on the bell tower of a church. Brick and stucco houses dotted the landscape surrounding the main shopping area. However, the retail outlets had no recognizable names. It appeared no chain stores were allowed.

Homesick, she missed Los Angeles and the apartment near the Ventura Freeway. Even with the smog, the traffic, and the frustration it brought to her everyday existence, she understood how to navigate in the metropolis. It gave her a sense of security. Here in Sierra Creek, everyone lived in a fishbowl. People knew everyone else's business. She might as well be in a foreign country.

Still early in the morning, Sierra Creek had little traffic. Instead of engines reviving and blaring horns, birds tweeted from the surrounding trees, not something she often heard in LA. Today, the sky appeared bluer than any she remembered in her lifetime.

Her problems started after her boss fired her. Well, "let her go" as he'd said, for lack of business. Afterward, the dearth of openings in her industry didn't surprise her. Who needed to buy fine jewelry with money tight? The struggle to buy food and pay the bills was top of mind, not accumulating gorgeous trinkets.

Networking had produced no employment, and she realized there was nothing for her in Los Angeles. As a contributor to the finances of her disabled father's income, when this current employment opportunity came up, she snatched it.

Stay positive. This place is only for the short term. You'll be employed in the city again.

She easily maneuvered her German convertible through the empty main street and parked in front of The Hitching Post, a feed, tack, and clothing store, where she'd be working on Monday.

She stepped out of the car and was about to enter when an older, grey-haired man, dressed in jean overalls and a chambray shirt, nodded. "On Saturdays, we don't open for another hour."

He scanned her head to foot and wrinkled his nose as if he had experienced an odd smell, then continued lugging a bag of feed toward the front door. He turned back to her. "You looking for feed or tack?"

"Uh, no. I'm Lauren Walsh. Your new employee."

He scratched his head, then with surprising strength tossed the fifty-pound bag through the open doorway. "You are kind of overdressed for the job."

"Is Mr. Smith here?" She ignored his statement but adjusted her pale pink suit jacket and pencil skirt. "I—uh."

"The boss don't work on the weekend."

"Oh—I thought... Never mind. Do you happen to know the way to Amy Cameron's farm?"

"Everybody does. You staying there?"

If she answered yes, every person in town would know. Maybe they already did. She sighed and nodded her head.

"Well, drive down this street until you reach the highway." He pointed with his gnarled hand. "Turn left and go for about three miles. On the right, you'll see two mailboxes." He rubbed his chin. "Turn and keep going past the green farmhouse. You'll come to a Y. Take the left up the hill. Don't take the right, it goes to the chicken farm."

"Okay. Thanks, Mr.?"

"Jake—plain old Jake."

"Thanks, plain old Jake." She grinned at him.

"You're most welcome, Lady Lauren." He nodded and smiled. "And mind you watch for cows that might wander onto the road. You wouldn't want to scratch the beautiful car of yours."

OMG, cows? This really is the wilderness—or was he kidding?

Her car sped out of town and she continued down the local highway. The two mailboxes came up quickly. A tight turn off the highway and the road narrowed into a small country lane. The beauty of the open meadows and the leaves turning fall colors relaxed her. It might be good to take some downtime from the stressful city and enjoy the quiet countryside—as long as it wasn't for too long.

A gust of wind hit the convertible. Her hair flew in her face. Unable to see, she pushed it out of the way and looked up to see the air filled with squawking chickens and a huge man in the middle of the road waving at her.

"Stop!"

Lauren slammed on the brakes so hard the seatbelt jerked tight, preventing her from hitting her head on the steering wheel. The car came to an abrupt halt, inches from a handsome guy, tall, tan, and furious.

"What the hell are you doing driving so fast on this road?"

"I'm…." She screamed as clucking birds flew at her. Her heart thundered. She forced down the memory of her childhood fear of birds.

When the fowl surrounded the car, she honked the BMW's horn. The chickens flew closer and she continued to scream.

"Stop! The dammed chickens are already upset. Be quiet and stay out of the way until things are under control!" the stranger demanded.

A hen flew into the passenger seat. She shrieked and jumped out of the car and ran into the guy.

In tooled leather cowboy boots, blue jeans, and a navy T-shirt he glanced at her. "You damn near ran me down." He grabbed one of the birds off the hood of her convertible and let it go. Another flew at her and she shrieked.

"Quiet!" He snatched the bird away, holding it with one hand. "You're alarming the poultry. They're terrified. After all this yelling, it might take days before they lay again." He glared and his blue eyes flashed as he brushed his dark brown hair from his forehead. "Be calm around them. They're delicate—gentle if you'll

4

stop scaring them. After all, they've been in an accident."

"Me, scare them!" She scoffed. "Are you crazy?"

A car honked and more birds flew into the air, clucking.

He handed her the one he held and ran after a hen about to run across the road.

"Don't leave!" Breathless, she trembled. The chicken wiggled and tried to fly, while she gingerly held it away from her face, fearing it might peck her.

The farmer directed a car past the disabled truck and then came back to her. "I'll take that bird." With the fowl held securely in his strong arms, he jogged to the truck and put it in a wooden crate. The sign on the door of the flatbed vehicle read, "Edgar's Egg Farm."

Frightened, she watched the stranger collect the rest of the poultry.

She opened the door to her convertible and found a hen comfortably sitting in the jump seat. Another stood in the driver's spot. It pecked at her when she tried to shoo it away. She waved her arms, shouting, "Get out of my car!"

"Hey, enough! They're more afraid of you than you are of them."

"You want to bet?" she yelled in a voice she didn't recognize. "Take these out of my car!"

He turned from her.

OMG, she was making a fool of herself, but as a kid, a huge black bird had dive-bombed her and pecked at her. Though she'd only been six years old, the event still remained fresh in her mind. The bird chased her until her father rescued her.

The guy crawled into the back seat, grabbed the resting bird, and stood up from the car.

5

"Lady, next time drive more slowly around these roads. You might have hit someone!"

"Look cowboy—whatever your name is." She poked her index finger at his solid chest and glared up at him.

"Chance Williams." He grinned.

His mocking smile irritated her. "Mr. Chance, I don't need your comments about what I should do or how to drive."

"Williams."

"What?" She removed her sunglasses and stared.

"Williams. My name is Mr. Williams."

"Yeah, whatever!" She waved him out of her way as a chicken flew at her. "Keeps those birds away from me. I thought you had all of them."

"All but this Rhode Island Red."

He grabbed the frightened Red, took it back to the flatbed truck, and found a crate to put it in.

"Get out!" She opened the driver's side door, pushed a final chicken out, and sat down.

"You can leave, but go slowly." Chance Williams scowled at her. "Then drive off to the end of the world for all I care. Just don't speed on this road again!"

Chapter 2

The sign in front of the home said, "Granny's Organic Apples." Lauren parked in front of a white two-story farmhouse and rested her head on the steering wheel.

Still shaking, her cheeks burned. She sure didn't want to see anyone in her current condition.

The thought of turning around and going back to Los Angeles flashed, but the reality of her situation stopped the idea. A job waited for her here in Sierra Creek. There was nothing for her in LA.

She combed the last of the chicken feathers from her hair and applied pale pink lipstick. She must look a mess, she certainly felt like one. Ignoring her rapid heartbeat, she pushed back the images of the gorgeous farmer with his rude behavior and cruel words. She'd never been talked to that way before. *Drive off the end of the world.* She scoffed. "This *is* the end of the world."

How could circumstances do this to her? Out of the convertible, she checked her shoes and discovered chicken poo on her pink open-toed pumps. She bit back an expletive. Perfect, for a simply horrible day. She found a tissue and did her best to wipe it away.

With a deep breath, she grabbed her overnight bag from the car's trunk and walked up the driveway. *Whatever the place looks like, you have to take it. You have nowhere else to go.*

The owner of the Hitching Post had arranged for her to stay in the small cottage behind the farmhouse. The reasonable rent made it possible to send money back to her father.

A short woman about her age, twenty-eight, in white shorts and a blue plaid shirt, planted orange mums in the front garden. With a gloved hand, she pushed back her long strawberry blonde hair from her pretty face and smiled.

"Hi, you must be Lauren." She took off her gardening glove and extended her right hand. "I'm Amy Cameron—are you okay?"

"Yeah, only I was almost in an accident, guess it shook me up—a little." She forced a smile and hoped it appeared friendly.

"Oh, sorry to hear that. Do you need anything?"

"No—I'm fine."

"Come and I'll show you the place."

A kid of about six years old ran up and said, "Hi, I'm Bobby."

"This is my son." Amy hugged him.

"Hi, Bobby. I'm Lauren." She couldn't help grinning at the cute kid with red hair, the same color as his mother's.

"I have a pony."

"You can show her another time. Lauren must be tired and would like to see her rooms."

"Okay." He ran off toward the house.

"How about a cup of coffee first? I made a fresh pot of decaf."

8

"Thank you. I've had a long drive and..."

"No worries. I'll get the key. The cottage is up the driveway on the right."

The huge backyard had a lawn with a flagstone patio, a metal barbecue, and a wooden table and chairs. Behind it, a barn sat on the left and a white-washed cottage was on the right.

Appearing to understand Lauren wanted to be alone, Amy quickly showed her around the cottage and then gave her a key.

"Let me know if I can get anything for you or answer any questions."

"Thanks, I will." Grateful to be by herself, Lauren closed the door to her new home.

The small cottage had been newly painted and appeared to be in good condition. Still, it was different from the residence Lauren had lived in. Until now, she had been comfortable in a high-rise apartment, overlooking a traffic-laden street. Damn, she missed the noise and bustle of the city. She'd felt alive there. Still, with the possibility of making an income again...

"This is only temporary. Be grateful. You'll be back home in a short while," she repeated which was becoming her mantra.

She spun around the shabby chic living room with its wooden floors and white walls. A painting of a field of California poppies, in a white frame, hung over a pale green and white gingham couch, and a tan leather chair sat near the rhyolite stone fireplace. The side table looked handmade and was also painted white.

In the bedroom, a queen bed, dressed in white linen with pink and white gingham pillows, welcomed her—a serene space. On the way to the bed, she tripped over a pair of huge black rubber boots. "What the heck!"

She bit back a curse and tried to kick them out of the way. Did they belong to the last renter? She noticed a yellow coat and pants hanging on a hook near the closet. *Amy will know who they belong to.*

Though the need to lie down on the bed and sleep was strong, Lauren went out to her car to bring in her suitcases.

As she reached her car, a huge yellow fire truck drove up and parked across the road from the farmhouse. *Oh God, a fire.* That would finish off her wonderful day, she thought sarcastically.

The truck's door opened and Chance Williams got out. He stood taller than she remembered and more confident.

Weird. I thought he worked with the chickens.

"Are you following me, Mr. Williams?"

"No." He stared at her.

"Where's the fire?"

"No fire." He slammed the truck door and strode toward her. "I live on the farm."

"I don't think you're funny."

"I wasn't trying to be."

"You're serious? I thought Mr. and Mrs. Cameron owned this place." She shouted as she ran to stay with him as he strode up the driveway.

"They do." He stopped. "Hey, lady, if you have any questions, ask Amy or Wyatt. I'm in a hurry."

He turned his back, moved rapidly to the backyard, and entered the barn, the door slamming behind him.

"Jerk!"

Nonplussed, she'd forgotten to take her suitcases from the car. *Shit.* She ran back and grabbed them.

Exhausted after her long drive and now hot, frustrated, and embarrassed, she set her luggage on the floor in the cottage living room, slumped into the leather chair, and leaned forward with her head in her hands.

She didn't want to be here. Nothing looked familiar. Out of her element, she couldn't seem to do anything right and sure didn't feel welcome. Well, what had she expected?

No matter because in Sierra Creek she found employment and the ability to learn from one of the best silversmiths in the United States.

Her dream of starting her own jewelry company and selling to the high-end retail trade was about to be one step closer. If only she didn't feel so alone.

She dragged the largest case into the bedroom, threw it open, and rummaged in it to find her baby-doll nightgown. She needed sleep. *Tomorrow everything will look better.*

***

Chance trudged up the stairs to the attic above the barn. He opened the door and coughed from the dust in the stifling room. With the ceiling fan on, he threw open the window to let clean air filter into the area.

Today had been filled with unexpected experiences. The most surprising was his odd meeting with the woman in the cottage, not to mention the accident with the load of hens.

He shrugged and yanked the bedding out of his backpack and tossed it onto the bed's bare mattress. Then he stood at the window and scanned the area. All quiet in the rental. how was she settling in?

It didn't matter.

He grunted and faced the room. It was rustic at best. Nonetheless, with the opening of the lumber mill and the sudden influx of new people searching for rentals, no other option was available to him. He wouldn't ask a city gal to live in the unfinished attic.

The open beam ceiling and unpainted wooden walls were okay with him. There was a lot of space for his work table and a corner for the bed and the garment rack.

He'd recently settled in the cottage and was beginning to think of it as home when she needed somewhere to live. So, he'd volunteered to move.

Dressed in pink, including high heels, she was like cotton candy. He smiled, imagining the sweetness of a kiss she might deliver. Still, the woman displayed a temper. He'd held back a chuckle when she poked a dainty finger at him and called him Mr. Chance.

He rubbed his chin and pictured her, a beauty, he wouldn't deny it. Today, after a chicken landed on her head, he'd done his best not to laugh. Damn, she was sexy even with feathers in her hair.

Despite that, she wouldn't be in Sierra Creek for long. A few hot nights and dirty, dusty days, she would beat a path back to LA, where she could have a spa day and get her nails done. He knew the type.

He sat on the bed and surveyed the makeshift apartment. The bathroom with a sink and shower was utilitarian, but Amy tried to make the rest of the place hospitable.

A multicolored rug, a gray loveseat, a club chair, and a white-washed coffee table formed the living room. The hoped-for microwave and coffee pot were waiting on a shelf next to a wooden kitchen table and two chairs.

"Home sweet home." He yawned.

As he made the bed, and wondered what the new tenant was doing in the cottage, at this very moment.

He glanced out of the cottage and spotted his boots on the porch. His firefighter gear, pants, and yellow jacket hung over the railing.

Chapter 3

Lauren couldn't believe a week had almost gone by since she entered the small town of Sierra Creek.

Friday at six in the morning, she rolled over in bed and stretched her sore muscles. It appeared everyone on the apple farm woke at the break of dawn, as soon as the rooster crowed his cock-a-doodle-do. She groaned, covered her eyes against the morning light, and wondered if the Hitching Post carried blackout curtains.

When the cottage showed up for rent, she didn't realize it was on a working farm. Early in the a.m., the place buzzed with activity as it was harvest time for the apples. Farm workers shouted to each other, and flatbed trucks drove up the driveway.

Lauren saw little of Amy Cameron until the evenings. She worked on the farm and at the mill's preschool. Most nights, Amy invited her to join the family for dinner, but by that time, Lauren was too exhausted and usually begged off. She wasn't up to small talk. Instead, she went to bed after a quick snack.

During the quiet nights, with no traffic noise to lull her, sleep was elusive. Nevertheless, in the morning, birds singing their unrelenting songs dragged her from a restless slumber at the break of day.

Chance Williams' schedule seemed to vary. She'd noticed the fire engine at the farm at different times of the day and night. He'd waved at her a couple of times during the week, and she had introduced herself, but they never stopped to talk for more than a minute or two.

At work, she was on her feet most of the time working at the old-fashioned cash register or stocking the shelves with items she didn't recognize. Moving the bags of feed was way out of her league. She had experience in outside sales of high-end jewelry, expensive but easy to lift.

The townsfolk were friendly—even patient if she didn't find what they wanted. Some showed her where the item should be located and told her how it was used. For their help, she was grateful because the owner of the store had not bothered to help her. In fact, they had yet to be introduced.

The other clerk in the store, Just Plain Jake, as he called himself, was a kind man who did what he could to show her the ropes. By the end of the week, she called him Jake, and his name for her was Lady L.

Still, her anger at the unseen boss increased as the days went by. Discouraged, last night, she considered leaving and returning to SoCal.

Dad's words rang in her ears, "I know you don't want to leave home. If things were different…" Her father had faltered and they both understood nothing would change their reality.

She'd taken the position in the Podunk town to apprentice with the best silversmith in the nation, not to become a feed and grain expert or learn the ins and outs of tacking up a horse. Saddles, stirrups, bridles, halters, reins, bits, harnesses, martingales, and breastplates, were all words from her new foreign language—horse lingo. *Shit!* She was a jewelry designer, not a retail clerk.

After coffee and a bowl of low-fat yogurt, she went to shower, then dressed in white cotton pants and a blue T-shirt, the only thing casual enough for her new position. With a little mascara and a touch of lip gloss, she ran out of the cottage with her portfolio under her arm, hoping to. at last. meet her would-be mentor.

***

Lauren's first impression of the silversmith was disappointing to put the best face on the encounter. His name as a silversmith was renowned in the jewelry industry. A disheveled, unshaven, gray-haired man of undiscernible age, walked into the backroom of the Hitching Post and threw a highly carved leather saddle on the workbench.

"What you doing here, girl?" he asked in a gruff voice. "This room is for employees only. Read the sign."

"I…"

"The Ladies' room is at the other end of the store."

"I'm Lauren Walsh."

"I'm not good with names, but I never forget a face." His blue eyes narrowed. "I've never looked on yours."

As if he heard the confrontation, Jake ran into the area. "Boss, this is our new employee, Miss Lauren Walsh, all the way from Southern California. I'm here to say she's a mighty fine worker." He scratched his stubble. "Wouldn't have managed without her these last few days—you being called away and all."

"Well, go do your job. I'm not paying for you all to stand around."

Jake patted her on the shoulder and nodded toward the front of the store.

Lauren stood her ground. After days of waiting for Mr. Sullivan Smith to view her designs, the time had arrived, whether he realized the fact or not.

"I brought my artwork."

Mr. Smith wrinkled his nose and sniffed. "Well, girl, let's see what you got." He pounded his hand on the nearest counter. "Show me."

With lips pursed, he surveyed the carefully done sketches. On a few of the drawings, he stopped and scowled before running his index finger over them, but he never smiled.

She cleared her throat to ask a question, but he held up his hand and shook his head.

At long last, he glanced up at her. "Tell me about this one." He displayed a design she was particularly proud of.

Stepping closer, she said, "Uh, a freeform abstract, clean, simple, shiny."

"What will happen once the metal begins to tarnish?"

"I…not my problem. Someone will polish it or I could clear coat it to slow down the process."

His lips tightened further as the lines of his furrowed brow deepened. He grunted and viewed the rest of her portfolio.

She stood on one foot, then the other, as if waiting for the final reprimand from a father figure.

A few minutes later, Mr. Smith turned and faced her. "What do these pieces do?"

"Do?"

"Yeah."

That's a stupid question. "They look pretty."

"Okay." He scrubbed his hand over his sunburned face. He crumbled one of her sketches, dropped it to the floor, and shook his head again.

17

"Hey, girlie." He paused and pushed the rest of the drawing back into the folder. "Tell me why you want to work in silver?"

"Uh." She hesitated. "It's cheaper than gold. I can't afford gold," she admitted sheepishly.

"My God, you're in the mother lode." He coughed. "If you want gold, you could pan for it, or buy at it a decent price." He frowned. "Silver should be a choice, not the last pick."

When she shrunk from him, his expression softened—a little. "I like your honesty—silver *is* cheaper, but never think of it as second class. You want to know why I design in the silver metal right here in gold country?"

"Uh, yeah," she said, her voice trembling.

"Grab yourself a pop. I'll be in my workshop."

She put a shaking hand to her cheek, pleased he appeared interested in showing her his work. At the same time, she was relieved to have a break from his intense personality.

In the bathroom, she splashed cold water on her face and took a deep breath. "What next?" Could she deal with the angry man and his passion for silver?

Carrying bottled water from the drink dispenser in the store, she slowly entered the workshop. An array of photos of his designs for silver-decorated saddles, medallions, and jewelry covered the walls. He sat at a large workbench facing the entrance. A magnifier and lamp rested on the flat surface.

Before she could comment on his patterns, he pointed to a chair. "Sit."

"I, uh…" She did what he said, setting the water bottle on the cement floor next to the seat.

"Jewelry making is not just a craft. You are making a legacy. Use a metal you love, and don't try to make it what it's not."

"I don't get what you're saying."

"Know the attributes, whether copper, silver, or gold." Each is telling you something—listen."

He leaned toward her. "Take a look at this piece. Hold it and observe the weight." He handed her a medallion. "It's newly made."

Cold and smooth, nonetheless, the warmth shone in the design done in the traditional concho disk.

"Here is one in the same pattern. I made it twenty years ago."

She held the silver circle and turned it over. "Beautiful." The motif was the same, but the older one was darkened with tarnish.

"Does the patina spoil the medallion?"

"No, the opposite. The form is enhanced. I noticed parts I didn't pay attention to on the new one."

He nodded. "With silver, plan for the tarnish. Let it define and develop your jewelry."

"I..."

"Make sure your piece is one your buyer will want to keep and pass on to their heirs. If you can construct something useful as well as handsome, all the better. Anyway, find a theme and cultivate it." He stopped and stared at her, with narrowed blue eyes. "Think about what you want to convey before you draw again."

Without another word, he stood and left the workshop.

Stunned by Mr. Smith's words, she sat, frozen. Proud of her work, Grandmother's words echoed in her brain. "Pride cometh before a fall." She had been sure he would admire her designs.

A tear slid down her cheek. Why had she thought she had talent? Time to leave. There was nothing for her in Sierra Creek now. Retail jobs could be found anywhere, no need to stay in this jerkwater town.

Jake peeked into the room and cleared his throat. "Lady L, don't be discouraged. Smith's a tough old bird, but he took time with you. He sees your ability."

"But he…" She sniffed.

"Hang in there. Things will get better."

"Will they, Jake?"

"Depend on it." He grinned.

In the days since she arrived, Just Plain Jake hadn't smiled until now.

Did she dare hope he was right?

Chapter 4

Deflated and discouraged after Mr. Smith's negative reaction to her jewelry designs, Lauren went back to clerk at the Hitching Post. She had let herself dream he would endorse her drawings, and then help her make and market them. Why had she imagined such a fairytale? The biggest blow came when he crumbled a drawing, threw it to the floor, and told her not to sketch for a while.

She bit back a sigh and did her best to smile at the customers as they had done nothing to hurt her feelings.

Jake appeared to be aware of her distress and told her he could handle things in the store. "Lady L, why don't you take off early and I'll close up?"

Not planning to return, she said goodbye to Jake and walked out of the shop.

The sun remained high, the heat almost overpowering her as she walked toward the parked sports car.

Sweltering air filled the interior of her auto, but she sat in the driver's seat and pushed down a sob.

Her future and her plans melted away, no working with the master silversmith, no new home for her and Daddy, and no money coming in. She moaned and closed her eyes.

What do I do next? She shook her head and with a small cry, she leaned back in the seat, ignoring the rising temperature.

A raging headache pounded over her right eye. If only she'd thought to put aspirin in her purse.

Someone knocked on the window. "Open up. It must be one hundred and twenty degrees in there."

She glanced at a concerned expression spreading across Chance Williams' handsome face.

"What are you doing here?" She rolled down the glass.

"Hey, are you okay?"

"I'm fine—just tired." She hesitated. "You wouldn't have an aspirin, would you?"

"Yeah, in my truck." He scanned her, before touching her forehead. Surprised, she pulled away.

"Lauren, how long have you been in the car?"

"I'm not sure." She shrugged, finding it hard to remember. "I… For a..."

"I don't like your appearance. You need to cool down and find something to drink. It's easy to become overheated here in the foothills."

"I thought you worked with the fire department. Are you a paramedic too?"

"Part of the job." He opened her door. "Come to the ice cream parlor with me and I'll buy you a milkshake."

***

Chance steadied Lauren when she swayed on her feet.

Dry skin, hot to the touch, dizzy, and a bit confused, were classic symptoms of heat stroke. She was probably dehydrated.

She didn't appear to notice—not uncommon, many people he'd treated didn't realize until serious problems arose.

"I only need an aspirin." She pulled out of his grip.

"Lauren, how much water did you drink today?"

"I… I left my bottle of water at work. I meant to…" She frowned.

"No worries, but let me treat you to something cold. I'll pick up the painkillers on the way."

He thought she might refuse, so he took her arm and walked slowly toward the truck.

"Do you know Sophie Danelavich Hansen? She owns the ice cream parlor and is one of our best-known citizens. You haven't lived until you've eaten her ice cream," he added to lighten the conversation.

When he opened the ice cream parlor's glass door, the strong aroma of peppermint ice cream permeated the shop. Not to mention, the smell of the coffee that mingled nicely with the scent of mint and chocolate.

He gazed around the well-known room. Photos of milkshakes, banana splits, and sodas hung on the deep pink walls. Heart-shaped metal-backed chairs with red leather seats lined up in formation around metal tables. He was pleased to find the place wasn't too busy and the booth in the corner was empty.

Sophie stood behind the counter. A heavy-set, brown-haired woman, she waved. A white apron spotted with chocolate ice cream smears was stretched over the tan dress she wore. Except for her changing her graying hair to brown, Sophie appeared as she had when they first met.

"Lauren, take a seat in the booth and I'll give Sophie our order—what flavor of milkshake?"

"Oh, a scoop of strawberry is enough for me."

He frowned but left without contradicting her. Nonetheless, he returned with the ice cream she'd ordered, two large glasses of ice water, and a vanilla milkshake to share.

"Having a rough day?" Chance asked as he set the bowl of ice cream and two glasses of cold water in front of Lauren.

She quickly drank a glass of water and held the other one to her heated cheek. "I didn't think I was thirsty." She spooned ice cream into her mouth and sighed. "OMG, you weren't kidding about how good this is."

When she finished eating, he handed her the aspirin.

"Thanks." She smiled at him for the first time. "I didn't mean to be a bother."

"No worries. I was going here to grab a late lunch. They make delicious sandwiches too."

Sophie came to the table with a tray piled high with food. "Here you go Chance, ham, Monterey Jack cheese, and avocado on rye. I brought a sample of a new item we are considering. It's sprouts, cucumber, tomatoes, and vegan cheese with mayo and Dijon mustard, on rye, of course."

"Hey, you've outdone yourself—let me introduce Lauren Walsh from LA."

"Hi, you must meet my daughter, Vanna. She lived in Los Angeles for a few years. I bet you two would have a lot in common."

The bell on the front door tinkled and several people came in and lined up at the counter.

"I better get back to work. Hope to see you again, Lauren."

"Try some of the food." He slid a plate toward her.

She nibbled on the vegan sandwich and he noticed her color improved.

"Feeling better?"

"Yeah. I didn't realize how overheated I was." She took a drink of the vanilla milkshake he offered. "This place looks like a store from a classic movie." She scanned the room. "I think I've stepped back into the nineteen-fifties."

"I guess if you're used to the city, it appears strange."

"Chance, it's different for you, being raised here and all. But as my dad says, 'like a fish out of water,' that's me. I don't know the town's culture. Things are so slow, too quiet, too small. I'm fenced in with nowhere to go and nobody to talk to."

"You miss the dirty air, traffic noise, busy streets, fast food, crowded shopping malls?"

"You're making fun of me, but yeah, something like that. Not to mention Wi-Fi, movies, concerts… You wouldn't understand."

"What makes you think I grew up in Sierra Creek?"

"I… You're so comfortable and you recognize everyone."

"I've been living in the area for about two years." He finished his food and slid the plate from him. "I grew up in San Francisco. A much more manageable city than LA but a city nonetheless. Out in the avenues, there's enough traffic, cars, and buses, not to mention malls with as much crowding as I would ever want in a big city."

"You don't miss the urban bustle—places to go and things to do?"

"Not usually—no. I was searching for something special. I wanted a place to relax after…" He paused, cringed, then shrugged. "Anyway, this place was what I needed."

"I think my boss hates me."

Startled by the sudden change of the conversation, he observed moisture filling her eyes, but she blinked it away. "I came to Sierra Creek for the opportunity to work with Sullivan Smith."

He listened to her hushed tones as she spilled out her hopes and dreams and how Mr. Smith dashed them this afternoon.

"What are you going to do now?"

"I don't know—look for another job?"

"Not much around these parts. Did Smithy fire you?"

"Smithy?"

"Most people call him that."

"No. I'm still a clerk, but that's not why I went to work at the Hitching Post. I can be hired for retail sales anywhere."

They sat in silence, while he considered what to say. Did he want to become involved with this woman and stick his nose in another man's business?

He wouldn't normally think of doing so. Yet, Lauren touched something in him. He wasn't about to delve into why. Even so, he related to her determination to accomplish a goal. Her sex appeal didn't hurt either. *Don't go there.*

"Smithy is my uncle, my mother's brother."

"What!" She nearly choked. "And you let me go on about how mean Mr. Smith is? You might have told me you were related." She stood up from the table.

"Hey, Lauren, don't go." He reached for her hand.

"Leave me alone." She ran for the door and was gone before he could stop her.

"Shit!" *That went well.*

Chapter 5

There you go overreacting. Will you ever learn?

Lauren returned to her car and started the engine. It seemed she was determined to make a fool of herself in Sierra Creek.

She shouldn't have run out on Chance. Waiting for the painkillers to work, she sighed and rubbed her temples. He wanted to help her and she rewarded him by complaining, blurting out her whole story, and, what a jerk, Mr. Smith was.

In a small town like Sierra Creek, why didn't she realize people might be related, or at the least be acquainted?

In Los Angeles, a city of more than twelve million inhabitants, a person could live for years and be somewhat anonymous, with little worry the city would know their mistakes.

Her cheeks burned. She was going to stay in this small town because, truthfully, where else could she go? The job at the Hitching Post was her only source of income. So, she had better not fly off the handle again.

As the air-conditioner cooled the interior of the car, Daddy's words reprimanded her. She could almost hear him speaking. *Lauren, stop and think before you speak. Count to ten and you won't have to apologize.*

She sighed and wished she'd bitten her tongue rather than complain to Chance.

When she arrived home, his fire truck was parked across the road from the farm. Hoping not to see him, she quietly snuck by the house and barn and went directly into the cottage.

Hot and exhausted, Lauren entered the shower and let the water relax her muscles.

Wrapped in a towel, she made her way to the galley kitchen and poured a glass of cold apple juice. Sitting at the bistro table, she sipped the liquid and refused to consider the fact that she needed dinner.

Her smartphone signaled a text from Ben, a man she had dated before she left Southern California. Daddy had nicknamed him "Ben the boring." That wasn't fair. He was a good man, stable, reliable, attentive, and yes—boring.

She groaned. After the sudden loss of her mother when she was a teen and her father's debilitating rheumatoid arthritis, Ben had been what she thought she wanted, a nice man who caused her no worry and no stress—but also no passion or love.

"I'm fine, Ben." She sent the text, a lie, but…

"Lauren, ILY—lonely since you left."

She started to type, then stopped. She allowed an image of Ben to filter through to her mind's eye, average height and weight. His brown hair and eyes were—ordinary.

If she were honest, she hadn't thought of him even once since arriving in Sierra Creek.

"I took your father to his doctor's appointment today." The new text chirped.

"THX. On my way to dinner. TTYL."

Not true but... Ben wasn't family and Lauren felt a sense of resentment that he would be involved with her father. Dad's neighbor, Zoe, had promised to drive Daddy to his appointments.

Lauren's thoughts were interrupted by a knock on the front door.

Still in the towel, she shouted, "Hold on for a minute." and ran to grab something to wear.

***

While Amy waited for Lauren to return to the door, she glanced back to the house and wondered what her son, Bobby, was up to. She had promised to let him help with dinner. About to turn six years old, he was suddenly interested in learning to cook. She hoped the kitchen didn't become a mess. Still, she smiled at the thought he wanted to make food for the family.

"What is it?" Lauren peeked out of the door of the cottage.

"Hey, it's Friday. We always have a barbecue and I hope you will join us. We supply vegan dishes if you don't eat meat. I'll introduce you to our friends, just a few of us. Not a large group, so, don't worry about meeting a bunch of strangers."

"I..."

Amy observed resistance in Lauren's expression. "Vanna will be here. I thought you might enjoy knowing her. She lived in LA for several years and..."

"Uh, okay, thanks."

When Lauren didn't say more, Amy stood for a second, an awkward silence filling the afternoon. "We'll be in the backyard in about an hour. See you, Lauren."

She ran down the stairs of the cottage wondering if she had made a mistake trying to be friendly towards her renter. Maybe she should have ignored Lauren. City people appeared to like to be left to their own devices and were not always ready to mingle just because they happened to reside on the same property.

Well, being neighborly came easily and if Lauren didn't want to come, she didn't have to. Amy would understand.

***

The sound of laughter led Lauren to the patio behind the farmhouse. The heat from the late afternoon sun warmed the area. Generously decorated with potted flowers and an arbor with climbing vines, the setting was lovely.

She paused and scanned the group before joining them. The owners of the farm, Amy and Wyatt Cameron, were there, but Lauren's eyes paused when she looked at a beautiful, tall, thin blonde. The man standing next to her was equally gorgeous, tall, dark, and handsome. Love shone in their eyes as they beheld each other.

What would it feel like to care that much for a man? She had always chosen to date men who wouldn't demand too much of her time or too much passion.

An older grey-haired man sat in the love seat reading a book to Amy's little boy.

Amy introduced her to Grandpa Bill, Wyatt's dad.

Vanna and Manny Gordon, the other couple, were even more beautiful when Lauren got closer. There was something familiar about Vanna. What? She'd never met the woman, but still, she recognized her.

"Hi Lauren, welcome. Don't worry about the slow pace of this little town. It will grow on you." Vanna smiled, her perfectly white teeth glistening.

"I've seen you before, but..."

"My shampoo commercial. It leaves my hair soft and glorious." She flicked her blonde tresses back.

"That's it. OMG, Vanna, I can't tell you how many times I have seen that one."

They both laughed.

Lauren, what would you like to drink? We have microbrewery beer, non-alcoholic apple cider, or iced tea?"

"Iced tea, thanks."

Everyone offered hellos but didn't cross-question her, instead, allowed her to comment as she became comfortable.

The table was set and a lazy Susan held bowls of rice casserole, coleslaw, and corn on the cob. French bread and condiments were also available.

Over a dinner of barbecued chicken and steak, they sat at a round table. Before long, they were sharing travel stories and the traffic problems found in cities around the world. Grandpa Bill told of his adventures riding a camel when he worked in the Middle East. Bobby shouted, "I want to ride a camel."

Vanna mentioned her experiences on the Ventura Freeway and Lauren discovered she had lived only a short distance from Lauren's apartment.

The younger men were all on the rodeo circuit at one time and disclosed funny incidents they remembered.

Lauren relaxed and she found herself grinning. *Nice people.* The words popped into her head.

The dinner dishes were cleared away and dessert was about to be served when Chance wandered onto the property.

"Sorry to be late."

"Hey, man, no worries." Wyatt stood and shook his hand.

Amy handed him a plate and pointed to a spot across from Lauren. "Help yourself, plenty of food left."

Chance didn't acknowledge Lauren and she had the sense he was avoiding looking in her direction.

The conversation resumed, but because of her action this afternoon at the ice cream parlor, self-consciousness interfered with her pleasure.

She considered making excuses and leaving but decided it might call more attention to her than necessary. So, she sat in silence.

After a while, she agreed to meet Vanna for lunch and thanked Amy and Wyatt for dinner.

If only Chance didn't live so close by. He bothered and confused her. Emotions she didn't want to understand demanded to be deciphered. She tried to picture Ben, but instead, a vision of Chance kept interfering. Whether she wanted to admit it or not, a mutual attraction between them existed. Did he notice it too?

***

In the following weeks, she went to work but no longer expected help with her designs from her boss. She rarely interacted with Mr. Smith. Other than that, things went smoothly. She and Jake functioned well together and she began to be more competent in helping the customers. She even began to recognize the people who came in with some regularity and made sure she remembered their names.

Jake introduced her as Lady L and so that became her name at the store. She realized it was spoken with warmth. It seemed he had nicknames for many people, but only the ones he liked.

A regular date for lunch with Vanna at her mother's ice cream parlor was something to look forward to. Amy often joined them as well.

Much to her surprise, she began to realize the positive qualities of small-town living. She appreciated the nights on the farm with only the crickets to break the quiet.

She had done what Mr. Smith suggested and hadn't tried to draw anything since he told her not to bother. But last evening the desire to do so returned. She didn't have a theme for her jewelry, but at least the creative urge had reappeared.

Tomorrow was her day off. She planned to go on a long walk and take the sketch pad with her.

Hot in here tonight. Lauren rolled out of bed, pulled up the shade, and opened the bedroom window, hoping for a cool breeze. Except for an array of stars, all was dark until a light flicked on in the attic over the barn. *Chance must be home.*

In a while, he stepped out onto the landing, threw off his shirt, and stretched. The porch light lit his muscled chest and broad shoulders as he did.

"Whoa," she whispered.

As if he felt her staring at him, he glanced toward the cottage. She stepped back into the dimness of the bedroom. Did he see her?

***

Chance made out some movement at the cottage window—the bedroom. He understood exactly where Lauren was. He'd stared out at the stars from that very spot on many a warm night.

She probably thought he didn't notice, but the full moon shined on her curvy form, sending need racing through him. Not only her appearance, but something

33

else about her called to him. A strong-minded but vulnerable woman, she wasn't afraid to tackle life to achieve her goals. He liked that.

He didn't date anymore and hadn't been with a woman since his accident. He flinched remembering the day, fighting a raging fire, he'd been knocked down. Luck had allowed him to land face down, his hands under him. His buddy had not been so fortunate. Still, with his back and legs burned, he was not ready to show what flames could do to human flesh. With time, he might acquire the courage. For now, it was better to keep to himself.

He groaned and went back into the attic apartment.

Chapter 6

Going to be a scorcher today, as Jake often said when he stood in the entry of the Hitching Post surveying the main street.

The fact was, days were always scorchers during the summer months, but he appeared to enjoy stating the obvious. Lauren grinned. He'd been kind to suggest she take a look at the California wildflowers as ideas for her themed-based jewelry.

Never a gardener or someone with an interest in botany, it hadn't occurred to her. It should have, but her focus had been on her problems.

She'd stopped by the store to get her thermos and ask Jake where was the best place to find the blooming fields he had mentioned.

"Anywhere, Lady L." He wiped his neck with a kerchief. "Walk right out your backdoor. Amy Cameron's farm is filled with them. She's got over two hundred acres."

"I had no idea. Thanks, Jake." She grabbed her thermos and waved goodbye.

Foolish, but she had never glanced past the cottage, other than to stare down the driveway.

Back at the farm, she parked and took her sketch pad and Conte crayons, then made her way to a path behind her current residence.

***

The tall golden grasslands swayed in a warm breeze and the sun relentlessly beat down on her. She pulled her long hair into a plastic clip, glad she'd remembered to apply a heavy layer of sunscreen on her face, arms and legs before she left this morning.

She pushed her sunglasses to the top of her head and squinted toward a grove of oaks. There would be shade, but didn't wildflowers love full sun?

Something moved in the tall grass. Snakes? She jumped. Jake had given her a warning to be aware of rattlesnakes. They were cold-blooded and enjoyed bathing in the high temperatures on a hot day.

With her dark glasses in place, she stared in the direction of the shifting grassland. A man lay prone on the ground appearing to focus on—what?

Too far away to find out, she moved closer. Chance, a single-lens reflex camera in his hand, seemed not to notice her arrival until she unwittingly cast a shadow.

"Hey, you're in my light."

She moved and he took the shot, then swung into a sitting position and glared.

"Oh, I thought you were someone else." He scanned her, and a desire to touch him passed through her.

"Sorry. What were you photographing?"

"A Lupin. They grow all over this place."

She must have had a blank expression because he said, "A flower."

He handed her one.

"Beautiful."

36

"Lupin a genus Lupinus of leguminous herb. It means wolf." He hesitated. "Lauren, if you could see yourself."

"Well, I'm shocked. I thought it would mean something about the shape or the blue color of the blooms."

"That would make sense, but how often does life follow a logical path?" He chuckled.

"True, but..." She shrugged. "Still, it gives me an idea for a brooch. You aren't kidding me about the name—are you?"

"Nope." He stood and brushed off his well-worn jeans. For a second, she found it hard to take her eyes off him. Her glance ran up his body to his pecs, covered by a grey long-sleeved T-shirt, and they flexed.

He picked up his backpack and shoved the camera into it. Without talking it over, they walked toward the shade of the trees.

"Chance, how do you know so much about flowers?"

"My mother is a botanist. She loves indigenous flora." He adjusted the pack. "When I was a kid, she dragged me all over the Sierra Mountains while researching and cataloging plants. She wrote a textbook that's still used in universities."

"Wow."

He handed her a bottle of water from his bag.

"Thanks." She took a sip. "But you're a firefighter. Right?"

"Fourth generation, my dad, granddad and great-granddad."

"Nice to have footsteps to follow."

"Can be, but…" Chance frowned. "Do you have a list of flowers you're trying to find?" He changed the subject and she had the sense she had touched a nerve.

"To tell the truth, I don't know a thing about flowers or gardening. Most of my life I've lived in a high-rise building near the freeway and never thought about plants, except to buy them at the supermarket."

"Then what brings you out on this hot day?"

She took a gulp of water and told him her plan to find a theme for her new jewelry designs. Spewing out her heart's desire to make something important that would become an heirloom to be passed on from generation to generation, she couldn't stop talking. Lauren realized she was saying too much, but Chance listened so quietly it was easy to continue.

To her relief, he didn't pass judgment on her goals. Instead, he offered a couple of flowers on the property she might like to view.

Naturally, she was aware of the orange poppy. "Chance what is this pretty yellow flower?"

"A California Buttercup, Ranunculus Californicus. Here, let's see if you like butter." He held one of the little blooms under her chin.

"What are you doing?"

"If your jaw turns yellow, you like butter—yep, you do."

She laughed. "That's silly, but yes, I do."

"Lauren, didn't you do this as a kid?"

"Uh, no."

"Oh, a deprived childhood."

"Shut up." She laughed. "What was the name again?"

"Ranunculus…" He stopped. "You can say, buttercup. Most people realize what that is."

She sketched a quick copy of the small plant and took a photo with her smartphone. She bet it wouldn't be as detailed as his close-ups, but it met her needs.

He offered a chicken salad sandwich packed from Sophie's ice cream shop and she took half. "Thanks."

Sitting on a log, they shared their impressions of Sierra Creek. As they both came from a city, they had similar responses and fell into easy conversation.

"Do you always take photos of flowers?"

"I'm shooting them for a calendar. The profit goes to help burn victims recover. Every year there is a specific topic. This year's subject is wild flora."

"Could I take a look at your camera?"

"If you want."

She clicked through the pics and with her peripheral vision she saw him lean against a tree trunk. With his long legs in front of him, he crossed his muscled arms across his broad chest and closed his eyes. Even in repose, he exuded strength.

She glanced at the photos, pausing on a couple that were breathtaking. "Chance, do you have a favorite?"

"Uh." He ran his hand over his chin. "I guess the Baker's globe mallow. It's often the first flower to grow after a forest fire." He sat up and took the camera. "Here."

"What a sweet little pink flower. I've never seen one."

"I guess most people haven't." He stretched. "Sounds corny, but it signals renewal. Life after the devastation. After the fires in California, that means a lot to me. You understand what I'm saying?"

"Absolutely. I…"

His smartphone alarm went off. He took the call and frowned "Got to take off."

"A fire?"

He nodded, grabbed his backpack, and jogged toward his parked truck.

***

Perspiring, but pleased with her start on the designs for her new jewelry collection, Lauren walked toward the cottage ready to relax and have a leisurely dinner alone. A long shower and a streamed movie would close out the successful day.

Lauren glanced over at the barbecue area behind the farmhouse, remembering the night she'd met Amy's friends.

Someone gasped and Lauren squinted into the sun, then she shaded her eyes in time to see Amy fall on the flagstone patio, and not move again.

Chapter 7

Dropping her backpack, Lauren raced to Amy. "OMG, are you hurt?"

"I'm fine, a little embarrassed, but good."

"Let me help you up."

"I'm not usually so clumsy." Amy's face reddened, as she stood up from the stone patio.

"You sure everything is all right?" She led Amy to a seat at the outdoor table.

"I'm a bit queasy and for a second, I was dizzy." Amy stared back at her.

Should Lauren call for help? Chance was a paramedic, but he went to a fire. She doubted there would be more than a couple of medics in a small town like Sierra Creek and they might both be at the fire. "Amy, I can drive you to the hospital."

"Don't be silly. I'm fine. I mean thank you—oh, I need to share this with someone. Do you promise to keep my secret?"

"If you ask me to."

Amy gagged and closed her eyes for a second. "I'm pregnant."

"That's wonderful!"

"Maybe, but I don't want Wyatt or anyone else to know. I've lost two other pregnancies and I won't put my family through the pain again. Do you promise?"

"Of course. I only…"

"When I'm further along, and the odds of losing the baby are smaller, I'll share the news with everyone—but for now…"

"Whatever you say. You can count on me." She reached over and squeezed Amy's hand. "Can I get you anything?"

"Like I said, I'm good."

"I thought morning sickness came early in the day. It's supper time."

"It hits me off and on all day."

"Wyatt hasn't guessed?"

"No. A baby is so important to him. It broke his heart when I lost the last one." Amy sniffed and her eyes filled with moisture. "I've made sure he has no clue, not yet anyway."

"My lips are sealed."

"Thanks, Lauren." Amy took a breath. "Bobby is staying overnight with a friend. I think I'll go take a nap before Wyatt comes back."

"I'll walk you to the house."

"You don't have to."

"I want to." She took Amy's arm.

***

After dinner, Lauren sat on the porch of the cottage and watched the sky turn orange and pink as the sun set and stars came out, one by one. She'd never felt at peace before. However, the quiet brought a new sense of what was important. The talk with Amy had shaken her. Lauren considered Amy's goals and compared them with her own—so different.

It seemed Amy Cameron's life involved people. She owned an organic apple farm to deliver pesticide-free apples to stores and worked helping preschool children at the mill. Now, she protected her loved one against pain and loss.

Lauren's goals dealt with money and the need to be rich and famous, with no husband and no children to get in her way. Her cheeks flushed, heated by the thought that she was selfish. *I mean money is a beneficial thing, but should it be the only driver of your life?* She didn't want to think about it.

Isolation from her friends in So Cal caused these annoying thoughts. She went into the cottage, slamming the door behind her, and texted her Los Angeles crew to catch up on the news of their lives.

Afterward, she streamed a movie but fell asleep before it was over. She guessed she'd had too much exercise walking in the hills today.

She woke up worried about Amy. Was Wyatt home? Earlier, Amy had told her that the fire was behind the sawmill and her husband had gone to make sure all was well on the property.

Still wearing the clothes from the day before, Lauren slipped on a pair of sandals and went out to check the driveway for Wyatt's truck. Not there.

Amy was pacing on the front porch, staring toward the road, when Lauren joined her.

"Can I wait with you?"

"Sure. I'd like the company."

"How are you feeling?"

"Better, I was able to keep some food down. Lauren, thanks for your help this evening. I only wish…"

"No news?"

43

Amy shook her head and absently rubbed her stomach.

"No news is good news. Right?"

Amy stopped pacing. "Yeah, that's what people say." She paused. "I don't want to keep you, but if you would like to sit with me…"

"Amy, I'm happy to."

They sat in the twin rockers and talked. "I first met Wyatt when I was a kid and he was a teenager. Tall and handsome even then, I think I loved him the first time I saw him." She smiled. "But I didn't exist to him, only an annoying kid with huge glasses, gawking at him all the time."

"It must be nice to have that much history with a man."

"Hm."

The quiet night and cooling winds caressed the nearby trees. The hours passed, but the men didn't return.

At last, a truck engine roared, announcing Wyatt's arrival.

"Thank God," Amy sighed.

Her husband brought the smell of smoke with him when he came near. The odor of it hung in his hair and his blue eyes were bloodshot.

Amy rushed to hug him.

He pulled out of her arms. "I'm covered in soot."

"I don't care. I need a hug."

He nodded and held her to him.

"Lauren, thanks for staying with Amy."

"Glad to, is the blaze out?"

"Pretty much. The fire crew is mopping up."

Relieved, Lauren went back to the cottage, wondering what so much love for another person would be like.

In the middle of the night but unable to sleep, she went back to streaming a movie, though her mind wouldn't focus on the plot.

**

At two thirty in the morning, Chance parked the truck in front of the farmhouse and grabbed his gear. As quietly as possible, he made his way up the driveway, noting the house was dark, as expected.

Exhausted, his muscles ached, begging for sleep, but adrenaline still raged in his veins and he understood sleep was out of the question until it abated. He rubbed his eyes and stifled a yawn as he trudged toward his current residence.

The blaze had turned out to be larger than he'd expected. Only good luck and hard work, by all involved, kept it from taking over the mill and destroying the buildings. Thank goodness, as the lumber mill now employed many workers and gave the community sorely needed jobs. After tonight, creating a full-functioning firehouse became even more urgent.

He had come to Sierra Creek for a break from the big city and the high-tension blazes they fought there, no tunnels or multistory edifices to deal with in the small town. In this burg, he had the opportunity to build a crew from the beginning, making sure they would be able to control any emergency the team might run up against.

A glance in the direction of the cottage found a light on in the living room window. Strange. He hoped Lauren was all right.

An unbidden fantasy that she'd waited for him to return home safely sent a grunt to his throat. He'd better get a life before he made a fool of himself. A career woman through and through, during their conversation this afternoon, she'd casually mentioned her plan to stay single and didn't believe kids were in her future.

He hadn't responded to the statement but remembered glancing at her hips, thinking her form appeared to be built to carry babies.

Lauren won't last long in Sierra Creek. Don't invest any more time thinking of her.

In his attic apartment, he tossed his smoke-filled clothes in the hamper in the bathroom and slammed the lid closed. While showering, he decided to make a date with a local woman. Someone who wanted to marry and deliver lots of children. That was one of the reasons he'd decided to move here—to find a country gal. The opposite of Lauren—a fashion plate, with being the CEO of her own jewelry company that catered to the rich and famous her desire in life.

Did that make him a pig? He shrugged. His mother had a profession, and he supported her choices, but she always made time for her two kids.

With a towel wrapped around his waist, he left the bathroom. The window in the main room was open to let in a cool breeze. He stood and allowed the air to refresh him.

His attention turned to the cottage in time to see the lights go out and the curtain in the bedroom window pull back. Much to his disappointment, Lauren didn't stand there. He recalled the other night she'd glanced out and the moonlight had caressed her.

What was he thinking? "Valley Girls" were known to be fake and self-involved. He needed a down-to-earth

46

woman who would stand by her man. Still, he wouldn't deny his attraction to Lauren. However, he didn't think she was a standby-your-man kind of woman. So, why did he crave her?

Chapter 8

Before dawn, Amy woke and made it to the master bathroom in time to upchuck the late-night snack she'd had with Wyatt after he returned from helping put out the fire behind the mill.

She kneeled on the floor and held her head, hoping she wouldn't be sick all day. If the nausea lasted for hours, how was she going to hold enough food down to feed the baby? Did she dare ask Dr. Danelavich for help? Would he understand her desire to keep the baby a secret until she was past the time for a possible miscarriage? She sighed and carefully stood.

"Honey, are you okay?" Wyatt knocked on the door.

"Fine. I'll be out in a minute."

Momentarily, he would leave for work and he'd drop Bobby off at school as well. She brushed her teeth, rinsed her mouth, and made a promise to hold it together until they left. Then she would call the doctor and make an appointment to see him.

With a deep breath, she opened the door and forced a smile. "Morning, my love."

***

The flames screeched and the trees exploded around Chance. *I'm burning!* For a moment, he was back fighting the forest fire that had trapped him and his buddy.

Waking with a start, he threw back the covers and sat up. His heart raced and he gulped the early morning air. *Thank God it's over— only a nightmare.*

He wiped the perspiration from his forehead. How long was this going to happen? Would he replay this terror every time he went to a new fire?

Silence filled the attic, only the outside sound of birds in the grove of trees near the barn could be heard as they sang.

The pines grew close to the buildings and it concerned him. He couldn't deny they were attractive. Still, he should talk with Wyatt. After the blaze last night, Wyatt Cameron might be in the mood to listen. They could remove the stand of trees in a day or two, leaving a firebreak.

He decided to grab a quick breakfast in town and go to the sawmill to check the grounds now that it was light enough to find what caused the problem.

The volunteer firefighter was still at his post when he arrived. Chance was pleased to learn of the lack of activity during the night.

"Well done." He offered his hand to the guy who couldn't be more than nineteen or twenty. The kid was eager and a hard worker, so Chance put him on his mental list of possible recruits for a paid position on the team.

"Thanks, Paul, get some sleep," he shouted.

Chance spent the next hour checking for clues as to how the blaze started in the first place. He let out a grunt. The grove of pines grew too close to the mill's

49

buildings. When would people realize the trees were fodder for an inferno?

His boot kicked a metal cylinder. A singed tin of food. Too burned to tell what had been in the container. but foodstuff nonetheless. A broken pottery dish and wine bottle appeared to give proof someone had been camping there. He also found pieces of tattered canvas cloth, probably a makeshift tent, and the rubber sole of a sneaker. Did the man take off in such a hurry he didn't even put on his shoes, or might it be a discarded one?

Anger filled him as he realized this was another fire that might have been prevented by the simple removal of a few nonessential conifers.

Thankful no one was hurt, Chance walked to the mill. Wyatt and Manny had helped last night and he'd begin by informing them what he had found, then make suggestions to protect the lumberyard.

The other day he'd thought about leaving Sierra Creek, making for a more populous location where he could be less visible and have more job options.

Now, he began to think his advice was needed in this little village. Perhaps he'd stay at least until the proper improvements were complete. The townspeople must be made to understand the danger and the easy mitigation that might prevent a serious disaster.

A safety campaign became the obvious choice. Both Wyatt and Manny seemed approachable, so they'd be the first people he'd contact. The mayor and the local radio station could also be involved. A strategy began to hatch in his brain.

***

After being up much of the night, Lauren overslept. Ignoring her growling stomach, and thankful she had showered before going to bed, she brushed her hair and

50

forced it into a ponytail. A white tank top and navy-blue cotton pants were waiting in the closet.

Shit. Mr. Smith would never want to help her with the jewelry making if she kept coming in late. Though she had stayed up with Amy, he wouldn't care what the reason was.

Her car took the turns on the country road without a problem. Still, Lauren remembered Chance telling her to slow down. This wasn't a freeway. Today, she discovered no chickens on the road. She laughed, thinking how foolishly she had behaved over a few squawking hens.

A parking space at the back of the Hitching Post opened up. At the opportune moment, she pulled in, turned off the engine, and grabbed her purse.

Chapter 9

"**Is** Mr. Smith here yet?" Lauren shouted at Jake just as Mr. Smith stood up from behind the counter at the Hitching Post.

"Yes, Mr. Smith is here and in time to notice your tardy arrival," her boss replied.

She found it deeply annoying he talked about himself in the third person. Still, she said, "I apologize, Mr. Smith. I…"

He held up his hand to stop her from speaking. "This is the second late appearance. If you're tarty a third time, don't bother to come back. Your employment will be terminated at that point."

"But I…"

"Excuses don't work here, Missy. I don't demand much and I realize my workers come and go. They move to more important positions. However, if you are being paid by me, I expect a timely arrival. Understood?" He spun on his heel, then turned back. "You can make up for the tardiness by giving up your lunch hour."

But I'm meeting Vanna and Amy for lunch. The words died unspoken in her throat as Mr. Smith marched out the backdoor heading toward his workshop.

She struggled not to let a tear squeeze out of her eyes.

Jake appeared as shocked as she felt. "He had no call to talk to you like that."

"I was late, but…" she hesitated. "There was a fire near the mill last night and I stayed up with Amy, while she waited for Wyatt to return home."

He nodded. "Don't worry about lunch. I'll stay here with you."

"Oh, Jake you're so nice, but I don't want to spoil your plans."

He ignored her statement and instead answered with, "Lately, I don't know what's in Smithy's craw, but it wouldn't hurt to be a little early for the next few days. I mean if you want to stay working here."

"I do and I've tried hard to do a satisfactory job." She wiped her eyes. "But duly noted." She sniffed and pushed down the desire to go to the workshop and tell Mr. Smith where he could put his job. Not practical when she was about to transfer money to her dad's account—funds he depended on.

After her father's rheumatoid arthritis worsened, her dad took early retirement. Now living on a fixed income, the added money Lauren sent made an immense difference to his quality of life. She sighed.

Shortly afterward, Jake left to tell Vanna, she wouldn't meet them at the ice cream parlor for lunch.

He returned from Sophie's with a turkey sandwich on rye and a chocolate milkshake. He accepted no payment, only grinned, and said, "It's on me this time, next time it will be your turn."

"Jake, you're a lifesaver." She hugged him, almost overturning the milkshake in his hand. "Chocolate—yum. I didn't have breakfast."

***

Smith's behavior was becoming more disturbing. The man Jake remembered had disappeared. It became harder and harder to keep even part-time staff when Smithy yelled and belittled the employees.

In the last eight months, they had replaced three or four people. The word around town was to stay away from the Hitching Post if you wanted a job. That was one of the reasons they went all the way to LA for Lauren Walsh. They were more than lucky to have Lauren. She was way under-employed. Today, Jake realized she would leave if she didn't have more respect shown to her.

Last week, he'd gone over the books and found the business had picked up and not only because of the tourists. They came every year and were factored into the mix. Lauren's suggestions for displays and the logical grouping of supplies made shopping easier for customers and the displays of the boots and clothing available in the store increased sales to the women in town.

Lauren ordered, with his permission, pretty cotton blouses to go with the work jeans, not to mention colorful gardening gloves in pink and purple. She added a few cowgirl boots, as Lauren called them, each with embroidered roses on the side. They sold out in less than a week and were now on backorder.

The woman had a knack for retail and seemed to realize a customer's needs almost before they did. How many times had he heard, "Why Lady L, I never thought of that. I'm so glad you mentioned it. And Lady L, that is such a great idea, I'll take two."

Lauren had set up a table with coffee and tea for anyone who stopped by. He realized it'd be even more popular in the winter.

The folks in Sierra Creek liked her friendly style. If she left, the Hitching Post would go back to being just a feed store and that couldn't keep enough of the families coming in or the money flowing.

***

Chance left the office at the sawmill satisfied with arrangements to cut the conifers back from the buildings and to place nightlights in the grove to discourage campers. Wyatt and Manny arranged to introduce him to Mayor Breen. They thought the civic leader would be amenable to the idea of an ad campaign. It appeared the mayor liked anything calling attention to his town and to himself.

That worked fine for Chance. He never wanted the limelight. Getting the job done was all he cared about.

The phone rang. Chance answered only to hear Jake request he do something about Uncle Smithy.

Not a man to cry wolf, Jake was usually calm and steady, probably why he'd been able to work with his uncle all these years. Today, he was riled up. "The store needs Lauren Walsh and your uncle is going to chase her away."

Uncle Smithy's home was not too far from Amy's farm. Chance drove out of town, but at the fork in the road, instead of taking a left to the farmhouse, he drove to the right. He kept driving past the chicken ranch and stopped at a dirt lane that ended at his uncle's white stucco house surrounded by his unplowed twenty-five acres.

He turned the fire truck facing out to make it faster to leave should he be called to an emergency.

As usual, the brown wooden door was unlocked. He entered and called his uncle's name. The house smelled of cigarette smoke and rotten food.

"Chance." Mr. Smith faced him, no smile to greet him.

"Smithy, you've got to air this place out." He opened a window. "Don't you ever clean?"

Uncle Smithy shrugged. "Had a cleaning lady, but she up and quit on me."

"No surprise if you talked to her the way you did to Lauren Walsh today. What the hell are you doing speaking to her like that, threatening to fire the woman? She had a good reason for being late, but you didn't bother to listen."

"What do you know about it?" His uncle frowned. "Jake, that old busybody. I ought to fire him too."

"Yeah, that's all you need. Then who would run the place? And as we are on the subject of the store, why so hard on Lauren? I would bet she was beneficial to the business."

"Why are you sticking your nose in this? You never bothered about my other employees."

Chance hesitated. His uncle was right. Why Lauren? "She's a fine person and needs the money."

Smithy sat in his old broken-down leather club chair. "I should replace this old piece of junk." He scratched his neck and rubbed the stubble on his chin.

"Don't change the subject." Chance grabbed a dining chair from the table and faced it backward so he could rest his arms on the back. "What's going on? Why don't you like her? She's a city gal, but she has talent."

"The woman bothers me. Gussied up all the time. She smells sweet and the long wavy brown hair of hers... Lauren makes me uncomfortable."

"Why you old reprobate, she's young enough to be your daughter."

"If you weren't my sister's kid, I wouldn't let you talk to me like that," he growled. "I know she's a kid. I would never...but when she looks at me with those wide eyes of hers... Well, I don't like it." He stopped. "If I'd married, I might have a girl like her." He took a breath and let it out slowly. "She reminds me what I've missed, wife, kids, grandchildren. Instead, I got you, a damned disrespectful nephew."

Chance smiled at his uncle's statement. The man wouldn't admit he cared—no need, it was understood.

"Hey, Smithy, find me a beer and I'll help you clean up this place.

"You can grab one. You know where they are."

"Smithy." Chance hesitated." If you're smart, you'll apologize to Lauren or you will curse the day you let her go."

Chapter 10

Spent, after her confrontation with Mr. Smith, Lauren entered the cottage, dropped her bag on the floor, turned on the ceiling fan, and opened the windows. Still fuming, she marched into the bedroom, threw folded clothes from the dresser on the bed, and began to pack her suitcase.

Where was she going?

With the back of her hand, she wiped perspiration from her forehead. *Face it. You're stuck here.* She shivered as a drop of sweat ran down her neck into her bra.

It was understood her dad was unable to work, and he depended on her for financial help.

She sat on the bed and surveyed the room. It was a nice place and affordable. No matter what happened, if she kept her temper in check and got to work on time, would the job be safe?

Mr. Smith's words haunted her. *If you are late a third time, don't bother to come back. Your employment will be terminated at that point.* Had the mean old cuss realized how important this job was to her?

She'd worked with nasty customers like him. So, why couldn't she turn her bad-tempered boss into a friend or at least a good acquaintance? She grunted at the thought of dealing with him again. Nonetheless, she had to remember her goal—learn from the master silversmith, even if the man was a cranky, aging, knucklehead, he understood silver.

In the bathroom, she tossed floral bath crystals into the bottom of the old claw foot tub and let water almost fill to the brim. She threw off her clothes and stepped into the tub, sliding into the warm water with a sigh. As she leaned back her long hair became wet, but she didn't care. With nowhere to go tonight, it didn't matter.

Outside, birds tweeted cheerfully and the sound of Bobby's laughter echoed in the distance. How wonderful to be young and carefree. Well, she reminded herself she was still young, if not carefree.

Too often, she'd been told these years were the best of her life. If so, she didn't want to think about the next stage. Right now, she was miserable enough.

Slowly, the anger and tension of this afternoon began to float away. Decisions about her job would be considered before long. She closed her eyes and refused to let any upsetting notions come to mind.

She must have fallen asleep because she woke with a start when her smartphone buzzed. Ben. At this moment, she didn't want to make nice with him or fabricate sweet talk about her day. Well, maybe she would with Chance.

Whoa, where did that come from? When she was around him, he confused her with emotions she hadn't experienced before and didn't want to. Still, at the same time, she longed to be near him and couldn't help wondering what his lips would feel like pressed against hers.

Damn. Being Mr. Smith's nephew should be enough to warn her away from him. Plus, Amy had casually mentioned Chance had plans for a big family, wanted a brood of kids, and a country gal happy to stay home and raise them.

Lauren shook the bath bubbles from her body and stood up from the now cold water. She and Chance certainly had different goals for the future. So, there wasn't a reason to become involved with him—not that he would be attracted to her.

Wrapped in a towel, she dragged a comb through her tangled hair and thought of running her hand over Chance's muscled torso. *You're incorrigible.* She laughed. *He is tantalizing, but you'd be stupid to get involved.*

Her phone chimed again. Ben. She couldn't ignore him any longer.

"Hey, Ben, how goes it?"

"What about you? I haven't heard from you for days. You can't be that busy."

"Uh, is everyone in So Cal, okay?" How long could she avoid telling him she didn't want to give him a running account of her life? They weren't a couple. They only dated a few times.

Unsurprisingly, he had a different take on their involvement. She'd realized that but had taken the easy way out, thinking leaving would solve her problem concerning him. Out of sight, out of mind. Right? Or did absence make the heart grow fonder for Ben?

"Are you still there, Lauren?"

"Yeah. Can you call back in a few minutes? I just got out of the bath and I'm only wearing a towel."

"Uh," he choked, then recovered. "Sure, babe." Ben disconnected.

Not smart. He probably thought she was flirting with him.

***

Barefoot but wearing the blue jeans she'd bought at the Hitching Post Lauren pulled a white cotton shirt from the closet and buttoned it as she padded into the kitchen.

Not in the mood to cook, she popped a mac and cheese frozen dinner into the microwave and poured a glass of Amy's homemade apple juice.

As the food warmed, she sat on the couch, opened her sketch pad, and studied the drawings she'd made of the wildflowers on the day she and Chance took a walk together.

The lupin was perfect for silver stems and blue sapphire blooms. The sweet pink flower, what did Chance call it? Didn't she write the name down? Anyway, a silver log with a pink flower growing from it. She'd call it rebirth to designate the earth's ability to regenerate after devastation. *Yeah.* She liked that. But as she hadn't seen one, it was essential to take another look at Chance's photo.

Had he come home?

In the bedroom, the phone buzzed, but she ignored the call—it had to be Ben.

You're a coward.

Possibly true, but she couldn't tolerate another confrontation today. The notion of hurting Ben's feelings was distasteful, but not talking to him for days hadn't worked to deter him. Eventually, she'd inform him they were not an item.

The microwave dinged and she glanced up in time to see Chance pass her window on the way to his apartment.

After supper, she'd ask to look at his photos again.

After dinner, Lauren carried her dirty dish to the sink and was about to leave to visit Chance, when Wyatt and Manny walked by the cottage and jogged up the stairs to his living quarters.

So much for her conversation with him. In a wooden rocking chair, she sat down to watch the sunset. The peaceful view in front of her belied her anxious mood.

***

Still on the landing, Chance glanced at the cottage, then let his buddies in to join him for a meeting to discuss the plans for the fire station.

Too bad this session was tonight. He wanted to check on Lauren and find out if she was all right. It wasn't his business. Still, he had the sense his uncle needed her and she sure would learn from him if given the opportunity.

If only the old coot would lighten up and agree to teach her. Truth be told, Smithy could use a kick in the pants. He was in a rut, stuck doing the same items over and over, or so Chance had been told by those who should know.

If all went well, Lauren might inspire the old man to take a new attitude toward his silver work, before his jewelry business was run into the ground.

"Got anything to drink?" Manny broke into his thoughts.

"Soda and beer in the fridge." Chance went in and, grabbed a couple of cans of each and set them on the coffee table.

"I'll show you the designs for the firehouse. He rolled out the blueprints sitting on the table. "I didn't realize Sierra Creek didn't have one until I moved here." He grabbed a cola, held the can but didn't open it. "I assumed there'd be at least a small station."

"The old chief seemed happy to keep the ancient pumper truck at his ranch," Manny said. "When he retired, we parked the old vehicle here on Amy and Wyatt's farm."

"That's when Manny and I began to think…" Wyatt popped open a beer. "Now the town is growing and after the blaze at the mill, we decided to bring out our idea for a new structure to Mayor Breen and the town council. We discovered a couple of properties we thought might fit the bill. Did you have time to check them out?"

"Yeah. I shot a few pics of the lots that could work." Chance slid photos toward them. "Do you have a budget firmed up?"

"Not at this point. The town's accountant is still looking at the books, but Mayor Breen promised he'd email the total to me by the end of the week. If his mood is anything to go by, the funding should be generous." Manny pointed to the first property as he sat down on the sofa still holding the cola. "This one is a little further out of town, but it would need fewer improvements to prepare the land." He took a swig of his drink.

Wyatt bent over the table, scanning the photos. "I don't think anyone on the town council wants to be unprepared after the fire season California suffered last year—good photos, by the way." He paused. "Since you're the fire chef, I'd trust your judgment on locating the hall."

Chance rubbed his jaw in thought. "I appreciate that. I'd pick the land close to town. It will cost some to get the ground ready for building. Though God forbid, there was a fire nearby, placing it close would allow us to better defend Sierra Creek."

"Okay. Let's go with your suggestion." Wyatt set his beer can down.

"Fine by me," Manny agreed.

"I'll send the info for the council to examine." Wyatt leaned back in a chair, a satisfied expression on his face.

"I'm having lunch with the mayor, so, I'll fill him in."

"Perfect, Manny. Hey, is Breen buying lunch to make another pitch to encourage you to run for mayor when he becomes the county supervisor?" Wyatt asked.

"If he is, he's wasting his time and money." Manny shook his head and chuckled.

"Wyatt, you better watch out or this new Supervisor Breen might want you to join the town council. You're a famous rodeo star too," Chance joked.

"Yeah, buddy, seems you did your share of riding too."

Chance laughed. "Back in the day." He smiled, thinking about the first time he met Wyatt and Manny on the rodeo circuit.

"Guess we might need to watch each other's backs," Manny added. "Or we'll find ourselves in politics."

They all laughed.

"I'll grab the blueprints for the building. But if we want to buy a new hook and ladder truck, the specs will need to be amended to accommodate the larger vehicle." Chance pointed to the garages. "It's a small firehouse, but the place will have room for three trucks including an EMS transporter. Not to mention a dorm, bathrooms, kitchen, rec room, and lobby."

The conversation continued as they scanned the drawings and Chance was left with the impression this new station was supported by both men.

They discussed various points of the plan and each one found a designated task to do. Wyatt would contact the real estate company and begin negotiations for the plot of land they'd agreed on. Manny would deal with Mayor Breen and the council members to shore up the budget, while Chance worked to redesign the fire hall and search for new equipment. This included securing a hook and ladder truck that could do the job, but not break the bank.

When Manny and Wyatt left, a sense of optimism Chance hadn't felt for some time, began to lift his mood. When he was damn near killed in a firestorm, he'd questioned his desire to continue fighting infernos.

Tonight, he had learned the history of the blaze on the lumber mill's grounds and how vulnerable Sierra Creek would be should a wildfire start in the area. With that thought, his motivation to serve the community deepened.

For too long, he had been in a hospital bed as he struggled to recover from the burns received in the deadly blaze—a useless hulk. At that point, Chance wondered if he'd ever be able to return to any kind of career, let alone this one.

He opened the door, stood on the landing, and took a slow breath—nice to be useful again.

Out of the corner of his eye, he saw someone move. Lauren.

Still, in the lounge chair, she must have fallen asleep. Should he wake her?

Chapter 11

Suddenly awake, Lauren sat up from the lounge chair on the cottage porch. A chill ran down her back. Someone was staring at her. She gazed upward toward the barn's attic and Chance nodded from the landing.

"Lauren, you okay?"

"Yeah, it was sweltering in there." She glanced down and noticed one of the buttons of her blouse had come undone and quickly fixed it.

He sat on the top stair and stared at the sky. "I'm used to the fog coming in over the water at night to cool the air. Here it's clear and hot all night. Still, we wouldn't see the array of stars like this, otherwise."

"In LA the bright lights of the city prevent viewing too many." She hesitated. "Sounds silly, but I was surprised how dark the country sky is and the stars—I had no idea…"

"Truly a city girl."

"Well, maybe not a girl, but yeah."

"You miss the place."

She patted the seat of the lounge chair next to hers. "Join me?"

He did what she asked and leaned back in the lounger, with his long legs stretched out in front of him.

"Lauren, are you settling in?"

"Trying."

"It gets easier. Moving to this small town was a shock for me, coming from the San Francisco Bay Area."

"I feel like a fish flopping on a dry beach." She stretched out her legs and realized how much longer his legs were. He was taller than she had realized.

"You were a fish out of water," he suggested.

"You got that right, and talk about a city gal, I didn't even own a pair of jeans." She giggled, making light of the serious situation.

"I'm not a country boy by birth. I've lived most of my life in San Francisco but…"

"Still, you want to stay in Sierra Creek."

"I think so."

She thought he was going to say more, but he remained silent, for a moment then said, "Lauren, I talked to my Uncle Smith."

"I don't…"

"I realize it's none of my business." He hesitated. "I care for my uncle. I hope you'll give him another opportunity and stay at the store. He can be tough, but underneath he's a kind man—I think he likes you."

It appeared her expression of disbelief caused him to change the subject because he said, "Can you find the north star?"

"Uh…"

"Search for the brightest one."

"Over there?" She pointed.

"Yeah, Polaris, the north star, part of the Little Bear constellation (also known as the Little Dipper)."

"I've heard of the Big Dipper, but…"

"Yeah, most kids can locate that star. The other one is harder to find, but I used to sail, navigation and all."

"I sailed too." Relaxed, she shared her experience sailing a Sunfish. "Early on, I learned how easy it was to capsize, but the weather was hot. The water was fine." She laughed. "Growing up, we went to Balboa Island." She stopped. "Hard for me to realize I'm so far from the ocean."

"Have you been to the lake?"

"There's a lake around here?"

"Yep."

"OMG, I feel stupid. I knew about the river, but didn't think…"

"Hey, don't be hard on yourself." He faced her. "Let me show you. Is Sunday your day off?"

"Yeah."

"Great, I'll pick you up at noon. Bring a swimsuit." He grinned. "Well, it's getting late. I'll let you go to bed."

He jumped from the chair and jogged up the stairs to his apartment before she could say anything.

She stood with her mouth open, wondering how or if she had agreed to his invitation. In her mind, there was no future with a man who wanted to stay in the rural town and have a bunch of kids for his wife to take care of. No way.

Even so, he was damned handsome and charming.

Should she go with him or call it off?

Chapter 12

Two days until Sunday, Lauren's day off from work. Could she hang tough and face Mr. Smith today? He would be counting the minutes to make sure she arrived early or at least on time this morning.

Though exhausted, sleep had been elusive last night. Afraid she might oversleep she'd set two alarms but woke before they went off.

She made a cheese sandwich and grabbed a small container of strawberry yogurt for lunch. Today, she wouldn't be deprived of her break.

Though she arrived fifteen minutes before the store opened, Jake was already at work. This time she didn't ask if Mr. Smith had arrived, there would be no repeat of yesterday's disaster.

Jake paced as he talked on the phone. "You don't get it. We ordered early to be sure your product would arrive on time. Now you're telling me we're not receiving it."

He waved to Lauren and smiled warmly.

Jake always seemed easy-going—kind, but whoever was listening on the other end received his ire.

"People are in short supply of the feed. Livestock is waiting and we gave them our word they'd have it today." He paused and she assumed someone was speaking on the other end of the line.

He grunted and rubbed his chin. "Yeah, well, it better be on my doorstep by the end of the day."

More silence, as Jake appeared to wait for an answer. "Okay. If not, I'm staring at a card from your competitor who's been begging me to buy from him—yeah, yeah. All right, no later than six p.m. on Saturday. He disconnected. "Hell."

"Are you okay?"

"Right as rain. Lady L, but I don't like confrontations, especially with people who should keep their word. Once too often, that company isn't delivering on the date they promised."

"Oh," she said weakly.

"Relax, Lauren, I'll take care of it. Hey, I'm glad you showed up." He hesitated. "I wasn't sure if we had seen the last of you." He scratched his head. "Come on, it's a beautiful day. Let's enjoy."

"Yeah." She did her best to smile while she scanned the store, but didn't ask where Mr. Smith was. Instead, she put her things in the back room, including her lunch which she placed in the refrigerator.

One minute after the Hitching Post opened, Mr. Smith entered from the back storeroom.

Her stomach clenched and her hands shook. Maybe he would yell and tell her to leave.

She could sense his stare as she stocked a shelf, but Mr. Smith didn't speak to her.

He nodded to Jake and the pair went to a corner, presumably to discuss business.

She didn't see Smith the rest of the day. Still, she tensed every time a door opened or a man entered. Was it her boss ready to complain about something she'd done wrong? How long would she be able to handle the strain of working under such conditions?

In the few weeks, she'd worked at the store, Fridays and Saturdays had been hectic. This Friday was no exception and the hours slipped quickly by. With the day almost over, if she made it through Saturday, she'd have two days off to evaluate her situation.

What about Chance? He was expecting her to go to the lake with him on Sunday. At this point, the only thing she wanted was to stay in the cottage away from everyone. A pang of disappointment ran through her when she thought about calling off her date with him. That surprised her.

She planned the future as a single woman. Why start something? Even if he didn't want a brood of kids, he had a job that constantly put him in danger. How many wives of firefighters were now widows?

No, not for her. Early in her dating career, and after a loss, she had crossed off the men she wasn't interested in—firefighters among them.

Chance was damned good-looking, his blue eyes, wide smile, brown hair, and appealing physique, but as her dad often said, "Laurie, you don't marry the outside of a man. You marry the inside, his heart, his personality. We all eventually grow old and ugly." Dad had laughed. "But if a man's heart is kind, you won't mind."

Chance might be a great guy, but his career choice put him at risk. There had been enough tragedy in her life—no more. She'd text Chance and cancel their date.

***

After work, tired and stressed, Lauren walked up the driveway toward the cottage. With the fire truck nowhere to be seen, the muscles in her back relaxed—a little.

At some point, she and Chance would run into each other, but not tonight.

"Lauren, you're just in time." Amy waved from the backdoor of the farmhouse. "Vanna will be here in a minute. We're having a girl's night. The guys are meeting with the mayor. Bobby is staying with Sophie and Johnny—Vanna's mom and stepdad."

"Oh."

"Bobby could hardly wait. Sophie told him he could make his favorite sherbet. I'm on my way to the patio, with dinner."

"Let me help you carry something." Lauren took a tray loaded with food and followed her.

Amy sat down at the table. "I made salad and pasta for us." She took a deep breath. "Vanna is bringing chicken for the grill."

"I should offer something."

"Not tonight. You're our guest—but next Friday…" Amy smiled.

Lauren couldn't help but grimace. Everyone assumed she would still be here. Were they right? "Okay, next Friday."

"Help yourself to a coke or iced tea." Amy sat up in the chair. "Hard to find a comfortable position. Oh, I didn't bring out anything alcoholic, the baby, you understand."

"This is fine." Lauren took a can of cola. "Amy, do you want one?"

"I put milk in the thermos." She reached for the tray.

"How are you feeling, Amy? Still nauseated?"

Chapter 13

In the backyard of the farmhouse, Lauren waited for Amy to answer her question.

"I'm fine, I only threw up once today. The Saltine crackers help."

"What's this about Saltines?" Vanna stood in the yard, her hand on her hip, her blue eyes flashing and her straight blonde hair shining in the evening sun.

Amy grinned. "I'm pregnant."

"OMG, "I'm so happy for you." Vanna wiped a tear before as it ran down her face, then hugged Amy.

Lauren watched the joy in the two women.

"Did you tell Wyatt?" Vanna set her bag on the patio table.

"I'll do it tonight."

Amy explained that Bobby was her little boy from her first marriage. "After my son's birth, Bobby nearly died. He couldn't keep anything down, lost weight, and was way too skinny." She took a few seconds, then continued, "He cried most of the time and was inconsolable. I was frantic. My first husband blamed me for giving birth to a sickly baby he never wanted in the first place and walked out on us."

"Oh, Amy— but your son looks so healthy." Lauren pictured the energetic six-year-old redheaded boy, with a quick smile. She often saw him playing on the lawn behind the house.

"He is—now, but as a baby and a toddler, I didn't know he had celiac disease" She hesitated. "I gave him all the wrong food. I thought wheat bread and cereal was good for kids."

"Isn't?"

"Not if they have celiac."

"I never heard of it."

"Me either—back then."

"Amy, you didn't do anything wrong," Vanna spoke up.

"Yeah, but…" Amy rubbed her stomach. "With this baby, I'll understand what to do if he or she has celiac."

Lauren noticed the love in Amy's eyes as she rubbed her growing baby.

Vanna went to the barbecue and put the chicken pieces she brought with her on the grill.

Amy hesitated. "I pray this baby will be all right. I couldn't stand the loss of another baby," she whispered almost to herself.

Seated next to Amy, Lauren squeezed her hand.

"Come on. This is a celebration." Vanna popped open a soda and proposed a toast. "To the little one who will be welcomed by Amy and Wyatt and loved by all who live here in Sierra Creek."

"To the baby!" Lauren added.

"Thank you." Amy grinned.

The rest of the evening passed quickly. Lauren began to know the two women and understand each had struggled to find their way in the world, before settling in Sierra Creek.

With their encouragement, Amy retired early.

In the kitchen of the old farmhouse, Lauren and Vanna washed the dishes and put things away. They shared their experiences of living in Los Angeles and the San Fernando Valley. They laughed at the antics they'd seen from drivers on the freeways.

"Vanna, do you ever miss LA?" Lauren placed a bowl of leftover pasta in the fridge.

"Not really. Well, maybe the shopping." Vanna stopped cleaning the utensils. "I grew up in Sierra Creek with only catalogs to stare at. So, I loved the huge malls. Oh, it was hard to park and they were packed with people, but once I was in there—a wonderland."

"You're making me homesick." Lauren giggled.

Vanna turned serious. "Residing in a small town can be a culture shock. Still, the people will meet you more than halfway if you give them a chance."

Chance, an unfortunate choice of words, Lauren thought. He was one of the reasons she considered moving back to the city. A funny twinge stung her and emotion stirred deep within when she was near him. No other man caused such a reaction to flow in her. Certainly not Ben.

"Lauren, you all right?"

"Yeah, just daydreaming."

***

Chance parked and grabbed his backpack, then jumped out of the truck. He slammed the door and locked it. Then he rubbed the back of his neck. Damn, the meeting ran long. Mayor Breen appeared to take enjoyment in stretching out simple concepts to make them convoluted. However, Breen meant well.

Part of the way up the drive, Chance's boot kicked something and it skittered across the pavement. He bent down to find out what it might be. In the moonlight, he saw Lauren's name emblazoned in gold on the white album.

It must have fallen from her bag. He glanced at the cottage. A light flickered in the bedroom window.

Awake?

He moved quickly toward the porch, then hesitated. Had Lauren fallen asleep with a lamp still on? If so, no need to bother her tonight.

He started toward the barn but turned around. If she believed her illustrations were lost, she'd be worried.

Convinced, he rang the doorbell.

"Who's there?"

"Chance."

"Do you realize what time it is?"

"I discovered your art book. I…"

The door flew open.

Dressed in an oversized T-shirt and shorts, she pushed back her long wavy brown hair that hung loose and sexy, freed from the usual ponytail.

"OMG, Chance, I tore this cottage apart looking for it. I was frantic." Her wide eyes flashed with excitement. "Thank you!"

"I found it in the driveway." He extended the book to her and she grabbed it, brushing his hand when she did. Heat ran up his arm and a shocked expression raced across her face. She must have felt the electricity too.

"I wanted you to have it in case you were concerned."

"I wasn't concerned. I was crazy!" She breathed in deeply. "All of my sketches for the new jewelry line are in here."

He was about to say something stupid like, "Be more careful," when she stood on her tiptoes, touched his face, and kissed him full on the lips.

"Thanks again." She stepped back and closed the door in his face.

"Shit." Talk about crazy, that woman could drive him mad.

***

Wyatt yawned and put away his meeting notes. He entered the bedroom of the farmhouse and watched his wife sleep. Before Amy came into his life, he hadn't realized how much of a void there had been. A hollowness had filled his days, while he'd done his best to hide that truth with drinking and partying. Since their marriage, an inner contentment filled the empty space in him, all because of Amy.

She purred in her sleep and a smile spread across her face. Every day she became more beautiful. His body tingled with the need to fondle her small pert breast. Was it his imagination or were they larger?

He undressed and slid into bed next to her. She rolled over and opened her arms to him.

***

The morning light came through the curtains and sent a beam of the sun across the king bed. Wyatt never bought blackout drapes because he wanted the light to wake him early for the long work days.

Amy still slept, so he took a quick shower and then went to the kitchen to make coffee.

She was sitting up when he returned. "Thanks, but I think I'll skip coffee today. I'm feeling a little queasy."

"Are you sick? Can I get you something?" He sat on the bed and leaned close.

77

Without answering, blood drained from her face and she ran to the bathroom.

"Amy!" What would he do if she was seriously ill?

Slowly, she came out of the bathroom and grinned at him, her eyes filled with emotion. "Honey, I'm fine."

"You were gagging."

"I'm pregnant."

Stunned, he stared at her. "Are you sure?"

"Yes."

"Thank God—I shouldn't have touched you last night. If I did anything…"

"Wyatt, I wanted you. It's all right."

He gently hugged Amy, then knelt before her and kissed their growing baby. "Hello, little one. I'm your daddy. I can't wait to welcome you."

When he stood, she held his face with her hands. "I love you, honey. Our baby is so lucky to have you as their father."

Too full of love, he couldn't speak. He embraced her and the baby and said a silent prayer they both continued to stay safe.

"I want you, Wyatt."

Desire growing in him, he picked her up and stroked her enlarged breast. "It's safe?

"Yeah," she said breathlessly.

The backdoor slammed.

"Mommy, Daddy, I'm home from Sophie and Johnny's," Bobby shouted.

Wyatt sighed. "You rest. I'll go."

***

Saturday morning was hotter than usual. The Hitching Post wasn't open, but the place felt stifling. Lauren turned on the overhead fan. It droned and wobbled but did little to move the sweltering air. Jake

78

was in the storeroom searching for another fan to put near the cash register.

She wiped her brow and continued to stock the shelves with the new supplies delivered last night. Would her boss check to make sure she arrived as scheduled? Was she a fool to think his attitude toward her would change if she arrived early, or was she wasting her time?

Chapter 14

Jake returned to the salesroom displaying an expression of victory on his lined face and with a white plastic fan in his right hand. "I dug it out from behind a bunch of empty boxes waiting to be recycled." He placed it on the counter and looked for a plug.

"Super! I'll dust it before you turn it on."

The storeroom is so dark I didn't realize how filthy it is."

"Easy to clean."

In a few minutes, Lauren faced the breeze, grateful for small favors. "Thanks, Jake. Don't let me hog the cool air." She moved the oscillating fan toward him.

"Lady L, don't thank me. I should have thought of it earlier."

"Uh, Jake?"

"Yeah?"

"Do you think Mr. Smith will check on me?"

"He did."

"What!" Lauren spun around to face Jake and almost sent a box of silver medallions to the floor.

He caught them in midair. "Hey, no worries. Smith drove into the parking lot, stopped by your convertible, and took off."

"Well, I never…"

Her smartphone alarm jingled, signaling it was time to open the store.

"Off to the races." She jogged to the entry, unlocked the door, then flipped over the sign in the front window from closed to open.

Main Street buzzed with tourists in brightly colored shorts and shirts. Wearing sunglasses, they clustered in groups hovering over maps, probably debating the next destination to explore.

Several of them headed in her direction.

She stepped back and let them in. "Good morning."

They enthusiastically rummaged through the aisles of the store, laughing and talking loudly.

Many of the sightseers bought souvenirs of Sierra Creek, including photos and polished rocks from the area. The straw hats and Stetsons Lauren had ordered were also popular.

As the heat of the day increased, the little fan struggled to cool the room, but the people browsing didn't seem to mind.

Jake took care of the locals and left her to make small talk with the out-of-towners.

Lauren did her best to keep track of the sales, making note of the more popular items.

The store's inventory was recorded by hand. A simple app could solve the problem and save hours of work. Nonetheless, Jake spent a significant amount of his time at work ordering the same goods over and over. Almost immediately after starting there, she had suggested computerizing orders and he seemed interested. Still, Jake mentioned the boss resented computers and didn't like being forced to use them. He loved the old ways. Doing things by hand gave him the feeling of control and it seemed being the man in charge meant a great deal to Mr. Smith.

Not to be deterred, when there was a lull in customers, Lauren searched for the best cost and most efficient choice of software to do the job. It might be important someday, should the info be needed.

About five minutes after closing, out of the corner of her eye, she spotted her boss's truck driving down Main Street. She was bringing in the items displayed on the porch of the Hitching Post and was about to close and lock the entry. She smiled and waved, but he didn't and his pickup continued down the road. With a sigh, she flipped the window sign to closed.

The best thing about being busy was the day went quickly—not a moment to think about personal problems. She stretched her sore back and wished for a soft chair and a footstool for her aching feet.

She glanced down at the brown stain on the breast pocket of her white cotton shirt. She had done her best to remove the remains of the chocolate milkshake one of the kids had brought into the outlet. While his mother shopped, he'd wandered away and tripped over something. Lauren had prevented him from hitting the floor, but he'd sloshed the milkshake on her. Thank goodness, it hadn't landed on any of the new clothes his mother had been examining.

After they'd left, Lauren washed up and wrote a sign asking customers not to bring food or drink into the store and placed the placard on the front door.

Vanna had promised to meet her for dinner—a snack really, at the ice cream shop. Lauren stared at her stained shirt and giggled, recalling the kid's expression. A change of clothes was in order. Should she go to the cottage before meeting up with her friend?

The old regulator clock sounded on the half hour. She was already fifteen minutes late. She grabbed her bag and left as Chance walked by the store with a woman Lauren had never seen.

If Chance saw her, he didn't react, and neither did the unknown female.

They paused and talked for a moment. The tall, large-boned, blonde leaned close to him as if to hear what he said.

Lauren ignored the urge to interrupt the couple. What they were doing was none of her business. So, why did it irk her?

In the ice cream shop, Lauren leaned back in her chair and breathed in the sweet aroma of peppermint ice cream.

"Vanna, this place smells amazing—chocolate and peppermint, I'm so tempted to forget what I ordered and go with a chocolate fudge sundae." She glanced at her blouse. "I look like I've already had one." She laughed and explained what happened at work.

"Kids." Vanna grinned. "You should see me sometimes when I get home after working at the preschool."

"The poor boy was so upset. I thought he might cry. Such a cutie, I couldn't scold him. My fear was Mr. Smith would walk in and me with chocolate ice cream dripping down my chest, the little guy bawling and his mother all concerned."

"Oh, Lauren, what a terrible experience." Vanna burst out laughing, then stopped. "I'm sorry, but it's such a funny image."

"OMG, it was hilarious, now that I think back on it." Lauren laughed too. "Thank goodness my boss didn't arrive. I might have been fired on the spot."

"But you didn't do anything wrong."

"I ordered more products that appeal to women and children—I mean they sell, but they bring in kids with food and drink into the store." She glanced up when the bell on the ice cream shop door jingled. Chance and the blonde entered and sat at a table near the window.

"You're staring."

"Vanna, do you know the woman?"

"Never saw her before."

When Vanna left to retrieve their order, Lauren did her best not to look in Chance's direction. Why should she care who the strange female was? *None of my business.* Anyway, Lauren wouldn't be in Sierra Creek for long. Particularly, if Mr. Smith refused to help her. She was only in this small burg for his expert instruction in silversmithing and if he didn't give it…

Her friend set a huge green salad and half a Monterey Jack cheese sandwich on rye in front of her. "Bon appetite."

"Yum! Your chicken sandwich looks good too." While they ate, Lauren managed, without being obvious, to peek at Chance and his woman friend.

***

"Chance, your mom sends her love."

"Thanks, Bonnie." He forced himself to ignore Lauren sitting at a table with Vanna. "They have delicious food here, not only ice cream."

"Who's the female?"

"What?"

"The one with the long brown hair."

"I…"

"You're gaping at her."

"Uh, just a gal who lives in town."

"Pretty."

84

"I guess. Anyhow, I was hoping you might be interested in helping me find a startup team for the new fire station here in Sierra Creek."

"I'm interested."

"Fine. My proposal is to begin with a few experienced men—and women." He paused.

"No worries, Chance. I realize you're not a pig concerning women or I wouldn't be here."

He nodded. "Let me buy you some food and we can talk."

Over salad and sandwiches, he outlined the needs of the town.

Swiftly, Sophie brought them two huge chocolate sundaes. "On the house," she said proudly.

"Sophie, you're wonderful!" Chance made introductions, explaining Bonnie was a friend from San Francisco.

"Lovely to meet you—enjoy." Sophie rushed back behind the counter as people were lined up once more.

"A nice lady." Bonnie took a spoonful of whipped cream.

"Yeah, most of the residents of this place are."

"I'm willing to help, but your dad has more to offer than I do." Bonnie swallowed. "Chance, you and your dad make up?"

The noise in the room increased as more customers entered and filled the tables. Laughter surrounded him and the aroma of freshly brewed coffee wafted toward him.

"Chance?"

"I'm working on it." *Not really.* He hadn't talked to his father since their last blowup. According to his dad, he was making the biggest mistake of his life by moving from the Bay Area to his position in Sierra Creek.

"He didn't want you to leave," she continued, then dug into her sundae.

"No."

"He misses you." She licked her spoon.

"Bonnie, I…"

"It meant a lot to have you in San Francisco. He wants a Williams working there. Especially now he is close to retirement."

Chance didn't answer. What could he say? Dad was a stiff-upper-lip kind of guy. The kind of man who grinned and dealt with whatever life handed him. He admired that in his father and had tried to do the same. Still, he wasn't him. His dad couldn't or wouldn't see, Chance's wish to move from the large metropolis. Dad called it self-centered.

"Bonnie, how is the old buzzard?"

"Same as ever. It's going to be hard when he retires. The station is his life."

"Yep." Could be, then he'll talk to his wife. Mom had waited long enough for him to show her a little attention.

Bonnie finished the hot fudge sundae. "Good stuff. The best ice cream I've ever eaten."

"Sophie makes it in the back room."

"Hm—Chance, you good? Settled in?"

"Yeah, I think so." He stared at the melting ice cream. He should eat at least a portion of it. He didn't want to insult Sophie, so he took a few bites and then shoved it away.

"After the last fire, I was ready to slow down. This town suits me." He leaned back and gazed at Lauren sitting with Vanna at the other end of the shop. She appeared tuckered but still appealing.

"Busy little place." Bonnie nodded toward the area where several people were lined up waiting for their treats.

"Tourists." His focus returned to Lauren.

"Chance, why don't you go say hi?"

He shrugged. "Another time. I'll walk you to your car."

"Well, thanks for showing the property for the firehouse." Bonnie finished her sundae. "I'll think about your offer of employment."

As they got up to leave, Chance noticed Lauren glance at him, and then turn away.

What was she thinking?

Chapter 15

It was still hot when Lauren left the ice cream shop and reached her parked car. She took down the top and drove to the cottage, hoping she didn't run into Chance and his friend.

She was in luck. No one was home, not even Amy or Wyatt.

In the cottage, hot and sticky, she pulled off her shirt and tried not to recall the day of upsets and disappointments. It was bad enough the little boy had spilled chocolate all over her, but then she'd seen Chance grinning at a blonde—not that it should matter, but somehow it did.

The cool shower helped calm her nerves and the aroma of vanilla shampoo soothed her. Afterward, she quickly dried her hair and stepped into an old pair of shorts and a pale blue tank top, no bra, or shoes— freedom.

With a smile, she grabbed her sketch pad and sat on the couch to work on the wildflower drawings. In a while, it would be a matter of deciding how big to make the pieces and what gems were needed.

She had a few stones left from a previous set of jewelry she'd made and sold while still in LA. It was doubtful they would be right as they were more about bling than nature.

The gems were in the bedroom closet. She threw open the window before digging them out. If she turned on the fan now, maybe it would be cool enough to sleep tonight.

With the front door ajar, she sat cross-legged on the couch again and lifted the lid of the small box. As she had thought, the gems were wrong for this project. They were too much like city chic—not what she wanted as her signature nature pieces. In her mind she had a theme, a sort of the earth's renewal, using natural metals and semiprecious stones.

She leaned back and scanned the drawings. Her favorite was the small pink flower that Chance told her grew after a forest fire. It was the first sign of rebirth when the world appeared to be dead. It would be the symbol of her line—Rebirth.

She frowned at the flower she'd done. It wasn't a proper representative of the bloom.

Chance had a photo of one. Not only that, he would remember the name and the place where it was found. She glanced at her phone and was about to text him when she remembered he was with the blonde.

Shit.

No matter. She'd check out turquoise and lapis online as possible choices for other pieces. Both of them went well with silver.

Vanna had mentioned there were shops in a nearby town that carried specimens of all the rocks and gemstones from the area. It might be worth a trip to check them out. She liked the idea of actually holding jewels in her hand, to consider the weight and how light hit and refracted in each one.

"Lauren?"

She startled. Chance stood at the screen door.

"What are you doing here?" She covered her mouth. That didn't sound too friendly. "Uh—I mean, come in."

"If you're busy I can…"

"No, stay. I was working on my drawings. You're just the person I want to see."

"Really?" Disbelief sounded in his voice.

"Yeah." She stood. "Want a soft drink?"

He shook his head but entered.

"Hey, sit down. Don't mind me. I had a bad day. I'm better now. I needed to ask about a photo you took."

He chose the largest chair and sat down.

Without thinking how close they would be, Lauren sat on the arm of his chair showed him the sketch of the pink flower, and leaned toward him.

Chance stared and cleared his throat.

Suddenly aware he must have realized she was bra-less, she jumped up and handed the sketch pad to him. "That's the flower. I know it's not right, but you snapped a photo I think I could use."

He took the drawing and examined it for a minute before saying, "It's close." He rubbed his chin as his brow furrowed. "As I told you, this a favorite plant of mine. I have several photos taken from different angles. That might help."

"Great."

While they huddled over one of his shots, he made comments about what he had seen after a devastating fire in the Sierra Mountains. Pain radiated in his eyes as he spoke.

"That's horrible. I've seen the TV news reports, but I know they can't show the size of the destruction or heat of the inferno."

90

"No, you have to be there and be scorched by the heat—choke on the smoke and ash." He shook his head as if remembering. "After one fire, as I walked through the burnt trees, I was pretty low. All the work to put out the inferno seemed to be for nothing. That's when I glimpsed the flower…" He scanned her. "Unexpectedly, viewing the bloom made the struggle to fight the flames seem worthwhile—corny, still…"

"Not corny." She wanted to say something soothing but was at a loss.

He sat silent as he scanned the photo again. "Hey, Lauren, check out the leaves in this pic. They're just coming out and appear to be smaller than the ones in your sketch." He bent closer and smiled. "Of course, you may want to take artistic license—that's all good too."

"No, I want it correct and you're right. I'm glad you mentioned the leaves. Chance, I need your photos to make sure I perceive everything properly."

Lauren browsed in his gallery searching for more of the same flower. Pencil in hand, she began to draw, taking special care to make the proportions correct.

In silence, they sat near each other. She felt oddly comfortable in the quiet with Chance. Did he feel the same?

With Ben, Lauren kept up a steady stream of prattle and couldn't relax. Why?

"Here are all the photos of the plant. I set them up so you can view them from different angles." Chance broke into her thoughts.

"Perfect." She took the smartphone and made quick changes to her drawings. "What do you think?"

He grabbed the book and glanced at it. "I'm not much of an artist but…"

Together they discussed the needed modifications. She leaned back and smiled. "You have a wonderful eye for shapes and sizes. You caught nuances I missed."

"I've probably spent more time in the forest than you."

"You bet. For most of my life, a walk in the forest meant going to Griffith Park in Los Angeles."

"Never gone backpacking, hiking in the backcountry?"

"Nope. I didn't realize the appeal—until now." She glanced at his handsome face.

"I'll take you someday."

"Thanks, Chance—you sure I can't get you anything to drink?"

"I'm fine."

"Yes, you are." *Oh damn, that was an asinine thing to say.*

He startled but didn't respond. Was he amused?

"Lauren, what time shall I pick you up tomorrow?"

"Uh, what?" *Okay, now you sound stupid.*

"The lake. I was going to show you Silver Lake."

"Yeah, well," She hesitated. "there's a store in the next county. Vanna mentioned it has a large supply of polished minerals and gemstones available. It's called The Rock Hound." She paused. "I thought…I mean, as I only have Sunday and Monday off and the place is closed on Monday…"

"Whatever you want." He frowned and the room's vibe turned cold as he stood to go.

"Chance." She grabbed his arm, surprised by the strength she discovered there.

"Yeah?"

"I hoped you would come with me. I don't know the mountain roads and the truth is, I can manage any

92

freeway, but the two-lane mountain roads scare me and I might get lost."

"So, you need a tour guide—a driver." He shook off her hold. "You've got a GPS in your phone."

"Hey, what I said came out wrong. I want to spend time with you. I…" She stopped.

He took a deep breath "What time, Lauren?"

"You name it." Her shoulders relaxed.

He looked at his smartphone. "I'll be here at ten. Most shops open by eleven on a Sunday morning. It takes about an hour to drive to the town you want."

"Okay, and thanks for your help tonight." She reached out to touch him, but he stepped back, turned, and left the cottage without a backward glance. The screen door slammed as his phone rang. "Hi, Bonnie. Yeah, great to see you again too."

So, the blonde's name was Bonnie. Was Chance making a date with her too?

***

Lauren woke from a deep sleep when her cell phone rang. Two in the morning, who would be calling? It must be a wrong number. About to close her eyes, the annoying song she used to announce a call sounded again.

"Hello." She cleared her throat. "Who is it?"

"Lady L?"

"Jake?" Had to be him as no one else called her by that name. "Are you okay?"

"Fell off my damned horse," he groaned. "Need you to take over my shift tomorrow, but I hope…" His voice dwindled into nothingness as if he was in pain

"Jake."

Lauren heard something fall.

"Jake!"

Chapter 16

Chance sat up, fully awake at the sound of someone pounding on his door. He jumped from his bed, his heart thumping as if he was on the way to a fire. He yanked open the door. "Lauren!"

She stared, red-faced and breathing hard. Her glance dropped to his white briefs and he realized he should have thrown on a pair of pants before he answered the door.

"I'm sorry, Chance. I should go."

"Come in. I'll get dressed. You tell me what's happening."

Slowly, she entered but stood near the door, leaving it open. "It's Jake." She took a deep breath.

"Hey, calm down." He slipped on a black T-shirt, then pulled on jeans, socks, and black leather boots. "What about him?"

"He called me a few minutes ago. He's hurt"

"Did you call 911?"

"No. I didn't know what to do. I don't have his address and…"

"Lauren, breathe. You did okay. What did he say?"

While she explained, he checked with the hospital and discovered their only paramedic crew was out on another job.

"Unfortunately, the paramedics are busy, but I'll check on Jake. You go back to bed. I got this."

"No way! I'm going with you."

"It's not necessary."

"I want to." She stood closer. "When I came to town, he told me to call him Just Plain Jake. But he is not. He's kind and caring and has been wonderful to me." Left unsaid was the opposite treatment by Chance's Uncle Smithy. "I'm not staying here. He might need my help."

"You going like that?" She looked down and gasped, crossing her arms across her tightened nipples protruding through the thin cotton top. "Give me one minute."

She ran from the room before he could say anything else. He couldn't help smiling. She was a good friend. Did Jake know how lucky he was?

He grabbed his "go bag," and realized the small town of Sierra Creek needed another paramedic unit. With only one, even tonight they couldn't meet the needs of the residents. What if several serious incidents happened at the same time?

He had recently pressured the mayor and town council to increase the budget for the new firehouse. Was there enough in the pot for more paramedics?

Dressed in white jeans and a navy and white striped shirt, Lauren stood at the end of the driveway when he arrived.

"Better take your car, Lauren." He moved toward the fire engine. "Jake's place is about six miles from here on a two-lane road with no street lights, it's pretty dark."

"I wish there was a full moon."

"Don't worry. This old truck lights up like a Christmas tree. You won't have any trouble following me—if you still want to come along."

"I do."

"Hand me your cell and I'll put my number in your phone. Text if you need to stop."

"Okay."

***

Grateful Chance knew Jake's address, Lauren gripped the steering wheel and drove toward the small road that would go to her co-worker.

True to Chance's word, the fire truck did light up and was easy to follow.

Suddenly, she slammed on the brakes, her seat belt holding her in place as a critter ran in front of her vehicle's headlights. The fire engine continued on without her. She squinted to see as the animal ran across the road. The creature stopped, ran back, then turned again and disappeared into the darkness. Opossum? She couldn't be sure.

To catch up with Chance, she pressed hard on the gas pedal, afraid he'd take a turn off, and she'd miss it. She forced the car forward, searching for the lights of his vehicle. With a sigh of relief, she spied them.

How long would it take to travel six miles in the dark on the narrow road? Too long.

Why had Jake waited until the middle of the night before he made the call?

Did he think he could take care of himself? She remembered how difficult it was for her dad to admit when he needed help. *Men.*

She wondered if Chance, as a medic, would be more likely to ask for assistance. He appeared so strong and in command, she doubted such a problem had ever occurred.

He signaled the fire engine's intention to turn into a wide gravel driveway. Lauren signaled too and pulled in next to the truck.

The single-level farmhouse appeared dark and there was no answer when Chance pounded on the front door, and called Jake's name. Lauren turned the handle, but the door was locked.

Chance rushed toward the back of the house and she followed, running to keep up with him.

The backdoor stood open and the softly lit kitchen suggested someone had been there, but the room was empty. When they yelled Jake's name again, a groan came from the living room.

Chance moved quickly into the darkened room, and she searched for a light switch.

A fluorescent light fixture sputtered on, and she scanned the sparsely decorated room. On the pine floor leaning against a brown leather couch, Jake tried to get up.

Looking pale and weak, Chance encouraged him to lean back. "Take it easy. We'll check things out before you move."

"Watch for the broken glass," Chance shouted over his shoulder, and for the first time she noticed a lamp had fallen and smashed into pointed shards of ceramic scattered on the plank flooring.

She dodged the glass, but she was too squeamish to look while Chance rendered aid. Instead, she glanced at the beige walls and the brown leather chair facing a flat-screen TV. Next to it stood a bookcase filled with hardcover books. Above the furniture, black and white photos of people she didn't recognize, were placed in succession.

One photo caught her eye. A younger Jake, dressed in a dark suit, was grinning at a young woman dressed in a long white dress standing proudly next to him. His wife on their wedding day? Lauren had no idea he had ever been married. If so, where was his wife now?

"Now, hold still." Chance gave Jake directions, all the time explaining what he was doing. He checked him limb by limb, back and neck.

She thought he might, but Chance didn't ask about the accident or why Jake waited so long to call. Instead, he bandaged a cut on his face and then told Jake his ankle was broken.

"I'm going to set this in place for the trip to the hospital. Looks like you may need surgery."

Jake hissed a cuss word before apologizing to her.

"Swear as much as you need to. It must hurt like the devil." Lauren frowned as Chance worked to place Jake's foot back into the correct position.

"Effing!" Jake yelled.

"Got it. Take a slow breath. Easy, Jake. I'll wrap everything so we can transport…"

"I'm not going anywhere until I find my mare. Bess was startled by a rattler. It took me by surprise when she reared up. Not like her." He paused and grimaced.

"It's all right. Rest now. You can tell us in a while."

"No. I need to find my horse and make sure she's okay." Jake's face reddened when he tried to stand.

"Hey, sit back. I'll search for your horse."

Both Jake and Chance stared at her.

"You?" they said in unison.

"Lady L, she's a gentle mount, but my Bess is scared or she wouldn't have thrown me. I don't think the snake bit her, but I can't be sure. I…"

"I need to transport you—now," Chance interrupted.

"It's okay, I'll find her." Lauren did her best to smile. "I spent much of my childhood on horseback. The San Fernando Valley has stables and places to ride. It doesn't matter if you have a Western or English saddle, I can…"

"We were out in the woods when Bess reared and ran off," Jake interrupted. "I couldn't walk and had to drag myself back here to the house. That's why I called at this time of the night."

"Oh, my God."

"Lady L, the mare could be anywhere."

"We should leave the horse until tomorrow." Chance stood up and packed his bag.

"You go ahead and take Jake to the hospital. I'll find Bess."

"I don't like the idea," Chance protested, his expression turning grim.

"Go. I'm okay." She held up her smartphone.

"All right, but text me if you need me—I mean it."

She waved as the fire truck backed out of the large graveled area.

For the first time, she realized how dark the rural area was and shivered as a chill ran down her back. She hadn't even asked what the damned mare looked like. Still, Jake was depending on her. Could she deliver what she'd promised?

Chapter 17

Chance did his best to soothe Jake and assure him the hospital staff would take excellent care of him. Apparently, Jake had never been in a medical center of any kind during his rather long life. The thought of giving up control and letting others take over worried him and he said it out loud.

Not the first time, Chance had to calm a victim of a calamity. All too often, the people he tried to help were taken by surprise when sudden circumstances beset their comfort zone.

He radioed ahead and let ER know what he had for them.

At the small local hospital, the nurses were waiting and quickly brought Jake inside. Chance promised to talk to the doctor. So, he entered the emergency waiting room.

He pushed down the desire to go back to the ranch and find Lauren. Was she safe? He should have made her come with him. Still, by her expression and body language, he'd understood her mind was made up. He wouldn't be able to change her resolve.

Jake was his patient and Chance mustn't forget his first duty. A grown woman, Lauren could make her own way. If she managed to stay unharmed in the streets of LA with the high crime rate and such, she would handle the current situation—right? He had to be.

The acid in Chance's empty stomach increased at the thought of her being on the unfamiliar property, searching for a frightened horse who didn't know her.

He tried to convince himself he would worry about anyone in her situation. Not true. Yeah, he might have a minor concern, but not the gut-turning anxiety running through him at this moment. He had begun to care for Lauren. A determined career woman with no interest in beginning part of a family, she didn't meet any of his preconceived ideas of the female he wanted to spend his life with. All the same time, she aroused a desire in him so strong he couldn't deny it.

As expected, Jake needed surgery and would spend at least a couple of days in the hospital recuperating. In a larger clinic, there would have been a surgeon available in the middle of the night. But his friend would have to wait until the next morning. Again, Chance was reminded of the medical shortcomings of living in a rural location.

***

In the living room of the small ranch house, Lauren scanned the photos. What kind of horse was Bess, a quarter horse, appaloosa, mustang, or Arabian?

It didn't matter, because no other horse would be roaming the night with an empty saddle.

She should have asked which direction to search first. Lauren shrugged. Jake had said she could be anywhere. With a flashlight from her car's emergency kit, she walked past the barn and found what appeared to be a well-worn trail. An obvious choice, but would the mare think so?

Unseen in the trees lining the path, an owl hooted. Had she awakened him from his sleep? She stifled a yawn and was reminded that because Jake couldn't work, a day of work waited for her in the morning. She would be in charge of the Hitching Post on her own. With the hope Jake didn't suffer a serious injury, she tried to remember the important information he imparted while they worked together.

On Sunday, there'd be no leisurely day off with Chance taking her to find jewels for her designs. More than the end of the gem search was the loss of the time spent with him. The thought astonished her. He didn't meet her standards. He had a dangerous job, a mediocre income, and wanted a gaggle of kids—no, definitely not on her agenda.

Ben would be right for her—a safe job, a high income, and a secure future. She had been ignoring his texts. Tomorrow, she'd call him.

She was startled when the owl hooted again and a critter rustled in the tall grass near her. She couldn't recall ever being this alone. *Afraid of the dark?* She laughed at her foolishness. Totally by herself, no one could hurt her—except the horse, or a snake, she corrected her thought.

A snake? Her breathing quickened. What had she done trying to show off to prove she could do it on her own? *Stupid.* Now, she must come through and find Jake's mare or seem a bragging fool.

With the flashlight showing the way she ran down the narrow trail. She stumbled but caught herself before she fell. She glanced up to find the path opened to a meadow.

She waved the light over the area and the field appeared empty. The yellow grass must be at least waist-deep. Bess was nowhere in sight.

Damn.

Jake did warn her the mare might be anywhere. With due care, she returned to the beginning of the search and went in the opposite direction. As Lauren passed the barn, she snagged a handful of hay to offer as a reward if she found Bess and could get close to her.

The sky was still dark, and Lauren felt like she had walked for hours. The flashlight dimmed. It probably needed new batteries.

She rubbed her eyes and let out a yawn. No point in stifling it. She was by herself. Her muscles started to ache, demanding sleep. She twisted her back to release the tension and yawned again. The yellow grass was beginning to appear inviting. She might curl up and take a quick nap.

I'm done. If I don't find Bess in the next five minutes, I'm leaving.

She shook the light to increase the beam and scanned the ground. Nothing.

A horse whined.

"Bess?" Lauren walked forward to examine the area. A quarter horse stared at her; a western saddle was still secure on her back. The mare didn't look injured, but Lauren was too far away to be sure.

"Bess, Jake sent me." She kept her voice calm but firm. "I'm going to lead you home."

With small steps, she moved toward the horse. "You're a good girl." At first, she thought the mare might spook and run. Lauren held out the hay and said, "Bess, I brought you a treat."

Just close enough to reach the reins that dangled on the ground, she picked them up and then offered a part of the hay to the horse. Hungry, Bess took the food out of Lauren's hand.

She walked in front of the quarter horse, setting a slow pace to guide her toward the barn. Once, Bess tried to take the lead, but Lauren gently pushed her back to tell her she was the leader.

For what seemed like miles, they kept a slow pace and walked until Bess saw the barn. The mare pulled free, rushed to the building, and entered. Lauren jogged after her.

Bess went to her stall and ate. Lauren laughed with relief. The horse was happy to be home. She joined the mare and cooed sweet words and took off the saddle and blanket. She opened a gate so the quarter horse could go from the barn to the corral at will.

Thank God. She would let Jake know his precious Bess was home. Unexpected tears slid down her face. Until now, she didn't realize the amount of stress she'd been under.

"What's wrong? Are you hurt?"

She glanced up to see Chance coming toward her, emotion showing in the concerned expression on his face. When he got near, he brushed a tear from her cheek.

"Lauren, you're bleeding." He reached for her arm.

"I am?" She stared at a deep scratch. "I didn't feel it. I guess it happened when I stumbled." She tried to smile.

"Come to the truck."

It was an order. She was too tired to argue.

He cleaned the wound.

"Ouch. It stings."

"Sorry. It's important to make sure the wound is free of contaminants. The antibiotic cream has a pain killer that will help." With gentle strokes, he applied the ointment and a bandage.

"I was worried about you." He pushed her hair from her face and gazed at her.

"You were?" A flash of heat ran through her.

"Yeah." He bent toward her. Standing so near, she sensed he told the truth because his piercing blue eyes reflected his inner apprehension.

"I don't want anything to happen to you, Lauren."

"You don't?"

"No."

He took her in his arms. She let her head rest against his broad chest, closed her eyes and listened to his steady heartbeat as his powerful arms holding her up. Safe. No one else made her feel that way.

Bess whined.

Chanced pulled back.

"You found her."

"Yeah, Bess was miles from here and I brought her to the barn."

"Well, I'll be darned."

Chapter 18

Lauren dismissed the alarm on her phone. She was already awake and, in the kitchen, about to scramble an egg for breakfast before taking a quick shower and going off to work at the Hitching Post.

She had stayed awake much of the night hoping to talk to Chance and find out about Jake. She'd even walked down the driveway and discovered the fire engine was nowhere to be seen.

This morning, it still wasn't at the farm and she began to worry about Chance as well as Jake.

She took her plate with egg, toast, and orange slices to the deck in front of the cottage. She needed a strong mug of coffee. Better make sure she had time to stop at Sophie's Ice Cream Parlor and grab one on the way to work.

The engine of the fire truck sounded in the quiet Sunday morning.

Chance.

Lauren squelched the idea of running down the driveway to meet him and tell him how worried she had been. They were only neighbors. He had no reason to explain his goings-on. Still, she could ask about Jake.

The smell of smoke preceded him up the drive. In full gear, his fire helmet in his hand, his shoulders slumped. Though his blue eyes were bloodshot, his expression brightened when he saw her.

"Hey." He smiled.

"Hey, yourself." She grinned. "Was there a big fire last night?"

Chance walked to the railing of the cottage's deck and leaned forward. "A grass fire, I got the call after I left you. The blaze was too damned close to some houses. I had to call out a couple of the volunteers in the middle of the night."

"Dear God."

"We got it in time. A good thing someone saw the fire and called 911, or…"

"Come in and I'll make you breakfast. You must be starved." She couldn't believe she'd said that. If she hurried, she had just about enough time to get to Sophie's for coffee and make it to work as planned.

He hesitated, then nodded. "But I'll stay outside. Don't want to bring the smell of smoke into your home."

"Are eggs, toast, and orange juice all right?"

"Exactly what I need." He left the railing, moved up the steps to her deck, and sat down in a chase lounge with a sigh. "Thanks."

"No problem." She ran inside and realized she was still in her skimpy baby-doll pajamas. What must he think? If he noticed, Chance didn't mention it.

She rushed into the bedroom and threw on a white T-shirt and blue cotton pants.

She cooked three eggs over easy, toasted four pieces of pumpernickel bread from Claus Mueller's Swiss Bakery, and plated them. Enough food for a man as sizeable as Chance? She had no idea. With utensils, a glass of orange juice, salt and pepper shakers, and strawberry jam added to the tray, she returned to the deck.

"Sorry, I don't have any coffee."

"No worries. After I eat, I'm going to bed."

Their eyes caught and held for a minute. Was he thinking what she was thinking?

He stood and stripped off his jacket. His broad, muscled chest expanded as a deep breath stretched the buttons of his navy-blue shirt.

OMG. Don't stare.

Sitting forward, he dug into the food. She watched him in her peripheral vision. A warm sensation arose in her.

"How's Jake?" She broke her mood before she did or said something incredibly stupid.

"A compound ankle fracture. He's going to require surgery and time to recover."

"That must be painful."

"Yeah. We don't realize how essential the ankle is until we can't use it." He finished his fourth piece of toast covered in jam.

"Jake's lucky you were there."

He shrugged. "My job." He stifled a yawn.

She took the tray. "Go get some rest."

He stood and nodded, then touched her cheek with the back of his hand. "Thanks, Laurie." He picked up his gear and left.

Laurie. No one ever called her that.

For a moment, she forgot she was almost late for work and froze, staring at his strong back as Chance walked up the stairs to his place. She jumped when his front door slammed closed.

Shit. She'd promised herself to be on time, or early today. Was she already in trouble with her boss?

***

Even though Lauren drove her car too fast on the small country road leading into town and skipped stopping at Sophie's Ice Cream Parlor for coffee, when she arrived at the Hitching Post, Mr. Smith stood glaring at her.

She tried to smile at him, but couldn't manage it.

Instead, she thought of the best way to tell her boss what had happened last night and explain why she was late again.

Would it make a difference? She shook her head as fear of being fired ran through her.

"You're late, Miss Walsh!" Smithy's eyes narrowed as his frown deepened.

Turning away from him, she went to the workstation and began to do her job as if nothing unusual was going on. Still, her back burned as Mr. Smith stared. Oh, she didn't see him, but she sensed the intensity of his glare.

At last, a woman entered the front door and Lauren breathed a sigh of relief. The boss wouldn't fire her in front of a customer. Right?

Thankful the tourists were plentiful today, her boss needed help to run the outlet. So, she worked as if it was a normal day. She smiled and kept up small talk with each shopper, whether they were strangers or townspeople.

Lauren shivered whenever Mr. Smith glanced in her direction. She ignored his grim expression and did her best to carry on, showing people products they wanted and a few things they hadn't thought of.

Glad she ate breakfast; lunch was out of the question as tourists poured into the Hitching Post looking for souvenirs.

A flustered woman entered with two boisterous kids underfoot, but they left with a smile, the children dressed in cowboy hats and boots.

"Thanks for stopping by." Lauren waved as the woman left.

I'm a damned good salesperson. If I do say so myself. Jake had laughed at her when she'd ordered western hats and boots for kids.

She thought of the man who'd been kind to her and prayed Jake would be all right.

As the day went on, lack of sleep and coffee didn't help her energy level, but she pushed forward.

To his credit, Mr. Smith carried his weight by lugging the heavy feed bags into the store without asking for assistance. Anyway, being a girl, he probably thought she was too weak to be of help. Truth be known, Jake always managed that part of stocking the shelves. So, Mr. Smith might be correct.

At about two thirty in the afternoon, her boss snarled, "Girl, go buy some lunch. I'm tired of listening to your stomach growl—twenty minutes, no more."

She texted Vanna at Sophie's Ice Cream Parlor and when she arrived, was greeted with a turkey on rye and a steaming cup of coffee with a dollop of whipping cream.

She and Vanna sat at a corner table on the back wall. Unable to stop, Lauren spewed out the news of Jake's accident and the night spent searching for his horse. Now, she waited to be fired. Incapable of holding it back, a tear slid down her cheek.

"Lauren, does Mr. Smith know you were late because of what you went through with Jake last night?"

She shook her head. "The other day, he told me he didn't care what my excuse might be." She shook her head. "Mr. Smith said if he caught me coming in after opening, I could pack up and go. My job would be over."

"Lauren, no!"

"When I moved here, I hated this town. Don't look so shocked, Vanna. I didn't mean there was anything wrong with the place. It was me. I didn't understand, no shopping malls, no movie theaters, no fast-food restaurants..."

She took a deep breath. "How was I supposed to live in this Podunk place?" She hoped she hadn't insulted her friend and quickly added. "But now, I don't want to leave Sierra Creek. You've all been so nice and I'm learning to do without the things I thought were so important. Not to be corny, but I'm realizing what's necessary to enjoy life." Her shoulders slumped.

"Hey, Lauren, I lived in LA too. I know how vital the right car, correct clothes, and expensive zip code can seem to be. I bought into the game, the race to have the best, most luxurious, greatest—everything." Vanna frowned. "It all seems insignificant today."

"Yeah." Lauren forced a few bites of the sandwich down her constricted throat. "And just when I thought I got this small-town thing down, I blew it this morning."

"Did Mr. Smith tell you not to come back?"

"He couldn't, not until Jake is better, but after that..."

"I'm sorry, Lauren. Maybe things will work out."

"I hope."

People lined up at the counter and Vanna ran to help her mother.

111

Thinking of spending the rest of the day with a scowling boss, Lauren dreaded returning to the Hitching Post.

Buck up! She wouldn't be depressed or give up her dream. She came to Sierra Creek to learn from Mr. Smith and that was going to happen if she had anything to say about it.

Her phone alarm rang. She had three minutes to get back to work on time. With a "goodbye and thanks," shouted to Vanna, she sprinted out of the ice cream parlor toward the Hitching Post.

At the door, she squared her shoulders and forced a smile on her face. She was going to make Mr. Smith like her and recognize her talent—but perhaps not today.

The rest of the afternoon went by quickly with tourists filling the shop. Much of the day, her boss disappeared, but she managed to handle the rush of customers on her own.

Later, she closed and locked the front door and flipped over the sign on the window from open to closed. She scanned the shop, straightened shelves, counted out the cash registers, and left the amount for Mr. Smith, putting the register drawers in the safe.

Her boss appeared from nowhere. His expression was unreadable. "Take tomorrow off, but be here on time on Tuesday."

"What? Uh, yes, sir—thank you."

Mr. Smith left the room.

***

Lauren sat in her convertible with the top down and surveyed the downtown area. She rubbed her eyes and sighed. Her job appeared to be safe, at least for as long as her boss needed assistance. Dad would never know how close he came to not receiving the promised money she sent to him every month.

A kind man, but too often life was a struggle for Daddy. Keeping a job seemed difficult even before his rheumatoid arthritis became a serious problem. The most she would say about his employment record while she was growing up was spotty at best and dismal at worst. Her mother carried the load of supporting the family. A nurse, her mother had loved the work. Lauren couldn't recall her mom ever complaining about heading the household.

Lauren remembered the day, in high school, when a collision on the Ventura freeway took her mother from her.

Back then, Lauren had found a retail job after school and on weekends to help the family. She had planned to be further along in her career by this time in her life. But what was the saying about best-laid plans?

She shook off the thought. *Make it work, Lauren. You're not the type to give up—remember that.* She could almost hear her mother's voice.

With a sigh, she called the hospital and talked to Jake, relieved to find his voice strong. The poor guy put on a good front, but she sensed he was exhausted and in pain. She did her best to be cheerful and let him understand she missed him at the Hitching Post. She promised promise to visit tomorrow and would take care of his animals, not to worry.

As she drove toward Jake's home, a warm breeze caressed her face, sending the realization that summer was nearing an end. What would autumn bring?

At Jake's property, she spied a fire engine parked in the driveway.

Chance.

Chapter 19

Chance didn't need to turn around. He recognized the sound of Lauren's German car.

He got out, leaned against the fire truck, and waited for her. He hadn't planned on seeing her again. He'd told himself he didn't want to. Trim legs, firm breasts, gorgeous hair, and eyes that flashed, she was damned appealing. Despite that, she represented everything he didn't want in his lady, a self-absorbed, career first, family last, citified kind of a woman. Still, the thought of running his fingers through her long brown hair, then opening her mouth to let his tongue play with hers, sent heat to his lower extremities.

"Chance, aren't you going to say hi?"

He scanned her. Tight jeans and a loose blouse opened low enough for a man to wonder what it would be like to undo the next button and scan the flesh hidden by the cotton fabric.

"Hey, Lauren." His voice was husky even to his ears. "What brings you out here?"

"Probably the same thing as you—the animals."

"Yep. I wondered about Jake's cat. He puts too much stock in that feral beast. He treats it like a baby, but every man makes his own choice."

"Yeah, yeah, you don't want to look like a softy, caring about a kitty." Lauren grinned. "Your secret's safe with me."

Chance couldn't help chuckling. "Let's go see if the horse you rounded up last night is still here."

He couldn't resist hooking his arm in hers. When she didn't pull away, they moved together toward the barn.

"Lauren, hope my uncle wasn't too grumpy at work today."

"Well, I came in late, but I still have a job." She cringed. "I thought my goose was cooked."

"Hey, he's not too good with people. All the same, the folks in town are used to him, or so I'm told."

"I don't know if I can get used to him."

"The old dog has a bark that is worse than his bite."

"I'll tell him that the next time he growls and wants to bite."

He laughed again and she joined him.

"I needed that, Chance." She squeezed his arm. "You're nice to be around."

Damn. Against his better judgment, he wanted to kiss her.

He let go of her arm, quickened his steps toward the barn, and resisted looking back at her.

If Lauren noticed, she didn't say anything.

In the barn, he yanked down hay from the loft and opened a bag of oats for the horses.

"I'll find the cat, feed it, then make sure it has water and fresh litter," Chance offered. "You'll take care of the horse—right? By the way, Jake owns a stallion too. He's friendly enough, unlike many steeds I've met."

"You ride?"

"Yeah." He flicked away a wasp. "That's where I met Wyatt and Manny. We were all on the rodeo circuit together, remember."

"I never thought of you on a horse."

"Laurie, the bucking rodeo ponies agreed with you." Chance scratched his head. "I didn't last long on the circuit. My heart and my rump weren't in it." He grinned. "Still, Manny, Wyatt, and I have stayed friends. So, when the opportunity to work in Sierra Creek came up, I grabbed it."

"Chance, we should ride together after the work is finished."

"Might. The horses sure need the exercise." He rubbed his chin and imagined her in the saddle, wavy brown hair flowing behind her as the breeze brought color to her cheeks, then wondered if going with her was a smart idea.

"I better get started. I also want to stack a cord of wood close to the back door so Jake can grab it, even with the medical boot he's going to wear."

"Remember the kitty, Chance."

"It's on my list."

They separated to take care of their chores.

In about an hour, he finished his work and decided to go for a horseback ride with Lauren. Though they had different life goals, there was no reason not to be friends.

When he didn't find her in the barn, he went to the driveway and discovered her car was gone.

***

As Lauren drove from Jake's house, she texted Dad's neighbor. Zoe had sent a message saying Daddy was in the hospital. She gave no reason. Lauren thought of phoning her but doubted there was a cell tower anywhere nearby. The call wouldn't go through.

Anxious, her hands shook as she held the steering wheel and made a tight turn to the local highway heading back to town.

On Main Street, she'd find a strong signal, and then a call could go through. She'd have answers in a moment, assuming her father's neighbor picked up the phone.

She should have said something to Chance before she took off. At the time, all she thought of was reaching her father.

She sighed and drove faster.

At the Hitching Post parking lot, the phone signal was strong. Lauren tapped her contacts list and found Zoe's number.

As she feared, the phone rang and rang until it went to voice mail.

With a frown, she wondered if she should keep trying or go back to the cottage where Wi-Fi was okay but not completely dependable.

She redialed and waited.

A breathless Zoe answered, "Lauren? Oh God, I don't know what to do."

"Please calm down and tell me what's happened."

She listened as her dad's neighbor did her best to explain the problem. After a fall in the bathroom, Daddy couldn't get up. Zoe had found him and had the sense to call 911. He had been taken to the nearest hospital and was in the emergency room being checked over by doctors.

As she spoke, Lauren could hear Zoe's voice trembling. In a minute, she would be crying.

"You did the right thing by calling for help. I'm so grateful and sorry this landed on your shoulders, Zoe. I should have been with him."

"Don't worry dear. The hospital staff will take care of him."

"Yeah, of course."

"Let's think positive." Zoe sniffed. "Your father will be home in a little while."

"Okay. Please stay in touch." Lauren disconnected the call.

Was her father seriously injured? *Dear God, please keep him safe.*

With her phone in hand, Lauren paced the empty Sierra Creek parking lot. After an online search, she found the number of the hospital where her father had been taken. On hold, while the operator transferred her to the emergency room, she stopped walking and began to stress. He might not have taken a tumble if she still lived with him.

On a Sunday evening, most people in Sierra Creek were at home. She should be home too, in her condo in the San Fernando Valley. She'd been selfish to leave to work with Mr. Smith. If she had stayed put, she'd be with her dad tonight.

Guilt for failing Daddy struck her.

"Hello. Yes, I'm here," she answered and then listened, nodding her head as she did.

She sighed, sat in the driver's seat, and slumped forward, resting her forehead on the steering wheel. Dad was not badly injured, but the ER doctor decided to keep him overnight to be sure he hadn't sustained a serious concussion.

She notified Zoe and told her what she'd found out. Assuming all went well, and nothing new popped up concerning his health, Daddy would be home in the morning.

Lauren dialed the hospital again and the nurse on his unit let her talk to him. He sounded strong and told her to stay in Sierra Creek. Even when she offered to leave and drive back to LA, he wouldn't hear of it. "Do what I think is best, Lauren. Stay where you are."

Reluctantly, she disconnected the call.

"I was worried about you when you disappeared."

Surprised, she glanced toward the sound of the deep male voice. Chance stood next to her car, a solemn expression on his face, his blue eyes staring at her.

"You all right, Lauren?"

"What are you doing here? I don't want you following me."

"I didn't. I ordered a pizza from the Italian place and parked to go get it." He frowned. "Not a lot of places to park a fire truck."

He started to leave.

"Chance wait." She jumped out of the convertible.

"Why?"

"Look, I—I..." What should she say to him?

He faced her. "Yeah?"

"Well, uh." She hesitated, wondering if she ought to mention her dad's accident.

"My food is getting cold. If you want to say something, spit it out."

"Go eat your damned pizza," she bristled. "I hope you choke on it." She got in her car, slammed the door, and drove from the parking space. In the rearview mirror, she saw a confused expression spread across his handsome face.

"What the hell? Lauren?" he yelled.

As she headed toward the cottage, Chance's angry voice lingered in her mind.

She'd taken her worry and frustration about her father, out on Chance, the person who'd been kind and not only that, the nephew of Mr. Smith, her boss.

Shit, Lauren. What's wrong with you?

At the cottage, she noticed Amy's car was gone. At least she couldn't say anything to upset her too.

In the cottage bedroom, Lauren threw herself on the bed and closed her eyes. Nothing had been right since the day she arrived in Sierra Creek. A Pollyanna, she believed everything would work out. But now, with Dad hurt, Chance angry, and Mr. Smith nasty, her urge to be creative had disappeared.

Adding to her distress, she insulted Chance at a time when she thought they were becoming friends.

In a large metropolis like LA, there are always new people to meet. If you made a mistake and burned an acquaintance, no worries, new people were available to take their place.

Not a possibility in Sierra Creek. Anyway, she didn't want to make other friends. Jake, Vanna, Amy, Sophie, and most of all Chance, were the people she cared about.

The sound of the truck's engine caught her attention. She sat up on the bed, totally alert.

Chance is home.

Chapter 20

The light was on in the cottage. Chance turned from the sight and jogged up the stairs to his attic apartment while balancing the extra-large pizza with one hand.

With the food set on the table, he threw off his coat, opened the front window, and stood waiting for the breeze to cool him down.

Lauren's behavior reminded him of his first impression of her, a self-absorbed bitch—though damned attractive. Today, emotional upset radiated from her. He ran his hand over his stubbled chin and sucked in a deep breath. Something had sent her into a tizzy. He'd experienced the same flare of temper when people were dealing with a fire on their property. Without a blaze, she didn't need to take her problems out on him.

No worries. She wasn't important to his life.

He grabbed a slice of salami and mushroom pizza and gulped it down. To enjoy the view, he usually ate the food with a cold beer on the small balcony while stretched out on a lounge chair. Not tonight.

His gaze strayed toward the cottage and Lauren. He grunted in disgust. No matter how appealing she might be, they were headed toward different futures—how many times did he have to be reminded?

He closed the window, sat at the table, took another slice of pizza, and chewed more slowly this time.

Tomorrow during lunch, he'd stop by Mel's Diner and ask the cute waitress who worked there for a date. Though not as good-looking as Lauren, she seemed friendly enough and liked living in the small berg of Sierra Creek. His intention: put down roots and build a family as well as a career in the town.

A rap on the door brought him back to the present.

Could be Wyatt wanted to discuss the Tuesday meeting with the architectural firm which would mean finishing the designs for the new firehouse.

Chance swung his tired body out of the chair, walked to the door, and yanked it open.

Lauren stood staring up at him, a tentative smile on her makeup-free face. Appearing fresh from the shower, her long hair looked damp. She wore a pink sleeveless sundress and stood barefoot, pink nails shining on her toes. Anger towards her dissipated. Desire replaced it.

"Can I come in?"

He cleared his throat and moved out of the way to let her enter.

"I'm having dinner. There's plenty. Take a seat."

She sat across the table from him. "I'm not really hungry. I. Well, I… Uh, maybe a slice."

He snagged a plate and handed it to her.

"Hm," She wiped her chin after one bite, then put the pizza on the plate he'd given her. "I was a total bitch tonight." She stopped.

If Lauren thought he would contradict her, she was mistaken.

To fill the silence, he offered her a beer. To his surprise. she accepted.

"I don't usually drink, but after today—sure."

She took a swig, coughed, then took a smaller sip. "Good."

"A local brewery in town."

As he watched her fidget, a strained silence filled the room.

"Chance, I should have told you I was leaving Jake's."

He gulped his pale ale.

"You aren't going to make it easy, are you?"

He shrugged.

"Okay, I'm here to apologize. I don't know why I yelled at you." She paused again. "I'm a mess tonight—I'm not excusing my behavior, but…"

Her hands were shaking and moisture filled her eyes. "At Jake's, I got a text from my dad's neighbor. Daddy fell and was taken to the hospital." She sniffed. "I tried to call Zoe, but there was no service at Jake's place."

He sat forward. "Sorry to hear about your father."

"I should've said something before I drove off. All I thought of was going somewhere my phone would work and find out how badly Dad was injured."

She stood and walked to the window. "Nice view here."

Surprised at the change of subject, he managed to say, "Yeah." He moved close enough to touch her. "Your dad, how is he?"

"Nothing broken, he has bruises and a slight concussion. The doctor is keeping him overnight in the hospital to be sure." She sniffed again. "I feel so guilty. I should be with him."

"What does he want?"

"Daddy told me to stay. He says he can manage on his own. Still, I can't stop thinking if I'd been home, he wouldn't have fallen. He has arthritis, you see, but won't use a cane and doesn't listen to me about being careful."

"Your dad is a man. Men are proud creatures." He hesitated, wondering what her reaction might be to what he was about to tell her. "Don't take that away from him."

She faced him, her hands flat against his chest. "What do you know?"

His muscles tensed at her touch as he reached for her, turning her face up towards his. "I was injured once."

"In a fire?"

"Yeah. Bedridden, powerless to do much for myself. I was useless. But my family understood enough not to force their help on me. They waited for me to ask and that let me maintain my pride."

"I only want to take care of him."

"I get it. But as a grown man, his job is to stand on his own. Don't rob him of the opportunity to prove he can still do it. Let him keep his self-respect. I may be wrong, but I think he'll thank you for it."

She reached up and caressed his cheek with her delicate hand, her eyes wide with emotion. "I don't know what to say—thank you."

Wrong time, wrong place, wrong woman, nevertheless, he bent down to kiss her, stopped before his lips reached hers. Still, heat coursed through him and by her expression, she had the same reaction.

Instead of pulling away, she leaned forward and clung to him, causing ripples of yearning to rage. "Lauren, it's late and we've both had a tough day."

"Yeah." She slowly moved out of his arms, then shivered.

He walked her to the door and flipped on the porch light, so he could watch her until she entered the cottage.

On his porch, moths flew way too near the heat of the incandescent light bulb.

The poor creatures didn't understand what they were doing, but he knew better. "Buddy, you're playing with fire."

Chapter 21

At the farmhouse, Wyatt smiled at Amy when she returned to the kitchen table. His wife was looking more and more beautiful and pregnant.

Finally, the unrelenting nausea had retreated and to his relief, Amy appeared healthy again. Now that she was able to hold food down, the doctor okayed her to return to work at the mill's preschool.

Early in the pregnancy, he had hidden his anxiety. Fearing they might lose the baby he'd concealed his concern from her. If Amy realized his apprehension, she never let on.

"I want to thank Vanna for holding down the fort alone at the preschool. I'm looking forward to seeing the kids again. I didn't realize how much I'd miss them."

"Bet Vanna will be happy you're back." He took her hand, held it, and became serious. "Honey, I won't be able to go to lunch with you today. Manny, Chance, and I have a final meeting with the architects."

"I'll miss you—but that's exciting. Are the designs all finished?"

"I hope so. Chance has the final say. The townspeople are lucky he's our new fire chief. The guy could've gone to a bigger community and made more money." Wyatt stood from the table and bent to kiss her, then patted her belly. "You two have a good day and Amy, drive carefully."

"I love you, honey."

"You too." He grinned. "More than you know."

On the way to the pickup, he waved at Chance, who was heading toward the fire truck. "See you at the meeting."

"Wyatt, do you have a second?" Chance stopped.

"Sure, what's up?"

***

Chance joined Wyatt in the pickup and took a deep breath. Where to start?

He was the new man on the block and didn't want to lose his friend's confidence. He needed his support. But something was going on in this small community and it could be dangerous.

"Buddy, what's up?" Wyatt sat back and waited for him to speak.

"I want to thank you for letting me be involved in the design of the firehouse."

"Naturally, we wanted your involvement."

"But that isn't the reason I need to talk to you." Chance rubbed his hand over his clean-shaven chin. "I don't know if you're aware of it, but in the outskirts of Sierra Creek, there have been three grass fires. The one the other night was near, Johnny and Sophie's place."

"I don't like the sound of that." Wyatt leaned toward him, possibly waiting for an explanation.

"Hey, long story short, I checked out each of the fires. They were all too similar. There was no campfire out of control, no Firecrackers from teens, and no dry lightning to cause them. I'm not an expert arson investigator, but there are signs that accelerants were used to set off the fires. That is suspicious."

"Chance, you're telling me—what?"

He avoided the question for the moment and instead asked, "Do you know of any other recent flare-ups?"

"Nothing in the open space." His friend began to say more but hesitated. Then he continued, "As you know, we had a fire at the mill. It was an accident. Still, we realized the volunteer fire department wasn't enough to protect Sierra Creek. So, we advertised and hired you."

"Well," Chance wiped the sweat from his forehead. "I'm not saying you have a firebug in the area, but it should be considered."

Wyatt frowned. "This time of year, the fields are damned dry and the trees are struggling without rain. I hate to believe a person would ignite a blaze on purpose, especially with the drought and lack of water available to fight infernos."

"I've made a plan for firebreaks in the community." Chance took a deep breath. "The people should do their share. We need the brush and shrubs cut away from the homes and barns. So, if there is a fire, we'll be better able to handle it."

"Manny and I can speak with Mayor Breen. Let's put it on the agenda for the town council meeting this week and make everyone understand what needs to be undertaken." He paused. "Chance, as fire chief, would you be willing to speak to the town officials mapping out a strategy to get the work done and explain the reasons?"

"Sure. Too early to mention the possibility of a firebug, but I'll suggest a plan to clear the underbrush to protect property and create a fireguard."

"Good. By the way, I hope you're wrong about a fire starter."

"Me too, but…"

Chance left the pickup and waved as his buddy drove out of the driveway. *Hell.* He wanted to think he was overreacting regarding a possible arsonist, but too many clues were pointing in that direction.

He wiped perspiration from his face. Even with the dried leaves falling from the trees, the heat of the morning felt like summer, but then, September was often the hottest month of the year. He threw off his flannel shirt and carried it over his shoulder, leaving only the light blue T-shirt he wore underneath.

The sound of the cottage door closing caused Chance to turn around.

"Hi," Lauren said a little breathlessly.

"Hey, you on your way to the Hitching Post?" He scanned her tooled leather cowgirl boots, tight blue jeans, and a white cotton shirt.

"I have the day off." As if embarrassed by his gaze, she pushed her golden-brown hair back and glanced away from him. "I plan to grab a few things from the store, then visit Jake's animals."

Realizing his stare made her nervous, he glanced down the driveway toward his truck, but asked, "How's your dad doing?"

"All right. He'll be home this afternoon. I talked to him this morning and he sounded like his old self again." She wiped the moisture from her eyes. "The doctor gave him orders to get a cane. He'll be fitted for it before he leaves the medical center. Hey, what about you?"

"Sunday and Monday are usually my days off, but I'm on my way to a meeting." Avoiding eye contact, he glanced in her direction. "Afterward, I could meet you at Jake's and we could exercise the horses like we meant to do the other day."

She looked surprised but seemed to quickly recover. "I'd like that. I could use the exercise too." She laughed.

Always so serious, that he couldn't often recall hearing Lauren giggle. It sent a ripple of satisfaction running through him and made him consider how to encourage her to do it again.

"I'll see you." He stopped short of saying "It's a date."

What was he thinking? He planned to lunch at Mel's and ask the pretty waitress out.

His phone alarm warned him he needed to hurry if he wanted to be on time for the conference.

An hour and a half afterward, he leaned back in the truck, took a deep breath, and stretched. Until this second, he hadn't realized how tense he was or how much it meant to him to view the architectural blueprints for the firehouse.

As expected, there were a few tweaks needed. Still, pleased the meeting had gone well, he had to give credit to the firm. They'd allowed his input. Wyatt, Manny, and Mayor Breen had okayed the design changes he recommended, putting their faith in his expertise. That meant a lot to him. Though it heaped a load of responsibility on his shoulders. Nonetheless, he'd come into the job of fire chief with his eyes wide open. As assistant chief in the Bay Area, he'd paid his dues. All he had to do now—not let Sierra Creek down.

With the consultation over, he decided to enjoy the rest of the day. Odd spending time with Lauren was part of his indulgence.

He tried to believe it was the opportunity to be on horseback again, after such a long absence, that pleased him. He shook his head. *You were never good at lying to yourself, or anyone else.*

The sun shone on the dry grass of the fields, making them appear like golden filaments and the heat increased as he steered the truck toward Jake's modest ranch.

As he expected, Lauren's car was parked where it had been the other night.

He found her in the barn, pitchfork in hand, tossing hay into the feeding trough.

"Hey, Chance. You made it." She grinned and pushed her hair out of her eyes. "How did your meeting go?"

"Fine." Spotting Lauren shoveling hay, it was hard to believe she didn't belong on a ranch. "Ready for a ride? We can let the horses eat after they cool down from their outing."

"Okay. The horses are saddled and ready to go."

"The stallion let you near him?"

"Yeah. Like you said, Chance, he's not so tough. I mean, if you're not afraid of him."

"Well, I'll be... Jake told me a woman couldn't get close to the ornery cuss, not to mention throwing a saddle on his back."

She leaned the pitchfork on the barn wall and put a hand on her hip. "I just told him I had ridden many a stallion, so, he might as well relax."

He laughed, imagining her giving the steed what for.

In the corral, she mounted the mare like an expert. He was reminded she had vaulted when she was a kid. *Damn, she must have been cute.*

"Whoa, boy. "He calmed his spirited horse before straddling the black charger. "Laurie, go out of the corral, to the left, and follow the trail."

131

Chapter 22

Lauren coaxed the horse out of the fenced pen and headed up the trail Chance had pointed out. He followed, letting her take the lead.

Her mount whinnied, probably surprised to be allowed to go first. She glanced back at Chance as he held the reins of his charger, probably telling the stallion the ladies were to go first. It pawed the ground with its front hoof, undoubtedly declaring that was not the usual way things were done.

"Laurie, ride to where the trail widens, then I'll give this boy free rein."

She waved and made an okay sign with her right hand.

He'd called her Laurie again. The sound of his deep voice sent a flash of heat spiraling in her. She didn't want to admit she liked him using the name—but that was the truth.

It didn't take much encouragement to inspire her mare. With a gentle nudge, she took off. Lauren grinned and realized the poor thing had been in the corral for too long.

Gripping the reins, she let the horse gallop and enjoyed the ride. She couldn't stop smiling, remembering she had been indoors as well.

After a bit, the thick forest lessened and the trail opened up.

The stallion snorted and rushed by, Chance appearing to urge him forward. As he and his mount hurried on there was no point in trying to keep up with them.

"It's okay." She patted her pony. "We'll catch up to them in a bit." With a leisurely canter, they made their way in the direction of the stallion and Chance. He appeared fearless on horseback and ready for anything that might be encountered. Was that why he was assigned the nickname Chance?

Shortly, she found him and the black beauty shading themselves under a pine tree.

"Hey, Laurie. I thought we could rest here and cool down."

"Sure." She dismounted. "I brought snacks for us."

"Great." He threw the blanket that had been rolled up on the western saddle and set it out under the tree.

With the horses tied to the lower branches of a spreading pine, she and Chance leaned against the trunk.

"Wow, long time since I've ridden." She rubbed her rear end.

"Got to develop your saddle muscles again, though they look fine to me." He winked.

She glared at him, then burst into laughter. "Nice of you to notice." A stupid thing to say, her cheeks burned with embarrassment.

He looked to be about to respond to her statement, but instead, he said, "You mentioned food?"

Afterward, the conversation was stilted at first, but while they munched on the banana bread Sophie now offered in her ice cream parlor, Lauren began to relax.

Chance had funny stories of his time on the rodeo circuit with Manny and Wyatt. He told of the moment he knew he wasn't meant to be a champion on the circuit. "The last time I was thrown off a bucking bronc and landed hard on the ground, I understood rodeoing had never been the right choice for me—time to leave."

"Were you disappointed?"

"Not really. In my heart, I always knew my life on the circuit would be a short one."

"Why do it?"

"Well, to be honest, to go against my family's plans for me—immature, but I wasn't much more than a kid." He wiped breadcrumbs from his lips. "Back in the day, I was right out of high school and wanted to experience life—excitement, danger."

"Is that why people call you Chance?"

"Uh, no. It stands for Chancellor, for my granddad. I'm named after him."

"Is he called Chance too?"

He chuckled. "No one would dare—hey, don't get me wrong, he's a great guy, but he demands respect—meaning we use his full name."

"I never met my grandfather. He passed before I was born." She shook off her disappointment.

Silent, she thought about how to brighten the mood. "You all remained friends after you left the circuit?"

"Yeah, the one good thing to come out of that misadventure—meeting them. Being an amateur, I was lucky I didn't break my neck." He grinned, before swallowing the last bite of bread. "They helped me find my current job."

"I don't mean to pry." She hesitated, wondering if she should ask. "If your parents didn't want you riding the circuit, what did they want you to do?"

He stretched, appearing unperturbed by her inquiry. "It was never a question. I would follow in the footsteps of the men in the family."

"Be a firefighter?"

"Yep, like the generations before me." He reached over and slid his arm around her shoulder. "Move closer. There's more shade near me."

She felt the flex of his muscled arm as he coaxed her to rest her head against his broad chest. Still, he didn't make a move on her as she thought he might. Instead, he seemed content to hold her.

Shortly afterward, she asked, "You want to know something odd?"

"Sure."

"Most people dream of being in wide open spaces." She stopped.

"Yeah?"

"It scares me a little. I mean, I've spent my life living in a high rise. When I looked out of my window, I faced another building of equal size. Rows of buildings, no panoramic views." She swallowed hard, fearing she was making a fool of herself. "At night the street glistened with twinkling lights in the nearby condos." She took a slow breath. "But here in the country, there's nothing to see, no people, no buildings, no lights. I'm not sure if I like it and it's so quiet at night."

"You're used to the city." He glanced at her with a kind expression. "I grew up in one too—San Francisco. This is a change for me as well. Don't worry, the country is an acquired taste. Give it some time."

135

Warmth spiraled in her as she stared up at him, wanting a kiss, needing it more than she believed possible.

He wasn't the type of man she'd planned to attract. Chance was dangerous to her life's agenda. Tempting, but he might get in the way of her best-laid plans.

The pressure of his lips on hers stopped all thought. Emotions she'd never experienced shot through her.

She sighed and leaned into his embrace.

Coming to her senses, she moved out of his arms. "The horses must be cooled down by now."

Lauren jumped up and walked toward the mare. "Guess we ought to move along."

"Whatever you say. With rapid movements, Chance folded the blanket and tied it to his saddle. "I wanted to show you something not too far from here."

"Okay."

As they rode side by side, he talked about the land and how much the surrounding acres meant to the town.

"Sounds like it does to you too. You're a convert from a city guy to what?"

"You tell me." He laughed. "Hey, the place I want to show you is next to the outcropping just ahead."

They galloped toward the rocks and dismounted, tying the horses to a manzanita bush.

"Does all this property belong to Jake?"

"We left his land before we stopped for a snack. This is county open space held for the community and is not for sale."

She scanned the area, with its large granite boulders and tall golden grass that appeared to go on for miles.

"I understand you don't like the rural scenery, but I thought you might have a change of heart if you saw this." He held out his huge hand and displayed a gem.

"OMG, it's beautiful! Such a wonderful color."

"Laurie, don't get too excited. It's a garnet, not a ruby. They can be found in this area. I dug this one out a few days ago."

"No way."

"Yep, there are garnets, amethyst, and even a rare diamond here in Gold Country.

"You're kidding."

"I'm serious. I read an old book that talked about the gems of the mother lode. So, I decided to search for them."

"And you discovered this beauty?"

"Yeah."

She held the stone up and stared at it. "The hue's almost as orange as the sun when it starts to set—amazing."

"That's the only one I've seen in that shade of red. My uncle told me they can be found in several colors, though deep red and brown are the most common."

"I had no idea."

Her dream of designing jewelry had all but disappeared in the last few days, a pipe dream from her childhood, she'd told herself. No one wanted her to succeed and why should they? Nonetheless, without the backing of some kind, she was doomed to failure. She ought to grow up, be realistic, and forget the fantasy. Despite everything, with the raw jewel in her hand, the desire to achieve her goal bloomed.

She smiled and handed the garnet back.

"It's yours, Laurie."

"I couldn't. You found it."

"When I spotted the thing, I thought of you and your designs." He closed her fingers around the rock. "Later, you can show me what you create."

"How can I thank you?" She held the rock to her heart.

"Hey, come on, I'll show you the exact spot where I dug it up. We might find more." He took off.

With her heart pounding wildly, she ran to catch him.

Chapter 23

Chance had never seen Lauren with disheveled hair and dirt on her cheeks, caused while she'd searched the ground on all fours looking to discover another garnet.

Such a different woman from the stuck-up one he first observed, dressed in a pink designer suit and high heels. Gorgeous, but somehow, he liked this Laurie better.

All had gone well today until he'd checked behind the granite outcropping and discovered remnants of a campsite. It appeared to be more than an afternoon picnic with a marshmallow roast.

A pile of empty charred food cans and several plastic wrappers suggested a longer stay. Could someone be living there at night?

The makeshift campfire was ringed by a few rocks but without a source of water, if the blaze got out of control the camper wouldn't be able to stop it.

A chill went through him, remembering the woodland inferno that nearly took his life. The blaze had started because of a careless vacationer.

He closed his eyes and shoved the vivid images out of his mind. Still, phantom pain rippled down his back where new skin had been grafted to replace his burnt body.

With a calming breath, he left the site.

He returned to Lauren and watched her brush the dirt from her jeans. No point in spoiling her day. This evening would be time enough to check and see if anyone came back to the encampment.

"Laurie, find another garnet?"

"No, but look at these crystals. Aren't they pretty? I think I'll design something using them."

"Nice." He grinned at her enthusiasm. She lightened his mood.

Lauren pocketed the crystals she'd found along with the garnet he'd given her. "This is astonishing. The earth is offering gifts."

"Since we're the guardians."

A startled expression formed on her face and she frowned. "I never thought of it that way. That's why you're a firefighter—to protect."

They returned the horses to the barn and he walked her to the convertible. He was about to say goodbye when she kissed him. "Thanks for the gem and the fantastic afternoon. I owe you."

"You don't owe…"

"Yes—I do. I planned to quit my job when Jake returned to work." She paused and scanned his face. "I think I'll stick it out—at least for a while." She grinned and drove off with a wave.

***

In the cottage bedroom, Lauren lay back on the bed and stared at the open-beamed ceiling. What a day. Never in her imagination would she believe she'd find gems in the open space near the little town of Sierra Creek—an unreal dream come true.

She reached into the pocket of her blue jeans and closed her hand around the garnet Chance had given her. Holding the stone up to the overhead light, it glimmered like an orange flame.

The gem had to be returned. It was too valuable to consider keeping it. After all, Chance was barely a friend, let alone someone to give her expensive gifts. All the same, she enjoyed holding the rock, even for a short time.

And what about Chance? If only he wasn't a firefighter.

She shook her head and recalled the promise she'd made to herself a few years ago. Only certain categories of men would be considered for a mate, steady men with safe and secure careers.

They didn't have to be especially attractive, exciting or well-built. The biggest concern was finding a guy who would come home to dinner every night and live long enough to grow old with her.

Refusing to recall the details of the time she'd let herself fall for a man with a dangerous occupation. she sniffed and brushed back a tear. A firefighter too, he'd died while battling an apartment inferno when a gas main exploded.

Hard to realize almost five years had passed. The grief had diminished, but the memory was still intense and the promise to stay away from that kind of hurt was strong.

Don't think about it. She wouldn't but understood there was no way to survive another similar loss.

Good old, boring Ben, was nice enough. His interest was in statistics and the accounts he managed. He held a risk-free position. Though perhaps a bit overbearing, nonetheless, he meant well and there would never be a worry about him while he was at work.

What more could she ask for?

Don't lie to yourself.

However, Chance scared her. He was too much like the man she fantasized about loving and feared losing.

She forced back the images of his intense blue eyes and easy smile, not to mention a touch that heated her. Longing for him had flared when he'd held her and now the desire to explore his body and soul flamed.

Still, the realization that he, against any natural inclination, ran toward hazards, terrified her.

He needed a woman unafraid of danger. Lauren wasn't brave. The death of her first love taught her once burned twice shy. She wouldn't invest her heart in someone who, at any moment, could die, leaving her alone and devastated. *I just can't.*

Startled at the sound of a knock on the cottage door, she ran to the front entrance and peered out through the window.

Amy stood smiling, her strawberry blonde hair framing her pretty face and an aqua blouse stretched across her pregnant stomach.

Lauren threw the door open. "Hi, Amy. Is everything okay?"

"Yeah, fine." Amy grinned and patted her belly. "Baby's growing like a weed." She laughed. "Hey, I realize it's short notice, but I want to invite you to join us for dinner, Vanna, Manny, Wyatt, Bobby and I will be there—maybe Wyatt's dad too."

"Thanks. I'd like that. Can I bring something?" She tried not to show her relief when Chance's name wasn't mentioned.

"We have things covered and only need your company. Say thirty minutes from now?"

"I'll be there."

***

Just before dark, Chance returned to the open space. The autumn breeze sent leaves swirling around him. He'd left the fire truck about a mile and a half from the campsite and made his way by hiking.

He tossed a sleeping bag on the ground near a large oak. Sound traveled far in the hills and this would be near enough to notice if anybody approached the campsite.

Birds stopped their songs and settled in the trees at sunset. The evening turned darker and the stars were visible, but the harvest moon outshone them with its orange glow. He wouldn't need a flashlight to follow any movement, human or animal.

As the hours went by, he stretched and wondered if he was wasting his time. Fighting to keep his eyes open, he stifled a yawn.

"Hell!" A silhouetted figure stood out in the moonlight and kicked a rock out of his way before moving forward.

Chance waited and sure enough, the man went to the makeshift campground and tossed sticks into the circle of rocks he'd seen this afternoon. Chance wanted to get a description of the guy, but a thick beard and a hat covered most of the stranger's face and hair.

A flame sparked and, with a lighter still in his hand, the male threw some crumpled paper in with the sticks.

"Hi, buddy." Chance moved closer.

143

"What the hell! Who are you?" The dude dropped the lighter and ran. The paper flamed, flying in the breeze and catching the bordering dry grass on fire.

Chance stomped on the flames with his boot and cursed. Damn, he wanted to grab the man but couldn't leave the small flare-up. With the wind, who knew where the flames might go if he left?

A few minutes later, with the fire out, he ran in the direction of the camper. The stranger was gone.

Why did the guy beat it? Chance scratched his head. Patrols need to be set up to keep an eye on this place and the open space generally.

Would volunteers be willing to join him on patrol? He rubbed his chin and thought for a moment. He might bring the idea up with Wyatt, Manny, and Mayor Breen at their next meeting.

Chapter 24

The days of September passed quickly. Much to form, the weather remained hot and the sky clear of any clouds that could bring rain.

When the farmers came into the Hitching Post, they expressed concerns about a continuing drought in the area and the cost and availability of water.

Lauren had never considered such issues concerning obtaining food. The lack of rain continued into October, and after listening to Amy's worry about her apple orchards, Lauren's ideas about the importance of precipitation changed.

Jake was back at work, and though he wore a medical boot on the mending ankle, he managed to do his job exceptionally well. Friendly, he made her work enjoyable and she looked forward to seeing him.

She wouldn't say the same about her boss. Mr. Smith had changed little since her arrival. On the odd day when luck was with her, Smithy grunted a hello, but no smile ever accompanied the greeting. She began to understand his personality tended to be grumpy and his bad mood was not necessarily aimed at her.

Vanna, Amy and Vanna's mother, Sophie, became her close friends. They met every Thursday for a girl's night out. Lauren admitted to them the get-togethers kept her sane after her boss had a gripe session with her. Also, they made her laugh, something she hadn't done often before arriving in Sierra Creek.

As the days flew by, she saw little of Chance and couldn't say if it was her choice or his. Even so, the afternoon they'd spent together blazed in her memory.

Vanna and Amy mentioned Chance had recruited firefighters to join the new team, and was overseeing the construction of the firehouse. It took most of his time.

Despite that, the other day, Lauren had seen him in a local café sitting at a window table with a pretty young woman. If he noticed Lauren staring, he didn't react, no wave or smile.

She wanted to return the stone he'd given her, but every time she went to his place, no one answered. So, she put the gem in her jewelry box and tried to forget her confused emotions regarding him.

Life moved on without Chance. She didn't use the stone he had given her. Instead, she utilized the crystals found on the same day. She designed a modern free-form brooch, with silver wire and prongs to hold an amethyst and the crystals in place.

Ben texted regularly, but she responded less and less. He offered to visit. She made an excuse and suggested a possible trip to visit Daddy in a month or so. They could meet then.

The hot weather continued and on a scorching afternoon, she went with Amy and Bobby to a favorite swimming hole.

"Come on, Lauren." Amy dropped a beach towel on the shore and slipped out of her blue and white sundress. Underneath, a blue swimsuit with a skirt made to accommodate her growing baby.

146

With Amy and Bobby's red hair shining in the sun, most people would probably realize they were related. Lauren wondered if the new baby would have the same color or the sandy brown hair of the father, Wyatt.

What would Chance's child look like? Whoa, where did that random thought come from? She shook off her T-shirt and adjusted the top of her red bikini.

The cool river surrounded her and the bikini darkened as the fabric became saturated with water. "Aw." Her body began to relax as she floated and watched the azure sky.

Bobby splashed her. She startled, splashed him back, and tickled him. They both laughed.

"I hope you don't mind, Lauren." Amy slowly entered the water. "He's being playful."

"Hey, part of the fun." She giggled and splattered him with water. He snickered and splashed her again.

Afterward, while Bobby played nearby, she and Amy snacked on carrot sticks and apple slices from Amy's farm.

Lauren stopped chewing and swallowed. "I heard you used to live in San Francisco."

"Yeah. I liked it, but it was so expensive. I moved back to Sierra Creek and the farm after Granny died." She paused, picked up a slice of apple, but set it down again. "That's when I got reacquainted with Wyatt."

"Was it love at first sight?"

Amy laughed. "I'm sorry. I'm not laughing at you, only the idea of our relationship being that easy." She glanced at Lauren "At first, I thought he was gorgeous but a real jerk. Only goes to show how wrong initial impressions can be. You could say we went through a few rough spots." Amy caressed her stomach. "Anyway, I'm happy now and love living on the farm with him."

147

"I never considered living anywhere but a big city."
Lauren hesitated. "Still…"

***

In the late afternoon, Lauren and Amy arrived back
on the farm. The sound of a chainsaw filled the air.
When Amy pulled on the hand brake, Bobby unbuckled
his seat belt and ran toward the noise.

"Bobby, wait! Don't get too close!" Amy struggled
with her safety belt and then rushed after him.

Lauren grabbed her own towel and swim bag and
followed them up the driveway.

"Wyatt!" Amy screeched, fear in her voice.

He turned and ran toward his son, catching him
before he could come too near Chance using a saw.

Wyatt picked Bobby up in his arms and tousled his
hair. "We should always stay away from anyone cutting
trees. It's dangerous, so we stay back! Did you have a
fun swim, big boy?"

"Yeah, Daddy. Why are you hacking the trees?"

"Chance and I are clearing the shrubs and trees from
around the buildings to make a firebreak."

"Oh. What's a firebreak?"

Lauren watched Wyatt with his adopted son. A
loving expression appeared on his handsome face as he
leaned forward to talk to Bobby. Amy came to stand
near her husband. He kissed her and patted her stomach.

In the private moment, Lauren didn't want to
eavesdrop and suddenly felt out of place. She waved
goodbye and went into the cottage.

Finally, the noise stopped and, to Lauren's relief, the
decibel level dropped. She showered, then tossed the
beach towel along with a few other items into the
washing machine.

Feeling relaxed after bathing, she dried her hair, dressed in jeans and a white tank top, then started the washing machine.

When the chainsaw started up again, she peeked out of the bedroom window. Chance, shirtless and wearing ear-muffs, handled the scary machinery.

Mesmerized by the sight of Chance wielding the chainsaw, she stood transfixed. His muscled chest flexed as he cleared the tree trunk of branches on a giant pine tree that grew near the barn. Unable to turn from him, she continued to stare as he cut the lower part of the trunk. He stopped, appearing to calculate how the pine would fall.

He made a second chop on the trunk and the tree toppled away from the buildings onto a wide path leading to the open fields.

With what looked like a satisfied smile, he cut the larger branches from the trunk, the saw vibrating in his huge hands. His chest glistened with perspiration and his well-formed pecs tensed.

Whoa.

He turned off the chainsaw and set it down.

As if he realized she was gawking at him, he grabbed and pulled on a T-shirt, then looked in her direction. Their eyes met. She smiled, waved, and then let the bedroom curtain cover the window.

A minute or two passed before the sound of the machinery began again.

Lauren pulled on her leather boots and went out to the barn. Chance was moving the logs he had trimmed.

"A shame you had to cut down such a beautiful tree," Lauren offered.

He glanced at her, an indecipherable expression on his face. "A sugar pine, funny, but I've spent my life trying to save trees. Here I am killing one—it *was* a beauty." He shrugged. "All for the good of the farm and to limit damage should a blaze happen."

"Can I help you?"

He stared at her hands. "The job is tough on the fingernails."

"Got some gloves?"

He reached into the back pocket of his jeans and handed her a pair of leather ones.

She slipped them on and found the glove's fingers way too long. "Tell me what to do."

"Grab the smaller logs and roll them onto the tarp over there. I'll drag it to the back porch of the farmhouse. After the wood dries out, Amy can use it in the house."

"Okay."

The work was harder than she thought. Still, at the same time, she began to gain strength, most likely adrenaline giving her energy.

"You've done enough for now." Chance touched her shoulder and grinned. "You're a great worker. Ever think of becoming a firefighter?"

"What?"

"Hey, Laurie, I was kidding."

"Oh." She giggled.

"Come up to my place. I'll make dinner. Frozen pizza."

She wondered if this was a sensible idea but followed him up the stairs to the apartment.

She remembered seeing him in the restaurant with another woman. And why not? Chance promised nothing, except dinner.

They had little in common and different reasons for being or staying in the small town. Even so, she couldn't deny she was drawn to him, but it didn't have to be a serious relationship. They could just be friends. Right?

"Lauren, I'll toss the pizza in the oven. Sit down and take it easy."

Chapter 25

Well, I'll be damned. Chance caught sight of Lauren sitting on his couch smiling at him. She was the last person he'd expect to be sharing dinner with.

He asked her, predicting she would decline. But here she was in boots and jeans, looking like she belonged in the place.

He rubbed the five o'clock shadow on his chin and wondered what would happen if he kissed her. He moved closer to her on the sofa. She noticed but didn't move away.

"The pizza is delicious." She held a half-eaten slice in her hand.

"I buy them at the Italian restaurant on Main Street. They'll make the pizza any way you want and freeze it for you. Easy, when I need something in a hurry."

"I've never been to that restaurant, but now I'm putting it on my list." She took another bite and licked her full lips.

He shouldn't have suggested she come to his place; Laurie was too tempting. There was no reason to get involved with a career woman who had no interest in having kids. Even so, tonight he didn't want her to leave.

The conversation had come easily when they were outside, but in the enclosed space, he could smell the aroma of her shampoo and it was difficult to ignore her appeal and keep his mind on their discussion.

Debating what to say next, he sat in silence.

"How are the townspeople responding to your ideas about clearing the trees and shrubs from around their homes?" she asked.

"All right, I guess, though no one seems to be in a rush to do the deed." With the neutral subject, he relaxed. "Vanna made a video message for the local TV station and social media. They showed the ad on the Sacramento TV stations as a service announcement." He sat back on the sofa.

"Great. She was an actress in LA, right?"

"Yeah, but she grew up in town. So, folks around here know and trust her."

"Nice."

"Mayor Breen thought I should do it." He chuckled. "I'm no actor."

"You're handsome enough to be one."

"Quit kidding."

"I'm not. You're as good-looking as any man in the movies."

Not if you could see my burn scars. Feeling awkward, he quickly changed the subject. "More pizza?"

"I couldn't. I'm too full—but thanks."

He encouraged her to talk about her jewelry business. She appeared pleased to discuss her plans and the designs for the crystals found when they searched for gems the other day.

"I'm so happy with how well the silver wire works with the amethyst."

There it was, the adorable grin and wide eyes that sparkled with glee when she smiled.

He moved toward her. Anticipating the sweet taste of her kiss as it mingled with the Italian spice from the food they had just consumed, he held her to him.

"Ouch!" She grimaced and pulled away.

He scanned her as a drop of blood ran down her arm. "Laurie, you're bleeding. You must have been cut by the branches."

"I didn't realize it—until now. She put her hand on the injury and grimaced.

"Hey, let's get you cleaned up." He disliked the appearance of the cut. Why hadn't he seen it earlier?

She stood and adjusted the strap on her tank top. "It's nothing."

"Probably, but I'm a medic, so…" He took her hand and led her to the bathroom.

In the small room, she stood stoic while he washed the wound. In his first aid kit, he found antiseptic and the tweezers he wanted. She began to shake when he pulled out splinters that had worked their way into the layers of her skin.

"Ouch," she whispered.

"I'm sorry, Laurie." He frowned. Many of the patients he'd treated were in much worse condition. Why did he react so strongly to her misery?

With butterfly bandages, he closed the cuts. "Does it hurt?"

She gazed up at him with moisture in her eyes. "I'm just a baby."

"No, you're injured. I shouldn't have let you work with me."

"I wanted to."

He gently pulled her into his arms and tenderly kissed her, then felt the rapid beat of her heart as she leaned against him.

With a sigh, she surprised him by returning his kiss, while she wrapped her uninjured arm around his waist and snuggled closer.

"Laurie, what are we doing?"

"I don't know. Just hold me."

He hugged her, then bent to stare into her eyes before increasing the pressure of his lips against hers. She opened her mouth and encouraged him to continue.

His breathing became ragged as his need grew when she began to move in rhythm with him.

Her hunger appeared to be as strong as his. It would be easy to carry her to his bed. Damn, his manliness almost demanded it. If he didn't like her, he might have. Except, he cared for her and wouldn't allow his powerful craving to cause him to take advantage of a friend.

No matter his yearning, everything was wrong. Their goals and their lifestyles were opposite—only their longing for each other seemed to be similar.

"Laurie."

She blinked and gazed up at him. "Chance." She stood on her tiptoes evidently ready to kiss him again.

"You're hurt, Laurie. I'll give you some Acetaminophen and bandages to take with you." He did his best to control the huskiness in his voice and sound professional if only she didn't look down and see his need. "Keep the cuts dry for a few days."

"Okay." She took a slow breath and touched her bottom lip with her fingertips. Her cheeks were reddened from his stubble, and a confused expression spread across her face.

Next time, he'd shave.

No! There won't be a next time.

***

Unable to sleep, Lauren rose early, showered, careful to keep her cuts dry, and dressed for work, then made coffee and toast. Last night, the memories of Chance had kept her restless and confused.

Laurie, what are we doing? Last night's question radiated in her this morning. They were certainly attracted to each other. But what were her feelings for him? Attraction was one thing, but marriage and kids were something else completely.

Hey, what's wrong with you? You're taking things too far. It was only a kiss.

Even so, it had sent desire racing in her, but to act on the longing would change her life and it was complicated enough.

She spooned strawberry jam on her toast and tried to eat it. With her dry throat, she choked and rushed to the sink for a glass of water.

Someone knocked. Hoping it might be Chance, she ran to answer the door. *Maybe if we talk...*

A tall, slim woman, with short blonde hair and big blue eyes, smiled at Lauren when she opened the door. Broad-shouldered, she carried her head high as if filled with confidence.

"Hi, may I help you?" Lauren asked, wondering what information she could have for this stranger.

"Dusty out here on the farm." The woman brushed off her navy slacks as she spoke. Then she glanced at Lauren, a quizzical expression on her pretty face. "Is Chance here?"

"No. I haven't seen him today."

"Oh, I thought..." She paused. "He's not in his place. His fire truck is still here and no one is home in the farmhouse either."

"Really?" Lauren stepped out onto the porch and glanced down the driveway. "I don't understand. He always takes the truck with him no matter where he goes."

"Yeah, I thought so. I'm Bonnie Brennen, by the way."

"Lauren Walsh."

"I know. Chance speaks of you."

Stunned, she gawked at Bonnie. What should she say to that bit of surprising news? She wouldn't ask what he said because the woman probably wouldn't divulge the conversation anyway.

At the sound of a vehicle's engine, Lauren turned in time to see Chance step out of a newer model jeep. He walked up the drive. So focused on Bonnie, she almost hadn't heard the car pull up. Annoying, but she had become concerned about Chance because he left without the truck.

"You're late. Where were you?" Bonnie demanded.

"Bossy, aren't you?" He laughed but never answered the question. "You already bought the uniform for the Sierra Creek Fire Station."

"Yep." Bonnie grinned.

Lauren was about to go back into the cottage as she was not part of the conversation when Chance called,

"Lauren, don't go. I want to introduce you to my assistant fire chief, Ms. Bonnie Brennen. We worked together in the Bay Area."

"Thanks. We met."

"I'm sure we'll become fast friends," Ms. Brennen said too quickly, then turned to Chance. "Shall we go, boss?"

"Bye, Lauren." He smiled and walked away with his new employee. Bonnie was talking to him as though they were best buddies and maybe they were. After all, she remembered observing them a few days ago at Sophie's Ice Cream Parlor enjoying each other's company.

Lauren grunted. Whoever Chance was involved with couldn't be any business of hers. Even so … Was it possible not to want a man for yourself and still be jealous if he showed interest in someone else?

Chapter 26

Lauren walked in the front door of the Hitching Post and found Jake already at the counter. He smiled and nodded toward the back of the store as Mr. Smith appeared.

"Lauren, go to my office."

Oh shit. What had she done now? On the way, she took a quick gander at the old regulator clock on the wall. Early. At least she wasn't late.

She halted at the door of his workspace and scanned the clean and organized room. The last time she saw the office it looked more like a hoarder's closet than a place to conceive metal designs or follow through with the work of bringing them into the world.

"Sit."

Without having to move anything off the tall stool, she did what she was told, her feet dangling unable to reach the floor. Suddenly, she felt like a school kid in the office for her bad behavior and was now waiting for punishment.

His expression was grim, should she say something like, good morning or looks like it's going to be a nice day?

Mr. Smith seemed to search for an object on his table, then turned back to face her. "I'm told you have talent—inventive designs."

"I..." She stared at her hands.

"Speak up."

"I try."

"Well, are you happy with your work or not?"

She glared. "Yeah. If I wasn't happy, I'd change them."

"All right, show me. If they are as first-rate as I've been led to believe..." He paused and scrubbed his scarred hand over his chin. "Let's not get ahead of ourselves. Do you have examples of your jewelry and your portfolio?"

"Not with me. They're at my house."

He sniffed, frowning. "Go grab them. Jake can watch the store, but don't take too long."

She stumbled out of the office, nearly falling, and, thanking goodness, she caught herself. What a fool she must appear. So sure, he had planned to fire her, the idea Smithy wanted to check out her work stunned her.

Who could have suggested her jewelry was high-grade?

Jake gave her a thumbs-up as she jogged out of the shop. He had to be the person talking the boss into allowing her to show her wares. How could she ever repay him?

***

Perspiration ran down Lauren's face. Was it hot in the shop or her nerves? She'd given her jewelry drawings to her boss before lunch. It was almost two o'clock. She hadn't seen him and didn't know if he'd stayed in his workshop or left the store. Did he take her portfolio with him if he went home, or had he left it unopened in the office?

Jake took off early for a doctor's appointment. He hoped to be able to remove his medical boot for good.

Mr. Smith had a note waiting at the cash register asking her to order winter styles for the women and children who now came regularly to check for new items.

What with the Hitching Post's online shopping, even she was surprised at how quickly the summer items had sold.

Certainly, clothes and shoes were best if tried on in person, and saving shipping costs was also a reason to use a brick-and-mortar retailer.

Close enough to the ski area, it was understood tourists made Sierra Creek a stop to and from the slopes.

In between customers, Lauren enjoyed searching the internet for the right items at the right wholesale price. Unsure of the budget, she ordered only a bit more than the previous purchases.

The clock struck six times and she rang up the last sale, wished a local farmer goodnight, and locked the front door.

In the boss's office, the lights blazed, but the room was empty. Her portfolio didn't appear to be in sight. She checked the parking lot and saw Mr. Smith's vehicle was missing.

Her shoulders slumped. He didn't bother to say he was leaving or give her a response concerning her designs.

With the store restocked and the cash in the safe, she turned off the lights and went to her car.

A headache pulsed over her right eye, so she closed her eyes and let her head rest on the steering wheel of the convertible.

Someone tapped on her window.

"Are you okay?"

She blinked and saw Chance, a concerned expression on his handsome face.

"I'm fine, just tired and hungry."

He opened the driver's side door. "Let's find some food. My treat."

"I…"

"Why don't we try the Italian restaurant? You said you'd never gone there." He held out his hand.

With a deep breath, and wondering if she was making a mistake, she took his hand.

***

"Feeling better?" In the Italian restaurant, Chance leaned forward and casually put his elbows on the table. The sound of Tuscan folk music played in the background and a hand-painted scene of what must be Tuscany filled one wall of the large room.

"I couldn't believe they had a spot for us, without a reservation. They called you chief."

He laughed. "I am Fire Chief Williams, so… Did you have enough?"

"OMG, the ravioli was amazing. I don't think I've ever eaten so many in one sitting." She licked her lips and thought about eating the last ravioli, then shook her head.

"Me too. I wouldn't have thought of pairing beef with white wine sauce, but somehow it works.

"I won't need food for a week," she joked. "I should walk off some of the calories."

"Let's go." He pushed back his empty plate and stood.

Warm air greeted them when they left the eatery. "Have you walked to the creek?"

"What does that mean?"

"Well, the town *is* called Sierra Creek."

"There's a real one?" She giggled. "I must sound silly, but I never thought about the name."

"I'll show you." They strolled down Main Street, stopping to admire the shop windows.

"Lots of Halloween decorations. I should put some in the Hitching Post."

"Amy could give you a pumpkin or two. I'm told she grows a pumpkin patch every year."

"Thanks. I'll ask her."

"We go to the end of the block and turn right."

She followed his instructions and came out on a residential street behind the main street. The sky was darkening and the lights of the homes twinkled on. She stopped to admire a three-story Victorian with a raised porch. "I love these old homes, but I'd be hard-pressed to find one in the San Fernando Valley where I grew up."

"They're impressive. San Francisco has the "painted ladies," as they call them. Unless you have a few million dollars hanging around, they're out of the question." He rubbed his chin. "Here in Sierra Creek, something like this is a possibility—assuming one was for sale, and this area is close enough to the firehouse too—the creek is over here."

She stared, surprised by his interest in the house, then peered down over the metal fence. "Pretty. Still, not much water." She watched the trickle meander over the rocks in the creek bed.

163

"Don't be fooled by the lack of water. It's only a stream now, but once the rain starts… I'm told it fills up and becomes a torrent."

They sauntered on, following the brook as the last ray of sunlight dipped behind the horizon.

A few people nodded to Chance and said, "Chief."

"Guess you're a celebrity," she teased."

"Yeah, that's me, a real big frog in this little pond." He chuckled. "Nice to be recognized though. It doesn't happen often in a large city."

"True. A person can go out day after day in LA and never meet anyone they know."

More conversation didn't seem necessary. For the first time in days, she was at peace. Worry about her job and her dad were at bay.

He held her arm as they continued walking. The lights of the town disappeared and though the fence stopped, they continued following the creek. It widened to a pond and Chance picked up a flat pebble and skipped it across the water. "Try it."

She shook her head.

"Laurie, didn't you do it as a kid?"

"Yeah, but I never could skip the darn thing. It just sunk. No matter, it's too dark."

"The moon is full, a harvest moon. Come on and try," he coaxed.

"Okay, you win." She laughed. "I can never make it skip more than once."

"Go for it."

"I'm not a child anymore."

"Won't you make an effort? For me, pretty please." He grinned.

"Stop." His smile was contagious because her smile spread easily across her face. She grabbed a stone and tossed the thing and it fell straight to the bottom. "Happy now? I told you I'm no good at this."

"Well, if you drop it into the creek. Think like a ball player—a pitcher. Choose a flat rock, hold it this way and throw it low." His stone danced on top of the pond four times before going under.

He found a rock and handed it to her. "Now, hold on like this." He positioned her arm. "Turn sideways and let go."

The pebble seemed to fly over the pond, bouncing three times before settling into the water.

"Wow. I can't believe that happened. I feel like a kid." Before she thought better of it, she hugged him.

He took her in his arms and kissed her on her cheek, then took her lips.

Reluctantly, she pulled out of his embrace. "Chance, we should go back."

"If you say so. I'll walk you to your car." Was that disappointment in his voice? Could she try to explain her feelings?

Chapter 27

After the walk with Lauren, Chance went back to his attic suite. He began work on the notes for the meeting he was to attend with Mayor Breen and the town council. A knock on the door brought him out of his thoughts concerning changes he wanted to mention.

He stood back, opening the door a little wider. "Dad, what are you doing here? Is everything okay? Is Mom all right?"

"Fine."

"Come in. Can I pour you a mug of coffee?"

"No." As he entered, his father's gaze swept over the room and a frown formed on his lined face. "Not much of an apartment for the fire chief."

"Sit down." Chance quickly picked up the laundry spread out on the couch. He dropped the towels and sheets on a chair.

His dad had turned greyer in the short time since he'd seen him, but he stood equally tall as Chance. His father was still well-built for any man, but especially one of his dad's age.

"Chance, I'll stand." He paused, staring. "So, this is what you left the Bay Area for."

"Did you eat?" Chance ignored the comment. "I can fry a couple of eggs for you."

"I stopped to eat on the way up." Never one to beat around the bush, his father continued. "I understand why you took this job. You want revenge on the forest fires that burned you and killed your friend. I get it, but come to your senses. It won't bring him back."

"Dad…"

"Chance, you don't have to be in this Podunk town." He frowned. "You had a promising career in the Bay Area until you volunteered to help with the forest fires." He barely paused to take a breath. "Son, I arranged for you to be interviewed for an important position that's right up your alley."

Chance remained quiet. After years of lectures, he knew there was more to come. All the same, how much was he willing to take now?

"The position is an assistant fire chief in a Silicon Valley station." Dad held up his hand. "Just talk to them before you say no. Opportunities like this don't come along every day. You want to prove something, but later in your career this opening will be gone."

"I appreciate what you're trying to do, but…"

"Damn right, it's only because of my job in San Francisco that they'd consider you. You're my kid, and our family name means something in the firefighting profession."

"It wouldn't be my abilities." Chance bristled. His worth was never enough. He always had to be more and better, but he would never be as good as the generations of illustrious ancestors who came before him.

"Look, son, that's not what I meant. I just happened to mention you to a colleague and suggested you might be interested in the position. And…"

"I'm employed as a chief."

"In this town." He wrinkled his nose as if he smelled an unpleasant odor. "The number to call is on this card." As usual, when his father didn't want to talk about an issue, he ignored Chance. Instead of more discussion, he handed him a business card. "Call or you'll regret it. I won't be here forever to give you recommendations."

There it was again, the idea that his dad wouldn't live forever, the old guilt trip.

"I realize you'll have to retire in a while and I appreciate what you're trying to do, but consider my situation." He cleared his throat and glanced at Dad, hoping understanding would be there. "I've promised the residents in this town, Podunk or not, that I'd help them. I can't leave the folks in the lurch with the job half done."

His father grunted. "They'll find someone else. After all, the place is small and only needs a fireman with minimal experience. The knowledge and skill you have is wasted up here."

How come his father was always so sure of everything? He displayed complete belief his decision was the right one and Chance's choice was the one to be avoided.

For most of his life, Chance had fought to find his place and make choices fitting his needs. A difficult task as his parents had a road map of the best path for him to follow. As a kid, he gave in rather than endure his father's bad temper—not anymore.

"I'll think it over." He stuck the card in his pants pocket, realizing he had no intention of applying for the job. He liked it here in the little berg. For the first time in too long, he had the sense he belonged, and his decisions were respected rather than demeaned and then dismissed.

"Thanks for taking the time to come up here to this Podunk town." He used the same description of Sierra Creek but with a sarcastic tone in his voice. Did his father notice?

"Chance, I hope you grasp I'm trying to do what is best for you. You can't live through another accident like the one you suffered. You're my only son, and you damn near died!" Father hesitated. "As the assistant in a larger firehouse, you wouldn't be put in that kind of circumstance again. Here with little help and surrounded by evergreens…"

A chill ran down Chance's back. He shook it off. "The next time I'm home, I'll take you and Mom out to dinner." He walked to the door, letting Dad understand the visit had ended.

When Chance peered out at him, his father squared his shoulders, then walked away without a backward glance.

He prayed someday his old man would understand his need to stand on his own feet and make his own decisions. Even though annoyance shook Chance, he loved his tough old man.

Back at the table, he organized the notes for the meeting with Mayor Breen and the town council. If he stated the issues with conviction, would they up the budget to adequately meet the needs to outfit the new station?

Enough for tonight. He set aside the work and yawned.

What was Lauren doing?

An image of Laurie smiling at him caused him to grin. Staying in the cottage, she was so close and yet out of reach.

***

Not wanting to be seen by the light of the full moon, a hooded man crouched under the canopy of heritage oak trees. Sometime earlier, his campsite had been discovered, and now he was forced to hide. Rage pulsed in him toward the man who had disturbed him.

Tonight, the land under him was rocky and though there was space enough to sit, he couldn't stretch out on the soft grass and gaze at the stars as he had before his camp was found.

With the thick foliage above him, starting a fire was too dangerous—no hot meal tonight. Anger flared at his situation. He opened a can of chili-flavored beans and ate them cold.

Someone should help him. Who? The asshole who chased him off his campsite? Not likely.

Life hadn't always been this punishing. His first job had come easily. It could be why he hadn't put much value on it. Back then, young, strong, confident, employment seemed to be his right. Lose one position, before he cared, he had another. The years flew by and now living rough wasn't fair. With a grunt, he threw the empty can and belched.

He didn't take drugs or steal. He drank a few beers, that's all, but even so, life shit on him… "Hell." He'd think about it tomorrow.

In his backpack, he searched for a beer. The cheap booze soothed him. Leaning against the trunk of an oak, he finished off the drink, belched again, and closed his eyes.

170

Sleep didn't come at first. Instead, flames appeared in his imagination and he warmed his body with the vision.

Damn, if it got any colder tonight, he'd build a campfire. Dangerous or not, the flames could be controlled.

***

Chance rose early and prepared for the meeting with the mayor and town council.

Last night, he'd planned his speech, pleased the meeting was closed to the public and understanding that the mayor was on his side. The realization helped him calm down. Also, Wyatt, Manny, and Mayor Breen would have his back during the question-and-answer session with the council members.

He decided to dress in his dark blue uniform, blazer, slacks, blue shirt, and solid tie. He wouldn't bring his hat. It was too formal. He wanted to look official but approachable.

In the parking lot behind city hall, he parked the fire truck and entered, taking the steps two at a time to the second floor and the council meeting room.

When he reached the open doorway, he was surprised to see a sign welcoming the town's people. Had he misunderstood? This was to be a private meeting. So, why the sign?

He peered into the green-carpeted, beige-painted, room and discovered the place was already partly filled with people. Some of the faces he recognized, others were strangers. He took a deep breath, then entered, forcing a smile to greet those who stared at him.

Crap. He'd been bushwhacked.

Mayor Breen rushed to greet him and shook his hand. "Sorry about the audience. The council members insisted the town be here to air their concerns," he said under his breath, a look of regret on his face. "Come and join us at the front table."

Rows of chairs lined up waiting to be filled, all facing the table. As he was introduced to the civic leaders, he could hear the buzz of neighbors greeting each other. He glanced up in time to spy Lauren, Vanna, and Amy come in together and sit next to Sophie and her husband, Johnny.

At least there would be a few friendly faces.

Breen nodded toward a chair. Chance sat down and did his best to look at ease, something his stomach didn't agree with.

By the time most of the room had filled with spectators, Manny and Wyatt still were not there. *Come on buddies, I need your backup.*

The mayor gaveled the meeting to order. When the room quieted down, he cleared his throat. "Okay, everyone understands why we're all at this meeting— put your hand down, Henry. There will be a chance to ask questions at the end."

People turned toward a gray-haired man dressed in a beige work shirt and blue jeans, his hand still in the air. "Yeah, okay, but I get the first one." Henry slowly took down his hand.

Breen tapped his gavel and continued, "I'm going to dispense with old business and go straight to the issue. I'm talking about the details of the new fire station and the needed equipment. The particulars are supplied in the handout on the seat of each chair. If you don't have one, grab a copy on the table at the back of the room."

A few of the folks got up, retrieved the flyer, and took it back to their seats.

"Peruse the information while I introduce you to Fire Chief Chancellor Williams. He comes from a family of honored firefighters and has spent years in the Bay Area working for units in San Francisco and the North Bay." The mayor paused. "I'd say Sierra Creek is damned lucky he agreed to move to our little village."

Polite applause followed and everyone stared at Chance. He scanned the room as expectant faces gazed back at him.

"Thank you for the kind introduction. I'm delighted to be here. My best to you for inviting me to your beautiful community. Because of Sierra Creek's governing body's foresight, this town has the opportunity to build one of the best firehouses in Northern California. Given the changes in the world's climate, the emphasis on fire safety is imperative to do so." He did his best to smile and sat down.

More applause.

"Now, let's begin," the mayor said. "There are many details, but to make it easy, the bottom line is the budget covers most of the firehouse requirements, building, and equipment. The only thing not priced in the final tally is the buying of a new hook and ladder truck. If you go to the bottom of the page, Mr. Williams has laid out a general cost of such a vehicle, only an estimate at this time."

"If you don't know the real cost, how can we decide about the truck? And…"

"Sit, Henry. not time for Q and A," the mayor interrupted.

"You said I could get the first one," Henry shouted back.

"If I might," Chance broke in. "Henry, you're right to wonder about the final price. The council has a general idea and when the choice is narrowed down, the exact total will be displayed for all to see. I would be happy to answer your questions then. But before we get too bogged down on that subject, I'd like to talk about the progress on the fire station and a plan to clear the brush and trees from our homes and businesses to protect them from burning."

He quickly ran through his list, then was about to discuss the firebreak, when Wyatt and Manny came into the room. The mayor waved them to the first row of chairs and removed reserved signs, obviously set out for them.

Afterward, Henry grumbled about adding any extra cost to the town's budget. A councilwoman asked for clarification on the details of the building and changes that might be needed. Another told him she had a friend who would like to become a volunteer firefighter.

Chance replied to all the questions, then handed out information on how and why to make a fire barrier. A lively debate ensued, interested in the cost, physical help with cutting a barrier around their property, and if the work was really necessary.

To his surprise, Lauren spoke supporting the idea of making sure firebreaks were done as soon as possible.

Manny and Wyatt promised to put a group from the mill together to assist residents who needed to clear an area around their property but couldn't do so by themselves.

Chance made a sign-up list.

With the queries answered most citizens congratulated and welcomed him. A few were less positive, saying they had gotten by without a new fancy home for the fire trucks and didn't find a need for one now. The mayor was quick to point out, that with climate change, times were different and the town must look forward, not back. That got another round of applause from the onlookers.

As the hour went by, Chance found himself following the movements of Lauren as she whispered to her friends and appeared to study the handout. Her long golden-brown hair was free and fell around her beautiful face. She brushed it back, glanced up, and their eyes caught. She smiled and her pink lips called to come and kiss them. He shook his head and turned away before he completely lost his train of thought.

The civic leaders didn't appear to notice. Instead, they expressed satisfaction with the meeting. The session was gaveled to a close with a promise to have an open house when the firehouse was completed.

People filed out of the room and Chance saw the waitress from Mel's Diner staring at him. He nodded but went to talk with Manny and Wyatt.

Lauren had disappeared without speaking to him.

Chapter 28

Lauren hurried back to the Hitching Post. She crossed her fingers, hoping Mr. Smith wouldn't be upset when he discovered she'd left the job in the middle of the day.

To her surprise, the boss was not at the store.

Jake smiled when she entered and asked how the meeting went with the mayor and all.

"Thanks for covering for me. I brought you a handout with info about making a firebreak around your property."

Jake grinned and set a twenty-five-pound bag of feed on the floor. "So, is Chance getting his truck?"

"I hope so. He was letter-perfect. Even when a man called Henry did his best to cause problems, Chance had answers."

"You like him, don't you?"

It felt more like a statement than a question. "Yeah, he's a great guy." Heat rose in her cheeks and she thought about turning away, but Jake had already caught her eye.

"Lady L, it's not what I meant and you know it."

"Jake, I…"

"He's a hell of a nice guy, and I see the way you two look at each other."

"We're friends."

When Jake's expression said he was skeptical, she added, "I don't date firefighters, no matter how nice they might be."

The brow over his right eye rose as he stared. "Never?"

"I was engaged to a firefighter when I was in college—he died in a fire."

"I'm sorry to hear that."

"Yeah, me too."

Jake left, walking toward the back storeroom.

She shouldn't have told him. It wasn't fair to Jake. She was taking her emotions out on him.

And how *did* she feel about Chance? Friend? Lover? She shook her head. *Don't exaggerate. The desire for a tall, handsome man in a uniform is just a craving. It should never be confused with everlasting love.* She'd given up that dream years ago. Running a successful jewelry business was now her focus.

Two customers entered the Hitching Post and she spent the rest of the day helping them and others hoping to buy something for the coming winter and to grab a few closeout items left from summer.

Jake busied himself stocking the shelves, then went home early, while she closed the shop.

She stepped outside, and after locking the front door, glanced down the street. *Darn!* She forgot her car was in the shop for a long overdue checkup and oil change. Amy and Wyatt promised to give her a ride home and she told them not to wait if she wasn't at the ice cream parlor at the agreed time.

She grabbed her phone. The battery was dead. *Shit.* She didn't charge it last night. "Wonderful!"

After jogging to Sophie's Ice Cream Parlor, she found the place closed. The sign on the door read, *sorry we missed you. Back at 8 AM.*

Yeah, she was sorry too. But it was her own fault. Now what? Even if she had a working phone, she could hardly ask Amy to interrupt dinner and come back and pick her up.

In LA, rideshare apps and private companies, happy to pick a person up, were plentiful. Sierra Creek didn't have a taxi or a bus, other than the one going to Sacramento early every morning and returning late the same night.

She closed her eyes in anger at her stupidity. Tired and frustrated, she gazed at her shoes. Heels, she seldom wore them anymore. Today, she wanted to appear well-dressed for the meeting. Foolish, as she only had to sit and listen. No one cared how she looked. Except for…Face it. She wanted to be attractive for… Don't say his name.

With feet swollen from standing at the cash register most of the day, she sighed. Only five miles, not that far to walk.

Ignoring hunger pains and wishing she had put on runners, she hiked up the strap of her bag and began her trek.

When she was rolling along in the convertible, the road to the cottage never seemed steep. Now, as she walked on the dirt shoulder, cars and trucks whizzed by way too close to her, shooting small pebbles at her. And what had appeared a mere slant, now seemed like a hill.

Couldn't be more than three-quarters a mile before her shoes were scuffed and dull. On the bright side, at least both the high heels were still attached. She straightened her skirt and continued.

Sweat dripped from her forehead. She wiped it away, remembering her attempt at a six-kilometer race in high school. She didn't come in dead last but close enough to realize running was not her thing. How anyone would think it was fun, she couldn't fathom.

Now, hiking in the hills searching for gems—a different story. That had a purpose, a goal, and an exciting result, if successful.

How much did her bag weigh? She grunted and moved the bag to her other arm. Tonight, when she arrived back at the cottage, the first item of business— take out any heavy paraphernalia not needed.

Lost in random thoughts, she almost didn't recognize the sound of the engine behind her. When she spun around, she saw Chance grinning at her from the windshield of the fire truck.

"Get in. I'll give you a ride home," he shouted out the window.

Chapter 29

Excitement ran through Lauren as she looked inside the fire engine, stopping at Chance, a curious expression on his face as he stared back at her, his blue eyes widening as he did.

"Need help getting in?"

"No. I got this." With a forced smile, she hiked up her straight skirt and hauled herself into the cab. Why was she nervous? He was saving her sore feet from a long walk and she was grateful. But this was his domain, and she was invading it. Somehow, that seemed wrong.

"Laurie, are you all right?"

"Yes." She responded too quickly and probably sounded angry, instead of relieved. With a sigh, she relaxed in the seat. "Thanks, Chance. My car is in the shop and I don't think my high heels could've lasted much longer."

"You should have called me."

"I didn't think. Anyway, my phone is dead." She scanned the inside of the cab. "I've never ridden in a vehicle this big. I'm used to my convertible. This must be hard to control." She had tried to think of something to say and ended up sounding stupid.

My Country Heart

An amused expression spread across his face. "It takes some getting used to. Better fasten your seat belt."

He reached over to help her adjust the shoulder strap to fit her. She jumped when he brushed her arm.

"You're nervous today." He secured the buckle.

"I guess I am. I don't know why." She smiled, but it was short-lived when he moved closer.

"Laurie, is that too tight?"

She shook her head and imagined her cheeks must be bright red with the proximity to him. He appeared more masculine surrounded by the steel machine encasing him. She glanced at his strong hands and thought how virile he looked and how much she wanted to kiss him.

"Ready?"

When she nodded, he started the engine and put the truck in gear.

Static filled the before a female voice came on the radio. "Chance, we got a 10-46 with a possible vehicle fire."

"Location?"

"From what I can tell, it's near where you live, only stay on the highway instead of taking the turn off."

"10-4, Bonnie. I'm on the way."

"Sorry Laurie, it looks like you're going to come with me."

"I…" She gripped the seat and held her breath as the fire engine pulled forward. Her heart beat rapidly, but she answered with a calm voice that belied the truth of her feelings. "Sure, okay."

Chance managed a glance at her before his eyes narrowed and his fists gripped the steering wheel. Then staring out of the cab, he frowned and appeared to scan the road ahead.

A few miles down the highway, she caught sight of a sedan, the front of the car in a ditch. "Chance, there, on the right."

He pulled up and parked a distance from the compact. "Stay in the truck." He grabbed his backpack and rushed toward the car.

She undid her seat belt and leaned forward searching for any smoke or flames near the vehicle.

A woman yelled for help, pounding on the window of the driver's side door.

Chance tried to open the door but without luck. Even from a distance, Lauren could tell the side of the car was dented.

"Ma'am, calm down. Are you hurt?"

"Help me!"

"Sit back and let me do my job. You're going to all right." He yanked on the door handle again. "Unlock your side."

"It is unlocked!"

By now, the middle-aged woman was hyperventilating, then shouting, "I have to get out. I can't stand it. I can't...Let me out!"

Lauren leaped from the truck, landing on her knees with a grunt. She picked herself up and jogged toward the scene.

"I said stay in the truck," Chance mumbled under his breath.

"I know her." She peeked into the window. "Irene, it's Lady L from the Hitching Post."

Irene stopped screaming and stared. "Lady L?"

"That's right."

"Dear God, you have to tell him to take me out of here. My seatbelt is stuck and I..."

"Irene, this is Chance Williams, he'll help you."

"Okay, but please hurry—I smell smoke!" Irene shrieked.

"Laurie, stand back. Irene, turn away from the window."

When the woman did, he broke the glass and leaned in to release the door. It wouldn't budge, so with a tool from his backpack, he pried open the bent door and cut the belt holding the woman in place. Irene screeched and clawed at him, trying to get out.

"Irene, stop! I'm helping you."

"Chance, something is on fire!" Lauren yelled as flames sputtered from under the car.

"Laurie, go back to the truck. I've got her."

Irene fainted.

Lauren felt the heat increase as the flames rose. How long before the car exploded?

"Chance!"

Chapter 30

Chance had barely set Irene on the ground next to the fire engine when the car exploded.

The heat increased and Lauren stifled a scream, praying Chance would be all right, when he ran back toward the vehicle, carrying a fire extinguisher with him. What would happen if the dry grass caught on fire too? Would the extinguisher be enough to handle that?

With her eyes wide open, Irene sat up and stared at the scene. "Dear God, my car's burning! I still have four payments to make on it." She tried to stand but fell back and grabbed her knee. Rocking in pain, she wailed, "What am I going to do now? How will I get around and get my grandkids from school?"

Stunned, Lauren wondered why the woman didn't see Chance risking everything to put out the blaze. Even so, she did her best to comfort the woman. Still, her mind lingered on Chance's movements as he attacked the fire.

The weather felt warm, but Irene started to shake. Shock? Lauren took off her blazer and put it over Irene's shoulders, then helped her lean back against a small outcropping of granite. "I know it's not too comfortable, but try and rest." She patted the woman's hand.

Irene gave her a weak nod. "Thank you. I'm fine." She winced and rubbed her knee again.

Lauren could see it was beginning to swell. "I'll be right back."

In the cab of the fire engine, she searched for a first aid kit. She had no medical training, but maybe there was something she might do to help the woman.

She left the truck empty-handed as acrid smoke blew toward her.

Chance returned and radioed from the truck. His voice was steady. For him, was it just another day at the office?

"10-78, Bonnie. I'm going to need help with a grass fire. Send an ambulance. The driver is hurt. Also, I'm going to need someone who can give Lauren a lift home."

"10-69. Eta five minutes."

The radio went dead.

Without explanation, Chance worked on releasing a hose and placing it in position.

"Laurie, move and try not to breathe the smoke," he shouted and pulled on a respirator.

The sound of an ambulance's siren blared as a red SUV pulled up, Bonnie in the driver's seat. A young man, dressed in a fire suit rushed to help Chance.

An ambulance parked, and a paramedic joined them. Irene was whisked away to the hospital.

The car flamed and the fire roared up the grassy knoll. Chance gave orders to send water onto the hillside as he struggled with the vehicle.

"Get in," Bonnie yelled at her.

"But…"

"Chance has it under control. Get in."

They rode toward Lauren's home, but the vibe in the truck was less than friendly. At first, neither of them uttered more than a few words. Though Chance's assistant didn't say so, she was probably annoyed being forced to play chauffeur.

Bonnie glanced at her. "Before you go too far, I want you to understand Chance is a good man. I don't want him hurt."

"What are you talking about?"

"Don't play dumb with me, Lauren Walsh. He cares about you and you are well aware of the fact."

"I hardly know him. So, I don't…"

"Why else would he tell his uncle to keep you in your job after you messed up? And why did Mr. Smith take a look at your drawings?"

"I…"

"Chance told him to."

"No. Jake mentioned my…" Lauren stopped. She had no proof it was Jake who asked Mr. Smith to see her sketches. She had only assumed it was. Had she made a mistake thinking Jake had put in a good word for her?

"As a firefighter, Chance needs a woman he can depend on. A solid female who won't let him down when he needs her. Someone fearless like he is. If you're not that kind, stay the hell out of his way, and let someone else have a shot." Bonnie pulled up next to the farmhouse driveway. "If you say anything to Chance about our conversation, I'll tell him you're crazy and he'll believe me. Now leave."

Shocked, Lauren stumbled out of the truck. Then with as much sweetness as she could muster, she said, "Thanks for the ride, Bonnie." Then, she slammed the door with all her might and walked away. Bonnie yelled something, but she couldn't understand it.

In the cottage, she dropped her bag, kicked off her heels, and slumped onto the sofa. With a sigh, she closed her eyes and rubbed her temples.

The last thing she expected was a lecture from Bonnie what's-her-face telling her how to treat Chance. I mean, it wasn't any of the woman's business. Plus, she and Chance were only neighbors and barely friends. Still, how far their friendship went sure wasn't Bonnie's concern, whether the woman worked for him or not. It didn't give her the right to monitor his personal life.

A little voice in her head said, "If you don't care for Chance, why are you getting so upset?" She ignored the question, dug in her bag and found her phone, and plugged it into the charger.

Before she could change her mind, she dialed Ben in LA. She needed a calm, maybe boring, but reassuring voice to tell her life would be slow and easy again. Was she looking for a refuge from her own feelings?

"Lauren, this is a surprise. It's been too long."

A reprimand? "I know, Ben. I should call more often. I've had so much to learn here on the job and..."

"Hey, you don't owe me an explanation. Anyway, things are okay. I arranged a regular poker night once a week with your father. So, I can make sure he's okay. Your dad keeps me updated with your progress out there in the boonies."

"Thanks for looking in on Daddy."

"I care about him."

Ben always said the right thing, or was he suggesting she didn't care enough, and he was scolding her? She didn't like the sound of that. Not to mention, it annoyed her when he called Sierra Creek the boonies. True, it was a small town, but the connotation of being nowhere and a useless place was far from the truth.

"Lauren, I think your career would be better served here in the city. Don't waste your time trying to get attention from the old coot who thinks he's more important than he is. After all, who, outside of the town, has heard of him?"

"How's your business doing, Ben?" She changed the subject before she said something she'd regret.

As she listened to him, it reminded her how much she detested his know-it-all attitude. Still, Daddy enjoyed his company and even encouraged the relationship between her and Ben. While he healed, Father needed a buddy. Ben encouraged him to follow the doctor's orders and gave her dad someone to talk to. She wouldn't interrupt that now.

Ben was still talking, but she hadn't listened. "I'm sorry, what did you say?"

"There you go again, Lauren—daydreaming. You're like a little kid." He hesitated. "I said come home for a while. Your father needs you and so do I."

She agreed to visit for Thanksgiving. Being it was October, Ben preferred Halloween. He laughed when she told him she had promised to help Amy with the sale of pumpkins in the pumpkin patch. "From expensive jewelry to pumpkins—how the mighty have fallen." He chuckled.

She didn't.

When the call ended, she threw her smartphone into her bag. It had been a mistake to reach out to Ben. Maybe he was trying to be nice, but there was nothing between them, except an obligation to protect her father from any upset, as his life was already in flux.

She should eat something. In the cottage kitchen, she stared into the refrigerator.

Was Chance safe? She had no appetite.

Chapter 31

The next morning arrived too soon. Lauren woke with a start. Still lying on the sofa, she sat up and noticed she was fully clothed from the previous day. She'd stayed up to watch for Chance and be sure he arrived home safely.

She glanced down the driveway and didn't see the fire engine parked in its usual space. Did he come back and then leave while she slept? Why did she care?

After a warm shower, she dressed in blue jeans, and a pale blue shirt and grabbed a stick of celery and a piece of buttered rye bread for breakfast. An odd combination, but it would have to do. She wouldn't be late getting to the Hitching Post. She rushed out to the driveway and remembered her car was in the shop. *Shit.*

"You're looking a little lost." Amy came up to her and smiled "I'm on my way to the sawmill, need a ride into town?"

"OMG, thanks. I forgot my car is being serviced and I don't dare be late to work."

"I have Wyatt's truck today. Jump in." Amy waddled to the driver's side of the pickup and Lauren realized just how pregnant Amy was.

"How much longer?"

"Feels like I might give birth today." Her friend grinned and rubbed her stomach. "Truly, I'm not due for a while."

Lauren leaned back in the passenger's seat. "Are you hoping for a boy or a girl?"

"Well, you know the old saying, a healthy baby. I just want the baby to be well."

Amy had been smiling, but now her expression turned serious and Lauren remembered Bobby endured celiac disease, so, certainly Amy might be concerned. Lauren changed the subject and later they were laughing as Amy told stories of the children at last year's pumpkin patch sale.

They discussed this year's patch and how she might help. She remembered Ben had made fun of the event, but Lauren looked forward to the day.

She told Amy of the car fire and admitted she was worried about Chance and wondered why he hadn't come back to the farm last night.

Amy glanced at her, then took the highway heading toward town. "No need to be concerned. He's fine. Wyatt told me Chance stayed overnight at the burn site to make sure he'd be there in case of a flare-up during the night."

"That's a long workday."

"Yeah, but Wyatt said Chance had hired a few new guys. After they're trained, his schedule should be better."

The pickup truck pulled in front of the Hitching Post with minutes to spare. She thanked Amy again and agreed to meet her and Vanna after work. Tonight, they would buy takeout and eat in Vanna's old apartment over the ice cream parlor. Time to make plans for the pumpkin patch and the Christmas Fair Amy had on the farm every year.

***

Chance stomped his boots and walked briskly up the driveway of the farmhouse. He coughed and squelched a curse. That damned fire engine appeared to be in worse condition than he'd been led to believe. With good luck, the old pumper had been able to control the grass fire that started after the sedan caught on fire. Had the wind been blowing or the dry grass any taller, the blaze might still be a problem.

Did the retiring fire chief mislead him or was the man too old to keep track of the equipment and the needed updates? He hoped the chief hadn't hidden the truth to convince Chance to take the job.

Whatever the reality—too late now.

He smelled of smoke and wanted a shower ASAP. His growling stomach suggested food would be his first move. No dinner last night and so far, no breakfast; he couldn't wait any longer.

Before he tromped up the stairs to his place, he slowed his pace. Remembering Lauren's action yesterday, he wanted to talk to her and wondered if she was home. Was she snuggling under the bedcovers with her long brown hair loose around her?

Damn. He would never know because he needed to mind his own business and that was the way he wanted it.

Too tired to shower or eat, Chance threw off his smoke-filled clothes and flopped onto the unmade bed.

Sleep was elusive. Could he make good and keep Sierra Creek safe if the town council didn't foot the bill for the new truck and other required equipment?

191

If a big fire hit the small village, that pumper wouldn't do the job.

***

At the Hitching Post, Lauren tried unsuccessfully to ignore her rapid heartbeat. Why was she told to wait for Mr. Smith in his workroom? What had she done now?

She paced the area, then sat on a high metal stool facing his workbench. After months employed there and doing her level best, if her boss wasn't happy, it might be time to pack up and go back home.

The thought depressed her. She'd made friends in Sierra Creek and had settled into the little cottage, decorating it to make the rental her own.

Even the rooster that squawked at the break of dawn was welcome. She knew how many times he would crow and afterward, she'd roll over in bed and go back to sleep.

She was startled when Mr. Smith, dressed in his usual blue jeans and work shirt, entered and grunted. He ran his hand over the grey stubble on his chin and stared at her.

Why did she feel as if she'd broken school rules and was in the principal's office to find out how long detention would last?

A chill slithered down her spine. "It's cold in here." She glanced at the open window.

"Important to have good air circulation when soldering—remember that."

"Okay." An odd thing to say since, unless called in to be disciplined, the workshop was off-limits.

"Let's start."

She noticed her portfolio on his desk. He opened it, and thumbed his way through the drawings, putting them in three different stacks. He stopped at one sketch

192

and scratched his head, his brow creasing. He tossed the art paper to the floor, grumbling under his breath.

She sucked back a curse and waited.

Finally, he looked up from her drawings and gazed at her.

Why didn't he speak?

"This is the way I see it." He paused and scratched his head again.

"Yeah."

"I understand you want my opinion." He sniffed. "So, I put your handiwork in three piles."

She nodded, unable to trust speaking without showing her impatience.

"I've been told these are new since your arrival in our little town."

"Yes."

"Pile one has pretty pictures, but don't bother trying to make them in silver. Number two could be constructed, but to my mind, they are mediocre at best." He paused and sat at his desk.

She started to gather her things. No reason to stay and hope to apprentice with a man who thought her creations were mediocre at best.

"But these are outstanding," he continued, apparently unaware she planned to leave.

"What?"

"You heard me. I could work with these designs. This one is especially nice. You've captured the flower perfectly. The notes say to use pink quartz and silver."

"I…"

"You will need to set up a soldering station like the one I have, with clamps and a small vise." He pointed to the other end of the long worktable. "If you don't own everything, I can tell you where to buy them. When you work, both of your hands must be free."

"All right." He called her work outstanding. It was more praise than she'd hoped for and all because Chance had told his uncle to pay attention to her drawings. How could she ever thank him?

"Lauren, take off the pin you're wearing."

"I'm sorry."

"The broch, your design, I'm guessing."

"Yes, Mr. Smith." She handed it to him.

"Free form, a unique style." He turned it over. "Hm." He reached for the reading glasses perched on his head. "Hm, that's what I thought," he said to himself.

"What?" No longer aware of the cold breeze or his gruffness, she leaned so far forward she almost toppled off the tall stool.

As if he had forgotten she was there, he blinked, then recovered. "This join will not hold. If you de-solder and move it here, you'll get a better connection and it will last. This one won't. Also, your weld is too chunky. I can show you how to smooth it out and still keep the strength."

By now, she and Mr. Smith stood side by side inspecting the sketches and talking about where to fuse the metal and how to change the designs to accommodate a stronger bond.

Until Jake entered and mentioned it was near closing time, they continued working together.

"Set up your station tomorrow, Lauren."

"I will. Thank you, Mr. Smith."

"Smithy, that's what everybody calls me."

For the first time since she started working at the Hitching Post, her boss smiled at her.

Chapter 32

The breeze picked up, signaling fall was here and the nights could be damned cold even if the days were hot and sunny.

He pulled his thin coat tighter and tucked his head against the wind. Another bitter night awaited him. The leafless trees no longer offered the warmth and protection they had months ago. He sniffed and rubbed his nose with the back of his hand, then patted his right jean pocket. The money folded there was for a rainy day.

Scratching his bearded chin, he considered the options. The cold temperature last night had made it damned near impossible to get comfortable enough to sleep in the old sleeping bag. It might be time to use the stashed funds for a blanket to ease the nights to come.

He moved toward town and the main street.

***

Lauren was still grinning when she returned to the sales floor. Jake was filling a bare spot with feed, with fifty-pound bags for the next day. It appeared the store had been busy because many of the shelves were almost empty. He should have called her back to the floor.

Instead, Jake had let her follow her dream to work with one of the best silversmiths in the US.

"Jake, thanks for covering for me." She walked over and hugged him. "I can close if you want to go home early."

A blush reddened his lined face. "I wouldn't mind, Lady L. I want to check the corral at home. Don't want anything blowing away with high winds coming tonight."

Alone in the shop, she checked each aisle and moved to stock them as needed. Her mind wandered to Chance. Where was he now? Did she dare to tell him how much it meant that he'd made a way for her to follow her dream?

He must care a little about her or why convince his uncle to take a look at her designs? Bonnie had warned her. *Leave him alone. As a firefighter, Chance needs a woman he can depend on. A solid female who won't let him down when he needs her. You're not that woman."* She stopped working. Could Bonnie be right?

Lauren's goal was to start a company and grow it into a million-dollar firm. Was there room in her life for both Chance and her company? He wanted kids and said as much, not to mention he had a dangerous career. If something happened to him, she'd be a left a single mother.

Hold on. Her imagination had carried her away again. All she wanted to do was thank Chance for the opportunity to work with Mr. Smith.

She shook her head, finished stocking, and went to the register to cash out.

The bell on the front door tinkled. She glanced up and stared into the intense eyes of a bearded man in a tattered coat, a black knit toque covering his hair.

"Where are the blankets?"

A chill ran through her. Had she seen him before?

"Well?" His gruff voice startled her.

"Aisle five. Let me show you" Body odor greeted her as she walked by him.

She pulled out the warmest blankets but suspected they were probably more than he wanted to or could pay.

"I thought the store sold surplus blankets."

"Uh." She remembered Jake had mentioned some of the old timers liked them. This guy wasn't old but… Where did they put them? "Give me a second."

She dug in the storeroom and at last found a box marked "surplus."

With an army-green wool blanket in hand, she returned and discovered the man looking at gloves.

"Yeah, those are the ones I want." He set the mittens on the shelf and walked toward the cash register. "How much?"

Hmm, good question. She scanned his dirty clothes and the torn cuffs of the thin coat he wore. "We were going to get rid of them. They are kind of old, so, I can let you have it for ten dollars even." She grabbed the price tag from the blanket and tore off the amount, *twenty-four dollars and ninety-nine cents.*

He held up the fabric, scanned the wool, and then rubbed his chin. "Yeah, okay."

With a hand in his right jean pocket, he yanked out nine wrinkled dollar bills and four quarters.

She pulled out a brown paper bag with the Hitching Post logo printed on it, slid the blanket inside, and handed the package to him. "Do you want the receipt?"

He grunted, shook his head, and asked, "Where's the men's room?"

As the stranger walked toward the bathroom, he shoved the bag into a large backpack.

She counted and flattened the crumpled paper money and wondered if they were his last funds. She added the difference to the amount the guy gave her, so the cash drawer would balance.

The regulator clock on the wall struck six thirty. How long was the guy going to stay in the bathroom? Maybe she shouldn't have let him use it. If not, where would he go?

The customer returned without the toque, his longish hair was combed back from his bearded face, and his hands were clean. He also smelled better.

He counted out enough change, including five pennies, to buy a chocolate-covered granola bar and left without saying thanks or goodbye.

Lauren rushed to lock the door in case someone else wanted to shop after the store was closed but not secured.

Was she a fool for letting him have the item for less than the price? Her instincts said he needed a break. Though unlikely to ever be in a similar position, she hoped someone might do the same for her.

She glanced at the clock again. If she didn't hurry, she'd be late meeting her friends for dinner, but first, she had to pick up her car. That is if the repair shop was still open.

Chapter 33

Lauren looked forward to seeing Amy and Vanna for dinner. Still, tonight she ached to speak with Chance and thank him for his intervention on her behalf with his uncle.

The move to Sierra Creek had been hard, but the effort was beginning to pay off. For the first time in many weeks, her dream of learning from Mr. Smith was becoming a reality, and all because of Chance Williams.

Late picking up her car, the vehicle was left outside of the closed mechanic's shop with a note. *Ms. Walsh, pay me the next time you are in town. Thanks.*

Wow, only in a small town like Sierra Creek could she expect such service and trust.

She drove to the main street and parked in front of Sophie's ice cream parlor. Amy and Vanna were meeting her in the apartment above the shop.

After Lauren arrived, Vanna served Chinese takeout, while explaining the place was her home growing up. But now that Vanna and her mother had moved away, the two-bedroom residence remained furnished but vacant.

As they munched on fried prawns and rice. Amy and Vanna discussed their week and then turned to a possible fundraiser to help generate the capital needed for the hook and ladder truck. Amy had learned from her husband, Wyatt, that one of the town council members had refused to go along with increasing the budget for the purchase.

"When he hears the news, Chance will be so disappointed." Lauren frowned and pushed her plate away. Not one to be defeated, she suggested a fund-me-page to raise money. "I don't have any idea how much such a vehicle costs, but every little bit would help."

"With the horrible fire last year, I'm surprised the whole council didn't go along with the idea of buying a new truck," Vanna added, a distressed expression on her face. She wiped the moisture from her eyes and pushed her straight blonde hair back.

Lauren wondered why she appeared so upset about an old blaze but decided not to ask.

"Yeah, don't they read the news? With all the forest fires across the state, you'd think the truck was a no-brainer," Amy added. "The councilor might be penny wise and pound foolish." She finished her rice and took a sip of herb tea. "Oh, the baby moved." She rubbed her stomach. "I think the baby liked their first try at takeout."

Amy laughed and Lauren and Vanna joined her. Then they fell silent, savoring the warm tea.

Vanna came up with the idea of a concert with the California Cowboys, a band that had ties to Sierra Creek. Though now famous, the group often performed at The Barn, a local venue. She would approach them.

With everyone on board, they made notes and took turns discussing fund-raising ideas. Before long, a timetable was decided upon. Now it was a matter of running the plans by the Mayor and Chance for their okay.

"I'm pretty sure Mayor Breen will be up for it. He loves anything bringing favorable publicity to Sierra Creek—especially since he has decided to stay on as mayor, rather than run for the county board of supervisors." Vanna smiled. "Manny often remarks the man is always looking for good PR for the town. I think this idea would qualify."

At nine-thirty, Lauren excused herself and headed home to the cottage.

Odd, it was the first time she thought of the little house as home. Until this moment, she considered Los Angeles her home base, and Sierra Creek as only a pit-stop.

Could she live forever in this small rural village? What about her dad?

An inkling of an idea filtered into her brain. Though he was loath to admit it, as Daddy aged his arthritis worsened. He needed more help getting around. The other day, Ben had reported normal daily tasks, including driving, were getting harder for Daddy, though he would never admit the truth.

If he were nearby, she would help him. Even if he didn't ask, she could drop in on him to make sure he was okay.

In the front seat of her convertible, she contemplated a scheme. It might be her dad would enjoy living in Sierra Creek. He grew up in a small hamlet somewhere in Minnesota, so… With a residence situated in downtown Sierra Creek amid everything her father required, no driving would be necessary. She could suggest wanting her father nearer. Yeah, that might just work.

Hmm, I wonder if Vanna and Sophie want to rent out the empty apartment.

Lauren's newly tuned car sped toward home. The fire truck sat in the usual spot when she arrived at the farmhouse.

Jogging up the driveway, she glanced toward the attic suite and noticed the light blazed in the front room.

Excited, her heart beat rapidly. The desire to hug Chance and tell him all the events of the day surged in her.

With ease, she ran up the stairs to his suite and knocked. When he didn't answer, she knocked harder.

The door flew open and Chance stood there with pants and boots still on but bare-chested. She reached out and hugged him, feeling his warm skin and powerful muscles underneath. "I had an exciting day. I wanted to tell..." her voice faded as she scanned his startled expression.

"Hey, who's at the door this time of night?" a woman shouted.

Bonnie.

"Oh, I didn't realize you weren't alone. I—never mind." Embarrassed, Lauren turned and ran down the steps. In her rush, she missed the last two stairs, falling on her hands and knees in the dirt.

"Laurie, are you okay?"

"Fine." Standing and ignoring the pain shooting through her knees, she did her best not to limp as she hurried to the cottage.

Inside, she leaned against the closed front door and took a deep breath. "Shit." *What a fool I've made of myself.*

Hobbling to the bedroom, she changed into her night clothes, and in the bathroom, she sat on the toilet seat and rubbed her right knee.

Humiliated, it never occurred to her that Chance would be entertaining someone tonight. With a groan, she cleaned the scratches on her right knee and applied antibiotic cream and a bandage.

Strong, handsome, and sexy, why wouldn't Chance be with a female?

Too restless to sleep and not wishing to think anymore, she turned on the television. An old movie flashed on the screen, a Western, but Lauren didn't know the film or care about the plot.

Dear God, what must Chance think of me? He and the woman were probably laughing at her right now. What irked her the most? Bonnie was the woman. Well, she couldn't say Bonnie hadn't warned her.

If Lauren was honest, in the back of her mind she'd hoped Chance had asked his uncle to take a look at her jewelry designs because he cared for her.

A headache throbbed over her left eye and she rubbed her forehead. *Damn.* She needed sleep to be ready for work tomorrow.

With a sigh, she stood and adjusted her blue pajamas with pink kittens dotted on them and turned off the TV.

She was about to extinguish the light when someone knocked on the door.

Chapter 34

Lauren opened the cottage door and found Wyatt Cameron on her porch. He scanned her, then appeared to be unsure if he should speak.

"Wyatt?"

"I'm sorry to bother you. I see you're ready for bed—Amy's in trouble. I'm taking her to the hospital. I wondered…"

"Oh, God. I'll watch Bobby. Go!" She grabbed her robe and ran after Wyatt.

Lauren's heart was pounding when she entered the back door of the farmhouse. Amy sat at the kitchen table, pale, a terrified expression on her face.

"Lauren, it's too early for the baby to come." She moaned and held her protruding stomach. "I can't lose the baby. I just can't!"

She rushed to Amy. Helpless to do anything, what could she say? She squeezed her friend's hand and promised to take care of Bobby. She wanted to tell her everything would be fine, but couldn't.

After Amy and Wyatt left, Lauren stared out of the living room window and noticed Chance's fire truck was gone.

Tiptoeing upstairs, she looked into Bobby's room. His red hair spread out on the pillow of his twin bed and a stuffed bear peeked out from the covers.

Such an adorable little boy, Lauren prayed he would never have to grow up without his mother as she had been forced to do. She pushed back a sob. Though it happened years ago, the memory of the day her mother died, in an accident on the LA freeway, was still raw.

It's over. Let it go.

Back in the kitchen, she made a mug of hot chocolate and carried it to the family room. She'd be close enough to hear Bobby, should he need her.

She took a sip of the sweet liquid and set the cup on the coffee table, wishing she'd grabbed her phone before leaving the cottage. Her only thought had been to go to Amy and Wyatt's home, so they could leave for the hospital.

Afraid to sleep because Amy's little boy could get up, she wandered the room, found a pack of playing cards, and played solitaire. Still, no matter how much she tried to calm down, her heart beat rapidly.

Strange how long the night can seem when waiting for someone. The dark lingered, refusing to move toward dawn. Still, no word from Wyatt. A regulator clock in the kitchen struck three times. She yawned—so much for a good night's sleep.

The sound of the fire truck caught her attention. *Chance.*

Dressed in a navy T-shirt and jeans, he pulled out a backpack from the truck, turned, and walked toward the farmhouse.

No need for him to see her again tonight. She moved away from the window.

A tap on the front door sent her running to answer it before the noise woke Bobby.

"Wyatt texted me," Chance said as he entered the house and went into the family room. "How are things here?"

"Okay. Bobby is sleeping. I left my phone in the cottage, so I couldn't text—didn't want to leave him alone to get it."

"Hey, it's fine. I'll tell Wyatt."

"How's Amy doing?"

"The doctor is with her." He sat on the leather couch. "You don't need to stay. I'll take over. Go get some sleep."

"I couldn't, not until I know Amy's all right." She dropped to the sofa next to him and tucked her legs under her.

"You took quite a fall this evening. Are you good, Laurie?"

She felt the heat rising in her as he stared, then she looked away. "About that, I'm embarrassed. I didn't mean to interrupt you."

"What do you mean?"

Damn, he was going to make her explain.

"Nothing. I don't mean anything." Her voice started to rise. "This is not the time or the place for this conversation," she whispered.

"There is no conversation. I asked a question and you refuse to answer," he whispered back.

"Chance, I only stopped by your place to thank you for talking to your uncle." She didn't mention hugging him. She leaned forward and drank her now cold chocolate milk. "I didn't want to disturb you and Bonnie."

"Hey. I don't know what you think we were doing."

"I…"

"We were working."

Without your shirt, she wanted to say but held her tongue.

As if he heard her thoughts, he continued. "When you knocked, I was about to shower after fighting a nasty blaze."

"No reason to explain to me."

"I'm aware of that, but wanted to—I like you, Laurie."

"You do?"

"More than like—if you'll let me."

She reached for him but stopped short.

He took her hand and kissed the open palm. "So delicate and still you create such beauty with metal." He pulled her to him and she went willingly.

"Laurie, I've seen too much ugliness. This harsh world needs beauty."

"Sometimes, I wonder if I should learn to do something else, a job that makes a difference."

"Don't ever think what you do isn't important. Laurie, it is. The world would be a harsher place without creative people like you."

As he bent toward her, she closed her eyes ready for his kiss.

Just then, the front door opened and Amy entered, with Wyatt holding her arm, appearing to steady her.

Lauren ran to her friend. "Amy, are you and the baby, okay?"

"Yeah, but I feel stupid. I made such a fuss. Indigestion, the doctor said. I guess the takeout food didn't agree with the baby after all." Amy laughed.

Lauren hugged her. "I'm so glad you're both fine."

***

After they said goodnight to Amy and Wyatt, Chance walked with Lauren to the cottage, then took her in his arms, brushing her long hair from her face and staring at her wide-eyed expression. "Laurie, go out with me on Friday night."

"I…"

He smiled. "You're so darned cute in those flannel pajamas."

"I like kittens." She grinned, appearing self-conscious as he gazed at her.

"I'll pick you up after work at the Hitching Post. Say six o'clock?" He kissed her before she answered, coaxing her full lips to soften and accept his. A sigh emanated from her as she leaned against him, yielding to his touch.

He didn't want to let her go. Still, he had the good sense not to rush a woman who, until now, he'd thought was not for him.

"Six is fine." She touched his mouth with her fingertips and left without another word, gently closing the cottage door behind her.

Damn, that is one sexy female and I'm not sure she realizes the fact.

Chance stood for a moment digesting his response to her. He shook his head and climbed the steps to his suite. Tomorrow couldn't come soon enough for him. Now, if only there were no emergencies to interrupt his plans.

Chapter 35

After many weeks of worry, disappointment, and upset, Lauren's daily schedule settled into a pleasant routine.

She worked side by side with her boss and the days went swiftly by. The soldering station he fabricated for her made fabrications easier and quicker to complete. Amazing, how a little adjustment in her method made all the difference.

To her surprise, he had a sense of humor and was filled with stories of his adventures as a rodeo cowboy in his early days. Because of his love of horses, he donated some of his silver designs to a yearly charity auction that benefited the care and feeding of old rodeo and race horses. She offered one of her designs and he seemed pleased to accept the piece.

With ease, she learned to help on the sales floor, then returned to the workroom to finish a project.

At the Thursday dinners with Vanna and Amy, they continued planning the concert with the California Cowboys, who were glad to help. The Fund Me Page brought surprising results and she looked forward to telling Chance.

Contemplating Friday night, Lauren relived Chance's kiss and wished for another. Busy, he had spent much of the week at the new firehouse, but in a while…

The only problem perplexing her was the continued communication from Ben. He kept her updated with too many texts about her father. Each one had a little jab about her not bothering to come to LA to visit Daddy. She understood Ben meant well, but it irked her that he implied she was not a loving daughter. She and Daddy spoke often. So, she didn't need Ben's input. Nonetheless, not one to start a confrontation, she let Ben continue to talk to her.

Friday morning was too beautiful a day to let Ben's interference stop her enjoyment of the day. Tonight, she would see Chance.

At the Hitching Post, just before closing time, Lauren rushed to the lady's room, took her hair out of the ponytail she always wore at work, combed her hair, and let it fall down her back. After applying a fresh coat of lip gloss, she glanced in the mirror and gazed at her happy expression. *Don't expect too much out of this evening. Remember you're only having a meal with a friend.*

Chance was waiting for her when she returned to the sales floor. "Ready to eat?" He grinned at her.

Heat rushed through her when he took her hand.

"You look great, Laurie."

"So do you." She grinned back at him.

The stroll along Sierra Creek's main street was somehow different with Chance by her side. People waved. She didn't recognize most of them, but many of the men shouted, "Hi, Chief." Or, "How's the fire hall coming along, Chief?" Another said, "The wife and I will be there for the concert."

"Thanks, buddy."

"Chance, I had no idea so many people knew you."

He shrugged. "Comes with the job." He paused. "Dinner at Mel's Diner all right with you?

"Sure."

Mel waved at them when they entered.

"How's it going?" Chance asked.

"Can't complain," the stocky man in a white coat and chef's hat replied.

A pretty waitress perked up when she noticed Chance, but seeing Lauren, she frowned and pointed to a table in the corner, facing the floor with a view of the street. "Will this do?" she asked. Lauren had the sense the waitress didn't care if it did or not.

"Perfect. Thanks," Chance answered.

"Humph." She tossed two menus on the table and hurried away.

The food might be delicious, but Lauren wasn't sure about the service.

"I hope you like burgers. Mel and his wife have been supportive of the new firehouse, so I want to… They also have salads—I think."

"No worries, I've been dying for a burger. In LA, my dad and I used to go to a local drive-thru every week or so and grab a cheese hamburger with fries. I really miss that."

Lauren read the menu. "Hey, Chance, Mel's Diner offers a Firehouse Burger. It includes two beef patties with chili, tomatoes, onions, and spicy fries. The proceeds benefit the fire station."

"You don't say?" He glanced at the menu. "Well, I'll be—that's the burger for me."

"Make mine the same."

211

A middle-aged woman with a pencil stuck in her hair came to their table. "Folks, what can I get you?"

"Two firehouse burgers and—Lauren, what do you want to drink?"

"A chocolate milkshake."

"Make it two shakes."

"Coming right up."

Lauren scanned the restaurant and located the younger server working on the other side of the room. The woman glared at her. Did the waitress have a crush on Chance? Lauren turned away and gazed out the window.

"Everything okay?" Chance held her hand.

"Yeah, better than okay." *When I'm with you.* The unexpected thought came unbidden. However, she would never say it out loud.

While they ate, small talk was easy and Lauren couldn't help recalling she'd often struggled to think of something to say to Ben. Surprising because she and Ben were raised in LA and had similar experiences. Perhaps it was his indifference to her life choices that bothered her.

"Laurie, is something wrong?"

"What? No, I'm recovering from the hot chili. My mouth is on fire." She grinned and drank the rest of her milkshake.

"I think Mel has a three-alarm fire going in these burgers." Chance stuffed his last French fry into his mouth. "You going to finish that?" He pointed to her plate.

"Help yourself. I couldn't eat another bite."

She grinned as he quickly downed her fries and finished off the rest of her milkshake too.

Afterward, they walked down the main street and turned the corner. A large gray wooden barn stood at the end of the street, country music blaring from the open doorway.

"You up for it?"

She stared at Chance. "Sure."

The volume increased in the bar and dance floor. Bales of hay lined the walls and people sat on them as chairs. There was a stage, but tonight it was empty and the songs came from speakers, placed here and there, sending the sound throughout the building.

"Can I buy you a beer or a glass of wine?" Chance whispered in her ear as a defense against the loud music.

His breath sent a shiver of desire slithering down her spine. "Uh—any California white wine is fine, thanks."

With their drinks in hand, they sat on a bale as far away from a speaker as possible. Chance sipped his coffee and explained he remained on duty tonight. "Once a roster of the fire station employees is set, I'll let the deputy chief take some of the control to give me a break."

"I have a stupid question." She hesitated.

"Go on."

"Well, do firehouses have poles?"

Instead of laughing at her as she thought he might, he nodded. "Yep, but only in the older two-story buildings. It started in the 1800s. In crowded cities, the space was limited, so they built up." He took a sip of coffee. "The new firehouse is a single story."

"Oh darn, I wanted to see you use the pole."

He nearly choked on his drink and laughed out loud. "You say the cutest things."

A quiet love song began and he put out his hand. "Dance?"

A tall man, but appearing to be sure of his movements, he held her to him. The heat of the wine flowing in her and the warmth of his taut body, with a sigh she rested her head on his solid chest and closed her eyes.

They moved to the rhythmic strains as if they'd swayed to the tune often. Of course, they never had.

"You feel good, Laurie."

His words vibrated through her. It sent an odd desire flowing within her. Did he experience it too?

A loud "down-home" ditty started and they left the dance floor and returned to their spot, only to find their wine and coffee removed and a couple of strangers sitting there.

"Must be a clue to take our leave. You ready, Laurie?"

"I'm fine with that."

He took her hand and led her through the ever-increasing crowd to the exit.

The lights of the town twinkled as they walked toward the parking garage behind the Hitching Post.

"It's beautiful here. Almost too pretty. It's unreal."

"A city gal is talking," Chance teased." I believe the folks in town take it for granted. They've never struggled with crowded streets with litter in the way when you walk to work or panhandlers or, well, you know."

"A city guy talking?"

"Yeah." He hugged her. "Could be why you're easy to be around. You get where I'm coming from."

Wishing they didn't have separate vehicles to drive home, she leaned against her convertible and gazed into his deep blue eyes. "Come to the cottage for coffee."

"I'd like to." His cell phone rang. "Chance Williams." He frowned, his mouth turning from a smile to a scowl. "Ten-four."

Lauren reached up and put her fingertips to his lips. "Chance, you don't have to explain. I realize you need to go."

"Give me a rain check on the coffee?"

"Sure." She wanted to shout, "Stay safe" but didn't.

Chapter 36

Pleased, and disappointed at the same time, Lauren dropped her purse, kicked off her shoes, then continued to the cottage's kitchen.

She rummaged in the cupboard, sure she recently bought decaf and it was hiding in there. Pushing the canned soup out of the way, she gripped the unopened bag. "Got you."

Waiting for the water to heat, she remembered the sensation of swaying in Chance's arms. Secure and safe, she hadn't wanted to let go. However, when the music ended, there was no other choice.

Was she ready to start something with him that could lead to…to what?

Too restless to sleep, she needed something to take her mind off Chance. With a hot cup of decaf, she curled up on the couch to stream a movie, no romances, maybe a Sci-fi or a thriller. Clicking on a movie service, she was about to make a choice when someone knocked on the front door and she went to open it.

"Chance!"

"Is it too late to take you up on the offer of coffee?"

"Come in. I just made a pot."

He wiped his boots and entered, still dressed in the jeans and blue dress shirt he'd worn at dinner tonight, with no smoke or ash on his clothes.

They walked to the kitchen.

"Cream, sugar?"

"Black."

"Is everything at the firehouse all right, if you don't mind my asking?"

He carried the mug and sat, with a sigh, on the sofa. "The building is coming along fine. It should be completed on schedule, but I have a lot of work to do with the recruits. It will be a while before I can delegate the running of the station to them, even for a short time. Bonnie is a little green in that area too."

"Oh."

"Hey, don't look so concerned. They're the best-damned group of firefighters in the state." He paused and gulped down the decaf. "Only they're not trained to make administrative decisions, not even Bonnie is ready."

"What will you do?"

He set the mug on the coffee table. "Instruct them and hope to find the right personality to take a leadership position." He stood and held out his hand. "Come here."

When she did, he put his arm around her and held her to him.

"I didn't have my goodnight kiss," he whispered in her ear.

"Oh, I..." When his mouth joined with hers, all thought disappeared. He increased the pressure and encouraged her to open and let his tongue play with hers. They moved together as if they were on the dance floor again, but this time they made their own music.

217

"Wow." She took a deep breath. "I've never experienced a kiss like that."

"Yeah." He leaned forward and ran his hand through his hair.

For a moment they didn't speak, silent as if they had to process what was happening between them.

"I never wanted to be involved with a firefighter again—not after I lost…"

"Yeah, I know. No way a career woman was for me. I always said I wanted a female to stay home and take care of the house."

"Now what?"

"Laurie, give me another kiss."

"OMG, I hoped you would say that."

***

October's heat continued and though the leaves turned deep autumn colors, it still felt like summer.

Chance got in his truck, started the engine, and drove toward town. The hot winds set him on edge as he recalled the damage a spark in the dry woods could do. If only the rain would come to lessen the danger.

Last year's fires had left California stripped of thousands of acres of forest, not to mention the loss of homes. Memories of the small town of Paradise, California raged. Years earlier, so many had died when the town burned to the ground.

He'd be damned if the citizens of Sierra Creek didn't have a plan to prevent such an event. What would happen if dry lightning struck in the underbrush or if an electric wire snapped? Linemen from the gas and electric company were helping him by checking the poles near town for possible problems, but there was more to do.

As he had told the mayor and town council, the plan was to clear around the outbuildings and farmhouses on the rural properties. Most of the owners had taken the idea seriously, but a few of the old timers saw no need to change their way of doing things and sure as hell didn't need a young guy from the city telling them how to prepare.

He gulped back a curse and rubbed the tension from the back of his neck. Maybe Mayor Breen could talk some sense into the elderly geezers.

At least the training of the recruits appeared to be going smoothly, and he now understood each firefighter's strengths and weaknesses.

He wiped his forehead and took a deep breath. The lack of a new hook and ladder truck concerned him but...

Today, he and Laurie would walk the acreage near the farms to check for brush that needed to be removed. She had asked to join him and he wouldn't turn down the offer.

After the other night at her cottage, his mind relived her generous response to his advances. He'd shared his private information. Things not talked about even with his closest friend, he told her stories of his childhood and his goals and dreams. In his arms, she'd listened quietly without comment or judgment. When he finished, she had glazed up at him and smiled.

Somehow, that simple act had been exactly what he'd needed.

In a hurry, he parked the truck behind the mayor's office and jogged up the stairs to find Mr. Breen.

Anita, the mayor's private secretary, sat primly at her desk. Grimly dressed in dark grey as usual, her dark mane in a tight bun, not a hair out of place, she stared at him when he entered the room.

He smiled his hello, but she didn't return it. The first time he met Anita, he thought she must be in a bad mood because of some recent occurrence. However, each time he saw the woman, her demeanor and attire were the same.

"He is expecting you, Mr. Williams. You may go in."

"Thank you."

Mayor Breen stood, adjusted the vest of his three-piece suit, and left his desk to extend his hand in welcome. "Come, sit down. I have some interesting news." He pointed to the chair facing the desk. "Coffee? I can ring Anita."

"Thanks, but I'm good."

"Fine. Fine—hot for this season." Breen wiped the sweat from his brow. "The damn fan is on the blink again."

Chance noticed the box fan wedged in the window of the hundred-year-old building, probably not enough decent wiring to handle air conditioning in the place.

"Well, here's the story. I talked to the town's accountant and I think we can scrape up some cash for the extra equipment for the old fire engine and a tune-up. I'd hoped to talk that stubborn ass on the town council into changing his mind and spring for the money needed for the new hook and ladder vehicle, but…" The mayor leaned back in his armchair.

"I appreciate you trying."

"Well, don't look so glum. We might work something out. I want the best for my little berg. I have for the last thirty years. Not going to quit now." He rubbed his chin and frowned. "Send me an example of the least budget you would require to buy one."

"All right."

"And don't lose faith in the girls, Amy, Vanna, and Lauren. They're planning charity events to help the cause."

"You don't say?"

"Yes, and so far, the Fund Me Page has raised an outstanding amount. You'd be surprised how many people, even strangers, care about firefighters and want to help."

"Well, I never…"

"Chance, the list of the fire apparatus you wanted is with Anita. She will take care of ordering them. I'll tell her to be sure the items are delivered to the new firehouse."

"Great—thank you."

"No worries, I've worked in civic life for a long time." The mayor walked Chance to the door and patted him on the back. "Problems tend to work themselves out. We'll talk again."

Chapter 37

Smithy took the day off from work at the Hitching Post to deliver his silver goods to the person running the Animal Fund Charity Auction. Lauren got the impression he enjoyed meeting with the guy as they were old friends from Mr. Smith's rodeo days.

He volunteered to bring her entry along as well. Odd, but she felt anxious. What if no one bid on the painstakingly designed pin? She cringed at the thought. How embarrassing would that be? *Nothing ventured, nothing gained.* At least she'd find out if she was any good at creating something people would want to buy.

Now that school was back in session, tourist visits slowed and business declined too. Jake needed the morning off and would return to the shop to relieve her so she could go with Chance in the afternoon.

Lauren paced near the front of the Hitching Post waiting for a customer to decide between two items. She was pleased to see Irene happy and recovered after being trapped in her vehicle on the side of the road. The recollection of the day Chance had rescued Irene still shook Lauren.

"The red shirt or the blue plaid? What do you think, Lady L?" Irene asked.

"They would both be beautiful with your hair and eyes."

"You always say the nicest things—my hubby says I wear too much pink and, well, red is close to pink, right? Maybe the blue, but I didn't really want a plaid. I don't know…"

"I have an idea, Irene. I'll be right back."

Lauren found the box of new items and held up a baby blue western-style shirt with abalone shell buttons.

"How about this one? It's new, not on the shelf yet. You would be the first to buy it." She held it up to Irene and told her to look at her reflection in the mirror.

"Perfect. I love it! Thank you." She hesitated. "And a special thanks for helping me the other day, Lady L, when my car went off the road." She wiped a tear from her cheek.

"Hey, I didn't do anything. I'm only glad to see you looking so well." Lauren hugged her.

When Irene left the store, she smiled and waved goodbye.

***

"Must be a hundred degrees," Lauren mumbled as she drove toward Johnny and Sophie's farm where she and Chance planned to meet.

Her lungs filled with the hot but clean air of the Sierra Nevada foothills as her car sped on the two-lane road.

She glanced at the deep blue sky and thought of the beige atmosphere so often seen this time of the year in Los Angeles.

The brakes shuddered as she brought the convertible to a screeching halt. A man stood in the middle of the road and stared at her much like a deer in the headlights.

"Do you need help?"

He glared at her.

When she opened the door, he ran off into the tall grass and disappeared into the forest.

Trembling, she sat and remembered the first words Chance had spoken to her when they met. *Lady, next time, drive more slowly around these roads. You might have hit someone.* He had frowned at her. *Drive off the end of the world for all I care, but don't speed on this road again.*

Would he care if she drove away and disappeared now?

As she continued toward Sophie's home, she made sure to keep the car's speed down. She considered the scruffy man in the road. He might be the same one who came into the shop and bought a blanket.

He had the worn backpack he'd carried into the store. She sensed everything he owned would be in the huge bag. Where was he headed? As far as she knew, there was nothing other than miles of forest in the direction he ran. Should she mention the man to Chance? And give him another reason to lecture her on driving carefully— better not to bring it up.

The fire engine was parked in the driveway of Johnny and Sophie's small white farmhouse.

Chance waved from the cab. "They aren't home, but we have permission to look around. Johnny also asked me to check out a shack on the border of his property and the open space." He jumped from the vehicle and slammed the driver's side door. "Ready to trek up the hills?"

"I'm wearing my hiking boots."

"I didn't think you owned any, you being from the city and all." He grinned.

"Didn't, until I started working for your uncle." She stuck out one foot. "See."

"Cute. I never realized boots could be—pink laces!"

"Yep, Vanna gave them to me. I'm a girl after all."

His eyes widened as he scanned her. "Won't argue that point with you."

"Good, glad it's settled." She laughed.

He chuckled and scanned her again. "Johnny managed to remove the trees close to his home, but a couple of bigger ones near the barn might be problematic." Chance continued to walk toward the other outbuildings.

"What about those bushes? The wood is such a pretty red color," she asked, glad to be on a safer topic of conversation.

"Manzanita. Here in the Sierra Foothills, they cut it down."

"But…"

"I don't enjoy taking out plants either. Still, the leaves are extremely flammable. The shrub can act like ladder fuel if it's close to a building or a large tree, setting them on fire while it burns."

"I never thought…"

"Johnny can take out the Manzanita and I'll get Manny and Wyatt to get rid of the bigger trees within a hundred feet of any structures." With a can of red spray paint, Chance marked an x on the pines to be cut down.

The sun beat down on Lauren as they trudged through the tall, yellow grass toward the next strand of pines. After a mile or so, she resisted remarking on the stifling heat.

Chance grabbed her hand to lift her over a rock outcropping. "Need a break?"

"Yeah. I'm roasting."

Relief flooded her when they stood in the shade of a tall conifer. The aromas of evergreen and aftershave wafted toward her. "Aah," she sighed and leaned against the tree trunk. "The air is so much cooler here."

"Hope your sweet little nose didn't get sunburned." He bent down and kissed the tip of her nose. "Laurie, you're beautiful."

His touch sent a shiver of surprise running through her. "Am I?"

"Yeah." His breath quickened. "Inside and out."

She opened her mouth to speak and he kissed her, leaning in to play with her hair while he increased the power of his embrace.

With her arms around his neck, even in the shade of the grove of trees, heat flared and her breath became ragged. Against her good sense, she was falling in love with Chance.

She pulled back from the realization and let the breeze fan her.

His eyes tracked her, but he didn't try to hold her again. Instead, as if he understood it was too sudden, he grabbed his backpack and yanked out a bottle of water. "Thirsty?"

"Thanks." She took the water and drank, wishing she was still in his arms breathing in his masculine scent and feeling the strength of his muscled arms.

Why was it that men who made her feel safe were the same ones who themselves were in the most danger?

"According to Johnny, the shack isn't too far from here." He broke her train of thought.

If she'd hoped the walk in the woods might be considered a date... After her response to his advances, Chance was all business. No complaints. After all, he didn't ask her to join him. She'd volunteered.

226

Chapter 38

"It's a cabin." Lauren observed "Rundown but…"

Scrub brush surrounded the dilapidated, greying building with its tar-paper roof. A towering pine stood behind the shack but offered little protection from the sun.

"And look at the view." Her breath caught. "I can see forever." She paused, scanning the area. "The person who chose to put the building here had an eye for beauty." She turned around to take in the one-hundred-and-eighty-degree panorama.

"If you glance to the left, that's Amy and Wyatt's farmhouse." Chance pointed. "Across the fields and the apple orchards."

"The house looks so small from here."

"We're up high. By the way, you were a real trooper climbing in this heat."

"Thanks—I wonder who built this."

"Johnny mentioned the original owner of the property built this hut for hunting season."

"Imagine a house up here—on top of the world." She grinned.

"Kind of isolated. I thought as a city gal, you'd want people around, traffic noise, and good shopping."

"Well, I do, but this is a daydream. Too good to be true." She frowned, and then the corners of her mouth turned up. "Let's go inside."

"Be careful, Laurie. The roof might not be stable. Hard to say when the last repairs were done—if any."

"Okay."

"I'll check around the back. You go in. I'll join you inside when I finish."

The front door was surprisingly heavy for the old rundown structure. Seemed it had once adorned a more important edifice. The handle turned easily, but the door squeaked and the bottom of it rubbed on the warped floorboards as it opened.

She blinked and tried to focus in the dark interior. Standing for a moment to let her eyes adjust after being in the bright sun, she sniffed the stale air and coughed at the lingering smell of cigarettes and decaying food. A single screenless window caught her attention. With a little effort, she opened it. Light poured into the room and dust motes floated in the room and were sent to dance on the accompanying breeze from the open window.

The space was larger than she first thought. Only one room, but with a fireplace and a makeshift dry sink. Not much, but if a bit of work went into the cabin…

"What the hell! Are you following me?"

Lauren turned too quickly, stumbled over litter on the dirty hardwood floor, and nearly fell. The stranger moved toward her and she screamed.

"Shut up, bitch!" His hand in the air, he continued toward her.

"Stop!" Chance's deep voice ordered, an imposing figure, filling the doorway, legs apart, his hands forming fists.

228

"I wasn't going to sock her." The stranger backed away. "The woman damned near hit me..."

"Get out!" Chance stepped closer.

"Hey, I..."

"Now! This is private property. Don't come back."

The stranger glared at Lauren, mumbled a curse under his breath, and ran from the shed.

When the man was gone, Chance pulled her into a tight embrace. "Did he hurt you? Laurie, if anything happened to you, I couldn't stand it," he whispered.

She held on to him like a lifeline, her heart thundering against his solid chest. "I was just scared."

With his strength calming her, she stood in silence listening to his steady heartbeat.

"Chance, I saw him at the Hitching Post and then again on the road coming here. He ran off, but I didn't think he might be going to this place."

"I believe he's been here for some time. I found the makings of a campfire behind the building and empty food containers. All it would take is one spark for him to start the brush on fire and the pines would go up too." Chance paused and took a slow breath. "With the winds, there'd be the perfect firestorm situation."

"Oh, dear God."

"The building will need to be knocked down."

"What about his things?"

"Laurie, you still care? He threatened you."

"I..." She stopped. "Well, he's human and obviously in trouble. No point in making things worse for him."

"You amaze me with your kindness."

She picked up a blanket, the one she'd sold to the guy. It still had the Hitching Post label.

Outside the front door, they piled the stranger's belongings and the cans of food found in the shack.

"When he comes back, this stuff is ready for him." Chance set the worn backpack down. "I added a business card to a displaced people's shelter. They might set him right, at least for a while. Families who lose their homes in a fire often use the services."

Before they left, Chance nailed the door and window shut and marked the house with a red X for demolition.

"Let's go home." He took her hand.

She liked the sound of that because more and more Sierra Creek felt like home.

***

The leaves of autumn fell but the weather remained hot and dry with no sign of rain. Lauren worked for days at the Hitching Post, side by side with Smithy. To her surprise, he was becoming a friend and she found herself looking forward to seeing him each day.

At the end of the week, Lauren packed up her work and left the store.

Parking in front of the farmhouse, she glanced at the azure sky. A pleasant routine had begun to set in, what with her employment and life on the apple farm. She enjoyed the rhythm of rural life without the big box stores and traffic noise. Morning walks before work increased her creativity and kept her fit. She didn't need anything else to make her happy.

That evening, Amy and Bobby were in the yard. Lauren waved and went to join them. She played ball with Bobby, then helped her friend rake leaves.

As Amy's pregnancy progressed, Lauren tried to do what she could to help around the farm, including gardening, something new to her.

Amy stopped raking and rubbed her back. "These days I don't have the stamina I used to, and I waddle like a duck when I walk," she joked. "None of my shoes are comfortable, so I wear my bedroom slippers. Look."

Lauren gazed at the faux fur-lined moccasins and back at Amy. "They must be comfy."

"Very." She giggled.

Her friend complained but also stated this was the happiest time of her life. Joy glowed in Amy's eyes as she spoke of her love for her growing family.

Lauren admired her courage, realizing Amy worried that celiac disease might be passed on to the baby as with Bobby. Nonetheless, Lauren believed the child would bring joy to all who knew the baby.

At the Friday night farmhouse barbecues, Lauren and Vanna now made the meals, though Amy insisted on baking the apple pies.

Since Bobby couldn't have wheat, Sophie always made a special frozen dessert for him and had begun to sell it at the ice cream parlor as well. One evening, Sophie mentioned she was working on an apple pie ice cream flavor. Everyone agreed it would be a hit.

The only downside was that days had gone by and Chance had not come home to his attic suite above the barn. Lauren had the impression he was avoiding her ever since their walk in the hills.

Amy mentioned he was staying nights at the new firehouse, though it was not yet finished.

He was doing his due diligence before having the crew move in; that's what she told herself. But in the back of her mind, other thoughts countered with the idea he didn't want to see her. They had become too close on the top of the mountain when he'd held her and whispered his concern for her safety. Did he regret his words? *Laurie, if anything happened to you, I couldn't stand it.*

231

Never mind, she didn't need someone to complete her life. She was, after all, a career woman. Right? So why did a void open in the pit of her stomach when Chance wasn't near?

"Daydreaming?" Amy interrupted her deliberation.

"Yeah. I'm afraid I do it a lot." She laughed without humor and picked up a broom to sweep the patio.

"Creative people usually do. Might be how you make such pretty jewelry."

"Thanks, Amy." She wanted to ask about Chance but couldn't think how to phrase a question without showing her confused emotion relating to him.

"How's your dad, Lauren?"

Grateful to talk about anyone but Chance, she explained her dad's rheumatoid arthritis and the problems it caused. "His reluctance to admit he needed anyone to care for him worries me."

"Wyatt's dad had trouble too and wouldn't accept Wyatt's or my offers of help. I guess it must be the age of these men." Amy paused. "In the end, Bill let us contact his doctor." She dumped a pile of leaves into a bin.

"Daddy can be stubborn." Lauren raked the dry grass and sent it into the bin as well. "I suggested he think about visiting Sierra Creek, a way to gently let him find out the positives of living in a less populated area where he might be able to function more easily." She stopped working and wiped her forehead with the back of her hand. "Living so long in LA, I don't think Daddy can visualize going anywhere else. I couldn't either until I moved here."

"Might be hard," Amy agreed. "Returning here after living in San Francisco was a real transition for me."

They worked in silence for a while, with only the sound of Bobby making engine noises for his car as he played on the patio.

"Truth be known, I've heard from Daddy's neighbor. He rarely leaves his apartment these days. His food and medication are delivered and he no longer visits his buddies." Lauren hesitated. "Zoe, the neighbor, does what she's able to, but the lady is moving back east and will be leaving in a couple of months."

"Oh. I understand why you're uneasy. No other family members in the area?"

"It's just my dad and me."

"Mommy, Lauren collected the eggs from the chicken coop all by herself today!" Bobby yelled as if he had amazing news.

"I sure did. Bobby gave me lessons on how to make the chickens move out of the way while I grab the eggs." She grinned. "Thanks, Bobby. I couldn't have done it without you."

"Hey, big guy," Wyatt shouted from his truck as he drove to a stop in the driveway, then came and hugged his wife and rubbed her stomach. "Everything okay?" He bent to kiss Amy before she could answer.

"Lauren." He nodded when he finished kissing his wife.

"Daddy, look what my car can do."

"I'm coming, Bobby."

"Amy, I'm going to take off and try to reach my dad on the phone." Lauren waved and left.

Chapter 39

In the shack, the squatter was shocked awake by the sound of a wood saw. The noise echoed in the hills and sent him clamoring to round up his belongings, including cans of food. Yesterday, he'd found the window and door nailed shut, but he'd shattered the glass window pane.

His heart thundered as his anger grew. Why couldn't he be left alone? Hadn't people taken enough from him? He spit the stale breath from his mouth and tried to tie up his sleeping bag. In a hurry, the bedroll didn't cooperate. "Hell!"

The broken window used as his entrance back into the building was still jagged with threatening shards sticking up. He didn't relish the idea of crawling over them. He cursed, knocked out the broken glass with a log, threw his stuff out, and followed them.

He landed with a thud on the hard, dry ground. On his back, he lay motionless, glaring at the blue sky. His breathing ragged and his heart booming, with a grunt he rose to a standing position and brushed off his jeans.

Where to go? His mind went blank. It appeared all options were now depleted. He wanted a beer and considered digging for one in his pack, but the buzzing of the saw coming nearer sent him into the forest at a run.

***

Early Friday morning, Chance met the head architect for a final walk around the building. It was with some pride Chance gazed at the product of hard work, able planning, and an experienced architectural firm.

The required changes and fixes had been completed, and the time had come to bring in the fire crew and open the place.

When the tour finished, he shook the man's hand. "It's better than I believed possible. This little town is in fine shape if a fire threatens the area. Can't thank you enough."

In his office, a place Chance had dreamed of having, he arranged for the new employees to move in and wrote out their work schedules. Mayor Breen needed to be kept in the loop, so he composed a letter informing him of the current situation. He inserted the budget required to purchase a new hook and ladder truck, more than Chance had hoped but worth every dollar in case of a serious firestorm.

As far as he understood, the money wasn't available, but at least the mayor and town council would receive the asked-for figures.

He certainly didn't mean to complain. This small town now had a state-of-the-art firehouse.

New bunks would arrive on Monday and the furniture for the day room would come too. Mayor Breen had lent him an old oak desk that had been in storage with the city. It was a bit worn from use, but Chance admired the workmanship. Earlier, Manny, whose hobby was woodworking, assured him that, with the right attention, the desk would serve him for many years.

The muscles in his lower back ached. He rubbed them and yawned. He needed some shut-eye after spending several nights on the narrow cot in the sleeping quarters at the firehouse.

A vision of Laurie came to mind. What would it be like to curl up next to her? He could almost feel her soft body. *Never mind.* Under those circumstances, he wouldn't be able to close his eyes, let alone get any rest. Still, he recalled her loving expression when she'd kissed him at the door of her cottage. *Enough.*

He shook his head. There was work to finalize. Dreaming about Laurie wouldn't get it done. The sooner he finished today's responsibilities, the sooner he could go home. He and Laurie needed to talk.

"Chance." Bonnie walked into the office. "Hey, I like your office." She stared but not at the room. Her eyes raked him like a radar beam.

He cleared his throat and shook away the feeling of being under a microscope. "What brings you in on your day off?"

"How long have we known each other?"

"That's an odd question."

"You going to answer?"

"Years. Why?"

She moved closer. A strange expression he couldn't decipher spread on her attractive face. He glanced down and noticed the top two buttons of her shirt were undone and a black lace bra peeked out.

"Bonnie, you're out of uniform."

"Yeah. It's my day off." She let her tongue run along her bottom lip.

Okay, now he was uncomfortable. He picked up his backpack. "Listen, I have to stop at the mayor's office and drop off some paperwork. So…"

"Chance, you must realize I care about you."

"Of course. We're good friends."

"Not what I mean and you know it."

"You're a nice kid, Bonnie."

"I'm not a little kid."

No, damn near five feet ten inches tall and well endowed, nobody thought she was a girl. But he considered her a younger sister. Even if he tried, which he didn't want to do, she couldn't be more than a pal.

"We might be right for each other. I understand your job and I'm not afraid of danger."

"Like Lauren is."

"You said it. I didn't. But since you used her name, she's weak and terrified of the work you do. When you need her, she won't be there for you. I would."

Anger rose in him. Why did he want to defend Lauren?

"Bonnie, this conversation is over. I need a team player, not personal advice. If you can't get with the program then…" He picked up his paperwork and left the room.

***

Mayor Breen had gone home early, but Chance delivered the paperwork to his secretary, Anita.

That evening, Chance stepped out onto the landing of his suite and stared at the cottage, dark and lifeless without Laurie. He sighed. For the first time, he realized how much he depended on checking to be sure she was there.

His plan to talk with her had been foiled when he came home early, but she was already gone. She'd departed for LA, left unexpectedly, and no one seemed to know her return date.

He considered asking why she left suddenly but held back. Locals didn't need to understand his desire to speak to her.

Truth be known, he struggled to define his response to her. He wanted Laurie, but how deep did his feelings go? Of course, she was beautiful. Bright and kind, she cared about people, including the man who'd frightened her. She wanted to do him no harm. That made her special in Chance's eyes.

An image of her, wearing pajamas and smiling at him, sent a wave of desire running through him.

As if to fight the sentiment, Bonnie's description of Lauren surfaced. *She's weak and terrified of the work you do. When you need her, she won't be there for you.*

Did her words have any validity?

He grunted, went inside, and returned to the work on his computer.

Where was Laurie right now? As a city gal, would she be coming back to this little village? Did LA offer more than Sierra Creek ever could?

With no answer, he forced his mind back to the task at hand.

Chapter 40

Los Angeles had a second-stage smog alert when Lauren's plane landed in the San Fernando Valley at the Burbank Airport. The air sat still and the sky hung like a beige ceiling over her head. Breathing deeply was discouraged and the heat was stifling. *Home sweet home.* However, when she thought of The Valley, it was always a clear spring day. Her memory could be so deceitful.

Worried about her dad, she looked forward to visiting him. She hoped Ben's text suggesting she come ASAP wasn't as grave as it sounded. Still, on the strength of his words, she had driven to Sacramento and taken the first plane to LA she could find.

"Lauren." A tall man dressed in dark slacks, a white cashmere sweater, even in this heat, and Italian leather loafers, smiled, his brown hair perfectly trimmed, his large brown eyes flashing.

Before she could respond, he swept her into his arms and kissed her hard on the lips.

She wiggled out of his arms. "Ben, stop. We're in public." What if this was Chance? Would she mind then?

Ben laughed and took her bag. "My car's in the lot." He pointed.

In his Mercedes sedan, she managed small talk, filling the air with unimportant details of her life in Sierra Creek and asking him about business, always a good way to keep him engaged.

In the circular drive of her dad's condo building, she grabbed her bag and jumped out before Ben could.

"Thanks for the ride. I'm in a hurry to check on Daddy."

As she started for the building, Ben yelled, "Okay, Lauren, but I'll be back to take you out to dinner."

The quiet lobby was the same as when she left. The older furniture and carpet still needed to be replaced. She didn't know why she thought it might have changed. No, she was the one altered, not the Lauren who left so many months ago.

When she entered Daddy's apartment, he sat in his easy chair as always and glanced up at her, a concerned expression on his face. "Lauren, what are you doing here? Did that jerk of a boss fire you?"

"No." She hesitated. "Daddy, how are you?"

"Fine. Why not?"

She bent down to leave a kiss on his unshaven cheek. "Ben said you were—never mind. I just missed you. So, I came for a visit."

Relief poured through her and her heart settled into a normal rhythm. Conversely, anger flared at Ben. His recent texts had sounded urgent. Clearly, a ruse to send her rushing to her father and bring her closer to Ben.

Daddy spent the rest of the day relating what he'd been doing since she moved to Sierra Creek.

She mentioned she and her boss were getting along.

After a snack, they watched old videos of her mother in happier times.

"I'll always love your mom. There will never be another woman like her." Dad hesitated and scrubbed his hand over his face. "But it seems so long since she left us—sometimes I'm lonely."

"Oh, Daddy." She held his hand and they finished watching the videos.

Lauren texted Ben and begged off the dinner date, telling him she wanted to make supper for her father.

Two days went by smoothly and she continued to put Ben off with excuses as to why she wouldn't be able to meet with him.

Her father used a cane now and was proud of his ability to move around. He told her it made him distinguished. Zoe said so. He grinned.

To Lauren's surprise, Zoe was still in town. But her condo was filled with packing boxes and much of her furniture was missing. It appeared the woman would be moving presently.

The night before Lauren's planned departure, Daddy sat her down, a serious expression on his face. "I need to talk to you."

"Oh, God. What is it?"

"Lauren, don't worry. It's good news. At least *I* think it is. I hope you will too."

"Don't keep me in suspense, Daddy."

He paused, and thencx took a deep breath.

"Tell me."

"Lauren, I've asked Zoe to move in with me."

"What! You mean like a girlfriend?"

He nodded. "Zoe said yes. That is if you don't mind."

Stunned, Lauren stood, mouth open but silent. She'd been so ready for a terrible medical diagnosis that she couldn't speak.

"Lauren, baby?" Dad started to leave his chair.

"Don't get up. That's awesome news. I'm happy for both of you." She hugged him and sniffed back a tear. "Zoe's a wonderful woman."

"Baby, you have no idea how worried we were. And with you and Ben being a couple, things will work out fine."

"Ben?" She hesitated. Her father's happiness depended on what she said next. *Hold your tongue. In a while, Daddy can discover you don't love Ben.* It's Daddy and Zoe's night. "Dad, I want to take you and Zoe out to dinner to celebrate."

"You're a first-rate kid, Lauren." He said, his voice relieved.

At eleven p.m., Lauren glanced out of the bedroom window to the Ventura Freeway. No matter how familiar, this was no longer her home. The smog, the traffic, and the crowds jangled her nerves. She longed for the peace and quiet of the Sierras and missed her newfound friends, including Chance.

Ben had dined with them and had insisted he pay for the expensive meal. It exasperated Lauren. She had wanted it to be her treat.

She sighed and got into bed in her childhood room. Tomorrow, nothing Ben did would matter. In Sierra Creek life would go back to her new normal. Ben could be left in Los Angeles where he belonged.

What about Chance?

Chapter 41

Smoke spiraled into the air and mingled in the tall pines near Johnny and Sophie's farm.

Chance drove the fire truck up the narrow road to the two-story farmhouse that appeared to be in the middle of a renovation. A metal barrel with flames reaching high into the blue sky burned in the yard sparks flying. He saw no one was in the area.

"What the hell!" Chance jumped out of the driver's side door to search for the person who started the open fire.

He had worked hard explaining the danger of open flames to the community. He put up posters talking about protecting the county from forest fires, and he'd attended public forums and town council meetings to clarify the problem. What did it take to get the message across?

A middle-aged man with brown thinning hair came out of the house, a bundle of sticks in his arms. He ignored Chance and tossed the wood into the fire. The flames spit sparks out into the atmosphere. One landed on the dry grass and Chance stomped it out with his boot.

At the same time, he held out his hand. "Chance Williams."

The man shook it but didn't share his name.

"What brings you to my property?" the man demanded.

"Your fire. There's an ordnance of no open fires and no barbecuing in the county. Too damned dry. One small spark can set the whole forest burning."

The man brushed off his jeans. Chance saw a bored expression spread across the guy's face. "You don't say."

"I do say. Usually, the rains start around this time of year." Chance paused. "This year, drought is being considered." He scratched his chin. "You from around these parts?"

"No."

After waiting for the stranger to give more personal information, Chance said, "Nice house, by the way. You have big plans in the works?"

"Yeah."

The fire continued to burn. Even so, Chance didn't want to start off on the wrong foot by writing the man a ticket. All the same, he needed to make it clear open flames would not be tolerated.

The stranger turned to go back into the house. To stop him, Chance offered more information about himself. It worked because when the guy learned they were both from the Bay Area, he mentioned his name, Mike Sullivan from Walnut Creek. He wanted a place to raise kids away from crowds and traffic.

The more they talked, the more he had the idea Mike might be trusted to cooperate. Especially now that he understood the hazard. The guy certainly didn't want anything happening to his new home.

Chance offered to buy him a drink and introduce him to some of the men in the area.

Mike agreed with a nod. "I don't know if this falls under your purview as a firefighter, but I've observed a scruffy-looking man with an old backpack camping at the edge of my property and Mr. Hansen's place."

"Yeah?"

"It's up near those large rocks." Mike pointed.

"I'll check it out."

They arranged to meet at the Mother Lode Saloon in a couple of days. When Chance left, Mike was wetting down the bonfire with a garden hose.

A fire road near the granite outcropping ended in a dirt turnout. Chance parked and headed toward the forest. About a quarter mile up the hill, the aroma of cooking chili beans greeted him. A crude campsite sat near a grove of sugar pines.

The place appeared to be unattended, but someone had started the food, so they must be nearby. A worn backpack, similar to the one seen in the shed, leaned against a tree trunk. Could this be owned by the same person who threatened Laurie?

At the crunch of pine needles, Chance spun around in time to see a man strike him with a rock. It was the last thing he remembered until he woke staring up at the tall canopy of evergreens.

He sat up and touched the bump on his forehead. "Damn!" The pack was gone, as was the man. The beans were burning on the dying fire, sending a putrid odor to mix with the scent of the fresh conifers.

He blinked to bring everything into focus before standing and putting out the campfire.

The stranger had gone too far. Chance would have to alert the local police and the forest rangers in the area.

245

The loner needed to be stopped before he seriously hurt someone and started an inferno that might do some extreme damage. He shuddered, realizing how easily a raging forest fire could start in drought conditions.

After being certain the fire was out and using water from the truck to make sure no sparks were possible, he returned to the firehouse. He grabbed an acetaminophen and went to work contacting the appropriate departments, including the local police and the US Forestry Service.

A paramedic assigned to the firehouse checked out his head wound and sent him to the emergency room at the small Sierra Creek hospital.

Chance thought it was unnecessary but followed the instructions to set the appropriate example for his crew.

Subsequently, the doctor cleared him to go home. He lugged his tired ass up the driveway of Wyatt and Amy's farmhouse disappointed Laurie's car was not in sight and the cottage remained dark.

The stairs to the attic seemed steeper tonight. He entered his place, dropped his belongings at the door, and without flicking on a light, stretched out on the bed and closed his eyes.

***

Before Lauren entered the taxi to leave for the Burbank Airport, Daddy waved and smiled from the condominium lobby. Zoe stood next to him holding his hand. Last night, she'd told Lauren of her love for him. The woman had cared for years but had waited for Daddy to give a sign he felt the same.

It was only about sixty minutes from wheels up in So Cal to a landing in Sacramento. By 10:00 a.m. Lauren had her bag and was walking toward the long-term parking lot and her car.

With the top down on her convertible, she breathed in clean air and headed down the familiar two-lane highway toward Sierra Creek.

At midday, few vehicles were on the road in the gently rolling Sierra foothills. The place was such a relief from the noise and congestion of LA County. Lauren's stress diminished and she enjoyed the sight of the California black oaks that stood strong and silent against the deep blue sky.

In less than an hour, the main street in town would be before her, then in a matter of minutes the turnoff to her cottage.

She hummed, something she rarely did as her voice wasn't good enough to let anyone hear it. All the same, in her open car, she sang along with the familiar tune playing from the mix of songs made for her travels. Life was sweet. Daddy was happy, so she could stop the sense of not doing enough to help him.

In the afternoon, she'd park and enter Amy's farm. If fortune smiled on her, Chance would be there too.

A road sign said twenty miles to Sierra Creek, and without being aware of it, she increased the speed of the convertible and took a turn too fast. Her car's back wheels slid onto the graveled shoulder. *Whoa.* She took her foot off the gas pedal, better to arrive a little late than to be in an accident.

Main Street bustled as it always did on a Friday at lunchtime. The Hitching Post's door stood wide open, and Jake had piled feed bags in front of the store as per usual. She considered stopping but thought he might ask her to work and she had other plans for the rest of the day. She hummed again, as an image of Chance caused her to grin.

She drove through the village and took the turn off to her home. Before long, she pulled into her usual parking spot in front of Amy's farmhouse. Disappointment hit her when the fire truck was nowhere to be seen. Still, in the middle of the day, it was to be expected.

Bobby would be in school and Wyatt and Amy working at the sawmill. Nearing her due date, Amy mentioned she might stop teaching a full schedule and begin to work part-time at the preschool.

Alone on the farm, Lauren carried her travel bag up the walkway toward the cottage.

"You're back."

She spun around and faced Chance, backlit by the sun.

"Why not? I live here."

"Thought maybe you'd decided to move back to LA."

She set her bag down and took a step forward, covering her eyes from the sun's glare. "Sierra Creek is my home now. I didn't think you would be here—no truck out on the road."

He moved a bit closer. "My day off. The second in command has it."

"Bonnie."

"No. She doesn't work here anymore."

"What?"

"Bonnie decided to move back to the Bay Area, where she came from."

"Really?" Lauren hoped her pleasure at the news didn't show in her face or voice, but she couldn't stop the corner of her mouth from turning up.

"I hired an old friend, a staff member from San Francisco, to take her place."

"Oh." She stood for a moment in awkward silence, sure when they saw each other again they would... What—leap into each other's arms?

"Well, I better..." Ready to walk to the cottage, she picked up her bag.

"I missed you, Laurie." He moved still closer.

"Did you?" She stepped toward him.

"Yeah—it's lonely without you."

He bent down and sent a whisper of a kiss on her cheek, then wrapped her in his embrace, while his kisses rained on her waiting lips. Gentle at first, but then he increased the depth and power. Her desire for him blossomed.

She gasped for air "OMG, Chance, I missed you too."

With his huge hand, he gently touched her cheek. "Good."

They didn't speak again, instead, he carried her bag to the cottage and they entered.

"Chance, all the days I was away, I couldn't stop thinking about you, I kept wondering what you were doing, if you were all right and..."

He sat on the sofa and patted the cushion near him.

Absorbing the aroma of soap, shaving cream, and man, she snuggled next to him and leaned against his broad chest letting his warmth engulf her. With emotions stirring, for a while it was enough to be in his arms, realizing he cared.

At last, he moved his arm from her shoulder and asked, "How long will you be in town?"

"What? I thought you understood. Sierra Creek is my home—for always."

"But what about your plans to start a business in Los Angeles? Do you honestly want to give that up?"

"I'm not. I can work here. I don't have to be in a city." She paused and scanned his blue eyes. "A funny thing happened the moment I got off the plane in Burbank. I realized everything had changed—didn't seem right." She took a slow breath. "But I was wrong. It was me. I was different. LA is no longer my home. Sierra Creek is."

"Laurie."

She gazed at him. "OMG, Chance, your forehead is bruised. What happened?"

Chapter 42

Lauren sprang from the sofa. "Chance you're hurt."

"Don't frown. I'm okay, just a bump." He stood and held out his arms to her, enclosing her in his embrace again.

"But…" His kiss silenced her and suddenly she couldn't think of anything but having more of him. She moved with his music as he brought their bodies together and they swayed in rhythm, holding on to each other as if the rest of the world didn't matter. For now, it had disappeared—only they existed.

She closed her eyes to allow one sensation, the response to his touch and the beat of his heart throbbing against her body.

"Whew." Chance pulled away. "Laurie, if I don't stop now, I can't guarantee I'll be able to."

"Yeah." Her breathing was ragged and she couldn't say more. Her face flushed as desire burned within her.

She reached for him and the doorbell buzzed. Ignoring it, she ran her fingers through his hair.

The buzzing stopped, but there was knocking on the door.

"Better answer, Laurie," he whispered, so near to her ear that it sent a chill down her spine.

She managed to take a deep breath. "Right."

Lauren opened the door and peered out.

"Hey." Vanna smiled. "Am I interrupting?"

"Well, I…" Lauren touched her face. She must be bright red.

"Lauren, I'm checking to find out if you'll be at the barbecue tonight. I've got the meat and Mom, as usual, will make the dessert. You were on for salad." Vanna glanced into the living room and cleared her throat. "Uh, no worries. I see you're busy." She winked and pulled the door closed.

Chance came up behind Lauren. "Vanna's smart, and Laurie, I'm one lucky man."

***

Chance made a garden salad and a potato salad. When she expressed surprise, he replied that no one could be a firefighter unless they handled themselves in the kitchen as well. "I'm a remarkable guy." He grinned.

"Yes, you are." She acknowledged his statement but didn't laugh because what he said was true.

If only he stays safe. She shook the thought from her mind. Time spent loving Chance was all she needed to think about. Still, would she be strong enough to prevent him from realizing she worried every time he went to work?

They attend the barbecue with their friends as they did most Fridays. She and Chance played ball with Bobby and caught up on the news about the coming baby. Bobby stated that he would have a sister or a brother to play with when they weren't a baby, of course.

Lauren hugged Bobby and assured him he would make a wonderful big brother.

After dinner, she and Chance sat around the campfire talking with, Amy, Wyatt, Vanna, Manny, Sophie and her hubby Johnny. No subject off limits, laughter came easily and Lauren had the sense of an extended family.

Long-sought-after contentment filled her as she listened to the conversations, including the past adventures of Chance, Wyatt, and Manny on the rodeo circuit.

When the fire died down and the party broke up, Chance walked her to the cottage. Much to her delight, he accepted her offer to come in.

***

In the cottage, Chance declined Lauren's offer to sit with her on the couch. Instead, he sat in the leather chair across from the sofa. "We should talk."

"Okay." She leaned forward. "What about?"

Her inquisitive expression and pouting mouth nearly took him off the desired topic. His longing to take her in his arms almost overwhelmed him. He forced himself to glance away.

"I'm a firefighter, always will be." He stopped and turned to scan her pretty face, searching for a response. She didn't comment, so he continued. "I was attracted to you since the day you damn near ran me down."

"OMG, don't remind me." She blushed.

"But Laurie, I've never planned for any other career than a firefighter and I don't intend to."

Her eyes widened as she stared at him, then she blinked. "I know." In silence, her brow furrowed as if in thought and she gazed downward.

Was Bonnie right about Lauren? She didn't possess the courage needed to stay with him and be at his side when he might truly need her.

253

He exhaled and stood up. It would be easy to surrender his heart to Laurie, but he wouldn't unless she was willing to offer the same unconditional commitment to him as he longed to give to her.

Breaking the stillness, he spoke, "Hey, I'll understand if you don't want to be involved with another firefighter, after your last experience." He paused and noted her saddened expression at the mention of her past relationship. "Laurie, I'm not a fortune teller. I can't tell you what the future holds for me." He stared as she flinched at his words. "I make you no promise that I will never be hurt or kil…" he stopped.

When she didn't say anything, he wondered if he should leave the cottage. "No hard feelings, Laurie. I understand."

"What?" She shook her head as if trying to understand him. "Chance, don't go." She stopped. "I wouldn't want you to do any other job."

Had he misheard her? "You sure?"

"It's what you do—who you are. It makes you special. I'd never ask you to change."

"Oh, Laurie." He enclosed her in his embrace and breathed in her feminine scent. She held on to him and the sensation of her warmth sent hunger rushing through his veins.

But she hadn't seen what fire could do to flesh. His body was proof. What would be her response when she viewed the scarring on his back he'd worn since the inferno that came close to killing him? Would she be strong enough to hang around, knowing it might happen to him again?

On tiptoes, she glanced up and he kissed her. Nudging her lips open with his tongue. He entered her lush mouth and explored until she sighed and leaned into him, their bodies moving in rhythm with their fast breathing.

Without stopping the kiss, he carried her to the sofa and set her on his lap.

His hand ranged over her soft curves while she ran her fingers through his hair and down his back. She gasped and pulled out of his arms.

It was the reaction he'd expected—grieved over. "Chance?"

He set her down. "You might as well know the truth before we go on."

Bonnie's words rang in his head. *Lauren doesn't have the courage you need in a partner.*

He stood, tugged off his shirt, and turned so she could see the angry red scars on his back, then he faced her.

Laurie's hands flew up to cover her lips, her large eyes filled with tears. "What happened?"

He would tell her the truth as he understood it, something he hadn't shared with anyone. The relief at the idea of someone else realizing what had happened surprised him.

"My team had joined Cal Fire and the US Forestry Service in a bid to control a blaze threatening a small town in Northern California. We fought the forest fire and appeared to be getting the upper hand when over thirty miles per hour winds changed direction. The flames raged and we were all trapped." He grimaced and took a slow breath.

He didn't check for her reaction and she didn't speak, so he continued. "I can't tell you exactly what happened next. Except, I woke on my stomach in a hospital bed disoriented and in pain."

With her eyes wide, an anxious expression on her pale face, Lauren hadn't moved since he started to explain.

He added, "I was lucky. I fell face down and was burned on my back. My hands were under my body, so I have the use of them. Some of my fellow firefighters were not as fortunate." He swallowed hard. "I did a lot of soul-searching while I recovered."

"You decided to remain with the fire service," she said as a statement rather than a question, then moved closer to him. She reached to caress his face. "Does it still hurt?"

"Not so much—no."

"Can I touch them?"

He blinked, surprised at the question. "If you want to."

Like the whisper of butterfly wings, her delicate fingers touched the red skin on his back and chills followed the track of her movements.

"Chance, it's your badge of honor." She paused. "And I adore you for it."

Speechless, he held Laurie to him as his heart thundered with love for her.

"Chance, shall we?"

She took his arm, and they walked toward her bedroom.

Chapter 43

Lauren stood in her bedroom and smiled. "I see your need, Chance. I want you. At first, I fought against my feelings for you—I was afraid." She came closer. "I'm not anymore."

Still bare-chested, he didn't respond. Instead, he slid out of his jeans and boxers. He unbuttoned her shirt and let it drop to the floor, her cotton pants were next, followed by her lace bra and bikini panties.

"You're beautiful, Laurie. Not only your looks but your heart."

He carried her to the bed, and slowly explored her body, leaving a trail of kisses as he did. Her lips parted and his tongue explored while she pulled him nearer, her breathing accelerating.

Her desire for him caused impatience to flow in her. Then again, he understood what he was doing because her arousal increased beyond any reactions she'd ever experienced.

Gently at first, then with full force, he took her once, then again, and again. All she could do was hold on and delight in the explosion of sensations spreading out even to her fingertips. She called his name as he filled her.

Together they lay spent, still entwined as one, their breathing equally ragged.

She must have fallen asleep because she woke up to find him gone. Panic set in. First, she lost her mother, afterward her fiancé, and now Chance. Gasping, she sat up, her heart racing.

"Laurie, do you want eggs and toast with your coffee?" Chance shouted from the kitchen.

He didn't abandon me. She leaned back against the pillows and let out a quiet cry of relief.

Wearing only his boxers, he peered into the bedroom. "Eggs and toast?"

"OMG, Chance. I can't believe there's a bare-chested chef in my kitchen." She giggled. "You're a firefighter. Don't you realize cooking like that is dangerous?"

"It's all right. I know how to put out a fire." He grinned.

"Not mine." She winked.

"Breakfast be damned," he growled as he entered the room, closed the door, and joined her in bed.

***

Lauren found herself singing as she cleaned up the breakfast dishes. *Your voice doesn't deserve to be heard outside of the shower.* She laughed at the thought.

Chance was in his attic apartment reading reports received from the night crew. If all had gone as expected, he'd have the rest of the day off.

She glanced out the window to the beauty of the countryside. With leaves the colors of red and orange, autumn sent Lauren's creative juices flowing, or could it be the nearness to Chance, a man who believed in her ability, that caused such a response?

This morning, Chance seemed so easy-going and carefree. When they first met, she wouldn't have guessed his good nature. At that time, he'd sounded stern and without humor. Now she realized he might have been in pain from his injuries, not to mention, as fire chief, the pressure to make things right for the new firehouse must have felt overpowering.

If luck was kind to them, Chance wouldn't be needed at the scene of a fire and they'd be together today.

He entered the cottage, walked into the kitchen, and hugged her. His face was clean-shaven, his blue eyes sparkling like dark sapphires.

"My you're sexy in the morning, Laurie."

Wide shoulders, slim waist, and strong arms, "OMG, Chance was the sexy one."

He nibbled on her earlobe and whispered, "I have the afternoon off. Why don't we visit the rock shop you wanted to see in the next town? Afterward, we'll have dinner and a movie."

"Sounds wonderful."

***

A car's horn honked and Laurie ran out onto the cottage's porch as a Jeep pulled up the driveway and stopped. Chance learned out of the driver-side window. "Ready to go?"

"Be right there." She ran back into the living room and grabbed her leather bag and a jean jacket.

Holding the door for her, Chance stood aside and she hopped into the passenger seat. "Your car. Right?"

"Yeah. I don't use it much these days. I keep it in a garage at Smithy's place." He glanced at her. "You look great, Laurie." He backed out of the drive and headed toward the local highway. "That yellow shirt brings out the gold in your hair."

"It's just plain brown."

"Laurie, nothing about you is plain." He hesitated. "Your hair sparkles in the sunlight."

"That's the nicest thing anyone ever said to me."

They rode in silence. The scenery changed from barren hills to more woodland with a proliferation of black oaks. On the small two-lane highway, they met only two vehicles, both of them going in the other direction.

"Not much action around here."

"Tranquil country." He agreed. "Must make a teenager growing up here long for the big city."

"Probably."

A faded sign appeared on the road. It read, Calaveras City Pop. She could only guess the number as someone had used the plaque for target practice. She could only observe it had three digits.

In a little while, the insignificant hamlet of Calaveras City came into view, a monument to a time gone by. Nearly empty enough to be called a ghost town, rather than a city, the limited population carried on.

Near the end of October, a banner celebrating Summer Gold Rush Days still hung across the street.

"I wonder if it stays up all year to advertise the festival?"

"I'm told the shindig is known as a way to drink and have a good time without worry. Guess the resulting profits keep the town going until the next time."

Lauren surveyed the area. "I'm glad the retail stores are open."

Though there were few patrons on the street, clerks stood at the entrances of their outlets, most likely to greet anyone who might be cajoled into coming in to browse.

"Chance, search for a sign that says, The Rock Hound."

He glanced at her, then back to the main street. "There." He pointed to a blue and white sign over a building. By the architecture, back in the day, it might have been a one-room schoolhouse.

He parked in front and she saw "open" written on the door.

"Thank goodness. I thought it might say gone fishing or some such thing." She laughed.

"You wouldn't be too far off the mark. Except I think it is hunting season at this point."

"Couldn't prove it by me."

They entered and she found the retail space was larger than expected. Rows of tables filled the room, each one marked with the names of the rocks being displayed. She stopped and took a deep breath.

"Hello," a middle-aged woman with greying hair and thick glasses called.

"Hi, this place is amazing," Lauren answered. "I don't know where to begin."

"Well, everything is marked with the name and where the samples were dug up. I'd be happy to try and answer any of your questions."

"Thank you." Lauren turned to Chance. "Hard to believe this is here in such a small town. It's a candy store for me." She gasped. "You should see this amethyst!"

She roamed the room choosing items that would work with her designs and found a piece of flawless cut crystal. *Gorgeous.* The stone could be placed in a creation she'd wanted for her brooch. She shook her head and put the crystal back on the table.

"You don't like it?" Chance held the gem up to catch the light.

"I love it." She leaned closer and whispered. "Too expensive. Anyway, I'm here on business, not to buy something for me." She moved toward a table marked turquoise.

In thirty-five minutes, Lauren had the stones she needed, including the turquoise and a card from the store's owner. The woman promised to ship other stones to her as needed and would give her a dealer discount.

Chance asked to pay, but Lauren declined. "This is a business expense." Still, she kissed him. "Thanks for the offer."

They left the store with her new possessions and she scanned the street. "Chance, let's go into that antique store."

"Okay." He followed her.

A case of antique bottles and mugs were on one wall and Victorian furniture filled the middle of the room.

She watched as Chance discovered old Daguerreotype and tintype photos of firefighters dressed in full gear from the past. A horse-drawn pumper wagon showed the equipment of the late eighteen hundred.

"Whoa, those were brave men—to attack an inferno with that apparatus." Chance grimaced.

"These pictures would make a wonderful exhibit at the new firehouse." She examined one of them.

"I never thought of putting something up to decorate the hall, but that might be a good idea—if you'd help me.

"Happy to."

He bought all of the photos with the understanding she would aid in their placement.

The day went by quickly and the township proved to be more interesting than she had thought possible.

They read about the beginning of the city. To her astonishment, she discovered Calaveras was a Spanish word meaning skulls.

There was a myriad of mementos concerning the California gold rush and information about how the discovery of the yellow metal changed the state.

The forty-niners, men who came to get rich by digging for gold in 1849, were pictured. Most of them went home broke but possibly a little wiser. Others stayed and built new lives in the West.

Afterward, Chance took her hand and they walked toward the jeep. "Laurie, ready for dinner?"

"I'm famished."

Chapter 44

Weeks sped by without a snag. The job at the Hitching Post continued to go well. With Smithy's okay, Lauren and Jake settled on a system that allowed her to work on her designs and still help in the retail space. She ordered warm winter clothes for men, women, and children then helped with the account books and sales. Jake chose to be in charge of feed and tack.

In the afternoon, when possible, Vanna and Amy met her for lunch. On the odd occasion, Sophie joined them.

Amy's pregnancy progressed nicely and she spent more time at the farmhouse and fewer hours teaching at the preschool. Lauren helped Bobby when she could and got to know him as a sweet kid.

Evenings, when Chance was not staying at the firehouse, were spent together, talking and watching movies.

Lauren learned the schedule at the firehouse and made plans to have a tour.

The days passed and there were no fires in the area and she was grateful. When November came in without rain and the climate was still warm, Chance gave the impression of being nervous, as if waiting for a shoe to drop.

Lauren took a deep breath. Today was Friday and the barbecue would be at the usual time. Chance had spent the last couple of nights at the station. Tonight, he would be home on the farm.

Having learned red was Chance's favorite color, she'd bought a red cardigan to go with her black shirt and jeans. Red flats completed the outfit. With her long hair tied back, she left the cottage to help Amy prepare dinner in the farmhouse kitchen.

On her way to Amy's house, a bird flew by, gliding on the wind currents. Without fear, Lauren followed the progress as it moved toward the rolling hills. Odd how beautiful everything appeared to her. When she first arrived in Sierra Creek, the stillness upset her. The empty hills seemed desolate and exposed. Today, she saw their quiet allure and appreciated the view.

Lauren knocked, then opened the backdoor to the kitchen.

Her friend glanced up from the stove. "Hey, I just put the apple pies in the oven. The grill is going and I started the steaks. Do you mind, I forgot to set out the hot dogs and buns?"

"No worries, Amy. Sit down and rest. I'll take care of it."

***

From his position on the hill overlooking the farm, everything appeared quiet. The man stared at the bucolic scene. The farmhouse, the barn, and even the chicken coop appeared to be in perfect order. The home stood whitewashed and ready for a camera operator to take photos for a postcard.

He grunted. Some people had all the breaks. He'd worked as hard as the owners of this place, but all he had to show was squat.

In a matter of weeks, the weather would turn to wind and rain. He shivered at the thought. He might as well face facts. He didn't want to spend the winter without a shelter.

Hell. He'd made plans before the asshole firefighter had the shed knocked down, leaving him nowhere to live. He swore under his breath, remembering the fireman who discovered his campsite after he set it up in the forest. He shouldn't have hit him so hard with the rock, but he'd been pissed off.

The aroma of the grilling meat on the barbecue caused a rumbling in his empty stomach. Laughter from the woman who lived in the cottage caught his attention as she left the farmhouse and walked toward the patio in the backyard.

He glanced at her. She was a tasty dish. He liked her but wanted the food she carried more. Right now, all he needed was a meal. He rubbed his stomach and sniffed.

When she went back into the house, he considered swiping the steak off the grill. He shook his head and gave up the notion. It might be possible to get cooked meat into the woods without being seen, but right off the fire, it would burn his hands.

A packet of hot dogs sat on the table next to the buns in an unopened plastic bag.

His mouth watered at the idea of eating franks. Decision made, he slid down the embankment and ran behind the barn. Holding his breath, he sneaked a quick look around the corner and saw no one.

With the stealth movements of an athlete, he sprinted forward and made a grab for the hot dogs with one hand and the buns with the other. He spun around and almost tripped on a kid's toy car. He kicked it out of the way and dashed up the hill toward a grove of trees. His heart beating wildly, he reached the evergreens.

"What happened to my car?" a little boy cried.

He didn't wait to hear the answer. Instead, he moved deeper into the forest.

Even before cooking them, he ripped open the package of wieners and quickly ate one.

Afterward, he huddled near the campfire and drank his last beer. *Shit.* He couldn't go on like this. Something had to change.

***

Lauren woke with a start. Blinking into the dark room, she glanced at her phone. One thirty in the morning.

Someone knocked on the cottage door. The sound increased and she jumped out of bed, afraid something had happened to Chance.

Still wearing her short pajamas, she threw open the door to see Wyatt pacing on the deck, his expression grim. "Lauren, sorry to wake you again. Amy's in labor and not doing well. I'm going to take her to the hospital."

Lauren gasped but before she could say anything, he added, "I don't want Bobby to worry. Will you stay with him? He's asleep."

"Sure. I'll grab my slippers and be right there. You go ahead."

Phone in hand, Lauren entered the farmhouse as Wyatt helped his wife down the stairs from the second floor.

"Thank you for coming, Lauren." Amy smiled before wincing and holding her stomach.

"Amy, just take care. Everything will be okay here."

Lauren pulled back the curtain to watch the truck back out of the driveway. She said a silent prayer for Amy and the baby.

Suddenly cold, Lauren wrapped herself in a throw and sat on the couch. Sleep beckoned, but she refused. What if Bobby got up and needed her?

She stood, walked to the foyer and listened. Nothing. The stairs to Bobby's room seemed steeper than she remembered. But she trudged up them as quietly as possible.

The door to his bedroom was open and she peeked in, sky blue walls with a dark blue comforter covering a twin bed. With a stuffed bear in his arms, Bobby looked so small as he slept. Such a sweet kid. How different his life would become when the new baby joined the family. She hoped that when the baby was older, he and his sibling would become best friends.

She sighed. So often, she'd wished her mother had lived long enough to give birth to another child, a friend for Lauren.

Back in the living room, she ignored the urge to yawn, picked up her phone, and surfed the web.

She blinked and rubbed her eyes. Did she doze off? She searched for the smartphone and checked the time, five thirty am. The house was quiet until the sound of a rooster crowing broke the silence.

No texts from Wyatt. How long did it take to deliver a baby?

Was there time to jog to the cottage for an outfit before Bobby woke up?

The fierce eyes of a man stared at her, when she opened the back door, his hand was about to reach for the doorknob. She jumped back, but he blocked the slamming of the door with his booted foot. An angry expression on his face, his hands flexed into fists.

She wanted to shout go away but was afraid she would wake Bobby. She crossed her arms in a defensive posture. "You're the man I saw in the shed." *That's a stupid thing to say.*

Without looking from his face, Lauren backed toward the stove where she had placed a frying pan for breakfast. If she could reach it to use as a weapon...

He scanned her and she realized she was still wearing her short pajamas. Chills ran down her. "You can't come in." *Yeah, like you could stop him.*

His eyes followed her as she reached for the pan, then he appeared to notice the carton of eggs on the nearby counter. As though he had forgotten her, he moved toward the food.

"Get out," she hissed between her tightened teeth.

"Lady, relax. I'm not interested in you." He grabbed the eggs. "Where's the bread?"

She nodded toward the cupboard. "Take it and leave."

"I'm not going anywhere."

"But..."

"Out of my way. I want the eggs." He scanned her again. "Get the bread."

She wanted to run but wouldn't leave Bobby. "Hang on." She pushed past him, then covered her nose as his body odor wafted to her.

"After you eat, go away."

He dropped his worn backpack and slumped in a chair at the kitchen table. She thought he might have mumbled something, but she didn't ask him to repeat it. Instead, she turned to the stove.

Stay calm. Wyatt and Amy depend on you to take care of Bobby.

With two eggs and three pieces of toast finished, the stranger gulped down coffee from the mug she gave him.

"Times up—leave. Take some food if you need it and go." She hoped her voice sounded stronger to him than it did to her. Stepping closer to the backdoor, she opened it. "Now!"

"I belong here more than you do." He slammed the empty mug on the table. "Lady, who the hell *are* you?"

"I…"

"Where's Wyatt?"

"I'll tell him you came by." She tried not to tremble. "Please leave."

"Lady, *you* get out."

"I'm not going anywhere," she whispered hoping Bobby didn't hear them talking.

"I want to see Wyatt. Now!"

"Do you even know him?"

"He is my brother."

Chapter 45

Wyatt wondered how long before the doctor let him back into the maternity room with Amy. He glanced at the clock on the hospital wall. Six a.m. Amy had been in labor for hours. He rubbed his tired eyes and stared at the closed door. Should he go back in or wait? *Please, God, I'll do anything you want, just keep Amy safe.*

At six-thirty, Dr. Danelavich stuck his head out of the door. "Amy's a real trooper. Wyatt, you can come in and see her shortly." The doctor came out into the hallway. "The midwife is with her. I don't think we will need to wait too much longer for your baby—don't look so scared. Women have been doing this since the beginning of time."

The doctor's words held no comfort for Wyatt. Amy was his life and if he'd caused harm to her by wanting this baby…

At long last, the doctor allowed him entry.

"Amy, I'm here."

She gave him a weak smile.

He held her hand through a contraction. "Take a breath, Amy."

A random thought crossed his mind. At least Bobby's all right, but if something happened to the boy's mom,

Bobby would never forgive him. *Stop, no point in imagining the worst.*

***

At the open door of the farmhouse, Lauren stood her ground and glared at the guy. "I don't believe you're related to Wyatt."

With a grunt of disgust, the stranger yanked out a tattered magazine from his backpack and thumbed through the pages. "Here."

She snatched it from him and gazed at a full-page photo. There were two smiling cowboys, each holding gold championship belts. The caption read, "The Cameron Brothers, Wyatt and Wes." The magazine was two years old, but she recognized Wyatt. Even with a beard, she realized the man in the kitchen was Wes.

"I'll be…" She shut the door and sank into a chair. "Wyatt is with Amy at the hospital. She's having a baby."

A stunned expression crossed his face. "I didn't know."

She had no answer. So, she remained silent. Smoke filled the kitchen and she discovered the stove was still on. She rushed to grab the pan off the burner and open the window.

"I've been in the house before. I'm going to take a shower. Then I'll be in the downstairs guest room." Without a thank you for the meal, Wes left the room.

"Shit," Lauren said under her breath. What to do now? Text Wyatt? He had enough on his mind. And Bobby, he would be getting up in a little while. Not to mention, she needed to be at the Hitching Post in a few hours.

Vanna and Manny were away for the weekend. With the weather still warm, Sophie might be busy making ice cream for her shop. Lauren didn't dare tell Smithy she wanted more time off.

She washed up the kitchen dishes and debated what to do if Wyatt didn't return before long.

At the familiar sound of a fire truck's engine, she ran to the living room and peered out—Chance. *Thank goodness.*

Lauren ran out to the driveway to greet him. She explained her dilemma and Chance hugged her. "Take it easy. We'll work things out."

We. She liked the sound of that.

***

The Hitching Post cleared of customers as suppertime approached. Lauren finished stocking the jeans and shirts and Jake brought in the fifty-pound bags of feed and got ready to close.

She'd been distracted waiting to hear news of Amy and the baby, making focusing on the job difficult. No news was good news—it had to be.

One of her regular customers had mentioned that babies take their sweet time and not to worry. Easy to say, but the woman didn't see Wyatt's grim face last night.

Chance had talked to Wes and told him he could stay with him. After all, Amy and Wyatt deserved their privacy when the new baby came home. As it was Saturday, there was no school. Sophie had picked up Bobby and taken him to the ice cream parlor with her. When the time came, Sophie and Johnny would take him to the hospital to see his sibling.

Lauren sighed and let her shoulders relax. *It takes a village to raise a child.* Again, she was reminded that small towns were villages. People stepped up to help where required, often without being asked.

She needn't have worried about Bobby being taken care of when she went to work.

If only Amy would safely deliver her baby.

What would it be like to carry Chance's child? She gasped at the thought.

With a shake of her head, she recalled children were not on her list of goals. But love, that was a different story.

***

Home from work, the farmhouse appeared dark and the fire truck was no longer parked in front. Lauren seemed to be alone. She didn't want to think about where Wes might be.

As she entered the cottage, her stomach growled and she realized she hadn't eaten much today. She kicked off her shoes, dropped her bag on the coffee table, and went to the kitchen.

Later, carrying a cooked and plated frozen dinner, she sat on the sofa and booted her tablet. She swallowed a few bites of the mac and cheese as a movie streamed, but her mind wandered. Did Amy have her baby? Was Chance called to a fire?

He'd planned to be with her tonight. They had even picked out a movie to watch. She grinned, remembering Chance cooking in her kitchen while dressed only in his boxers. It seemed knowing how to put together a hurried meal was part of being a firefighter—handy for a partner too.

Don't go there. He hasn't asked. You love Chance, whatever his feelings. Admit it.

"Okay, I admit it." She shouted into the empty room. She laughed, realizing happiness had been a foreign emotion for too much of her life, but now things had turned around.

She dialed her father, wanting to share her joy with him. He had found a new beginning with Zoe. Would he understand Lauren's need to move on with a new partner?

"Hello."

"Daddy, I'm in love," her voice rose with excitement.

"Lauren, have you been drinking?"

"No."

"Certainly, you're in love. Ben's been mooning around my place waiting for you to come home."

"No, not Ben. His name is Chancellor Williams, Chance for short."

The phone went quiet.

"Daddy, are you still there?"

"I thought you and Ben had an understanding." Her father waited, probably expecting a response. "Lauren, you and I talked about this. He's a good match for you. A safe job, so, you'll never have to worry about him or go without—not with his position and his substantial earnings."

"But Daddy…"

"What does this Chance Williams do?"

She took a deep breath and squirmed in her seat as if in front of the principal at school when she was a kid. "He…" She faltered.

"Is he a gambler? A thief? What?"

"No." She laughed.

"Then why hide what he does?"

"I'm not." *All right, I might be.* "Chance is a firefighter. The Chief of the Sierra Creek Fire Department."

"No! Not again!"

"Daddy, I…"

"Didn't you learn anything? We've had enough deaths in this family, first your mother, then your fiancé!"

She tensed at her father's anger.

"Lauren, baby, I believed you would never consider another fireman. You can't replace Danny, no matter how much you want to."

"I'm not trying. They don't look or act anything alike. Chance isn't a daredevil. He's older, more serious—careful."

"Baby, say what you want, but they both take the same risks and fires don't care who they burn."

Remembering the scars on Chance's back, she winced and accidentally knocked over the plate of half-eaten mac and cheese. *Shit.*

"You're my daughter, I can't see you unhappy and alone again. This is too much." Her father hesitated. "Lauren, after your fiancé was killed, I didn't think you'd ever smile again."

"I know. I'm sorry you're upset, but falling in love isn't a choice. It just happens and I…"

"I don't want to talk to you until you think about Ben. Give him the opportunity he deserves." Her father disconnected the call.

"Daddy!" She sniffed and wiped a random tear. All of her life he had supported her choices, whether it was a university or a career, it hadn't made a difference. She always depended on his encouragement—not today.

She wasn't angry. Hurt would be a better description of her emotions. She slumped forward and put her head in her hands. *Daddy, I wanted you to be happy for me.*

The movie continued to stream on the tablet's screen, only white noise to her as she wondered what to do now.

Her dad appeared to be frightened for her. She understood since she was scared too, but that didn't change her love for Chance.

A text pinged her phone. *Sorry about tonight. Called to a brush fire. CUT X Chance*

Life with Chance meant plans made, then changed at the last minute. Would she adjust to the upheavals of that kind of life and still be happy?

The problem wasn't caring. Love for him filled her heart and soul. The debate involved whether she had the courage to be the woman he needed, or should she bow out for his best interest and let someone else... The thought of another woman being with Chance—impossible.

She remembered a quote her mother often cited. It went something like, "Everyone is tested, but courage doesn't mean you don't get scared." Her mother would pause and smile at her. "Courage means you don't let fear stop you."

For the love of Chance, could she do that?

Chapter 46

Early Sunday morning, Chance glanced out the window of his apartment. Judging by the weather, he thought it felt more like July, perfect for picnics and barbecues. The month was November and there should be a chill in the air with the promise of rain in the near future.

The other day, the "D" word had risen louder in the grumblings of farmers in town. They had been spared last year, when rain storms arrived, late, but welcome nonetheless. Now a drought might be here and it caused farmers to consider their options.

Chance took a mug of coffee to his landing. The hot air brushed his face as he surveyed the area. Even so, the blue sky showed no sign of smoke coming from the hills, only a hawk scouting for small critters to bring home to the nest.

He breathed easier, leaned against the railing, and gulped down the last of the fresh brew.

Heat lightning was his biggest concern. If people worried about lightning at all, they thought about being hit by it. Though it could be deadly, the odds were against that because most people understood to go inside when they saw lightning.

The storms were most often found in the summer. It shouldn't be a problem in a normal November. In spite of this, nothing about this month appeared to be usual. He wiped the sweat from his neck. *Going to be damned hot by this afternoon.*

In weather like this, if lightning flashed in a remote area, it could trigger unnoticed fires that smoldered for days. They'd flare up, bursting into serious and difficult-to-fight wildfires in hard-to-reach areas. It might burn until the inferno made its way into a populated locale.

Chance rubbed his chin, and considered what to do next. He would check the area and make sure the underbrush and trees marked for removal had been taken out. The more he prepared for the event, he hoped would never come, the better.

Dry lightning was a firefighter's greatest fear, and scientists predicted climate change would cause more lightning strikes every year.

He took a deep breath and was about to go back into the suite when Laurie ran out of the cottage. He called to her. Seeming not to hear him, she rushed toward the farmhouse.

He left the mug on the railing and went after her.

As she started to enter the kitchen, he caught her. "Laurie, what's up?" She leaned into his arms and he held her to him. "Sweetheart, why the rush?"

"I got this text." She handed him her phone.

At 3 a.m. a baby girl, 7 lbs. 9oz, was delivered. Amy and baby doing fine. Home this afternoon. "Thank God."

"Chance, I was so worried." She paused. "I want to make sure everything is ready for them."

"I'll help."

They entered the farmhouse and found dirty dishes on the kitchen table. Moving further into the house, the smell of cigarette smoke wafted toward Lauren.

She opened the door to the downstairs bathroom and coughed. Cigarette butts along with wet towels were scattered on the floor. A can of beer stood on the washstand next to a razor and a bar of soap.

She wrinkled her nose. *Damn, Wes. He knew not to smoke in the house.*

Chance came up to her. "I'll take the bathroom. You can have the kitchen."

"Thanks. I sure didn't want… Well, thanks."

He rolled up his sleeves and she noted his muscled forearms and strong hands. The memory of his touch sent desire racing through her. Odd how sexy a man was when helping with housework. She hurried back to the kitchen and opened the window.

***

In an hour and a half, Lauren watched Wyatt drive the truck into the farmhouse driveway. He helped Amy and the new baby out of the truck.

His pride was undeniable as he held Amy's arm. She walked carefully up the drive, never taking her eyes from the bundle she carried.

In order not to wake up the baby, Lauren whispered, "Congratulations you two. Welcome home."

"Thanks, glad to be back," Wyatt responded while still gazing at his wife. The love for Amy that radiated from him was almost palpable.

They all entered the kitchen and continued through into the living room. The house took on a pleasant vibe that had been missing when Wyatt and Amy were gone.

Amy sat in the lounge chair and sighed.

Lauren set out a buffet on the coffee table and offered drinks, tea, coffee, milk and something stronger for the men.

"This is great! I haven't eaten for—I don't know how long." Wyatt rushed to the table and then glanced at his wife. "Honey, milk? Sandwich?"

"Is your newborn all right?" Chance spoke for the first time.

"Yes. She's fine," Amy assured him.

Chance nodded and sat on the sofa.

"You can see her if you want to."

Lauren moved closer. Amy unwrapped the blanket. The little girl had a bit of red hair like Amy's but unlike her hazel eyes, bright blue eyes the color of Wyatt's looked at Lauren."

"Amy, she's wonderful! The most adorable baby I've ever seen!" Lauren paused. "I didn't realize a newborn is so small."

She glanced up and discovered Chance standing next to her staring. Their eyes caught. A strange sensation ran through her. Lauren's heart pounded. If Amy and Wyatt realized, they didn't let on. Maybe they were too absorbed with their newborn.

Lauren cleared her throat and walked to the coffee table. "We have Swiss cheese or chicken salad sandwiches."

Wyatt brought Amy a cheese sandwich and a glass of milk. He gingerly held his daughter while Amy ate. Then she took her baby to her breast, a pink cotton blanket shading her.

"We named her Mary Louise after Amy's grandmother." Wyatt grinned. "Granny was a strong, loving woman—important in both my life and Amy's." He stood near his wife while he wolfed down a chicken

281

Reggi Allder

sandwich. "Bobby wanted a sister. So now our family is complete." He bent and kissed his wife. "I love you, honey."

"You too, sweetheart."

He grabbed more food and leaned back in a club chair.

"Lauren, thanks for cleaning up the house. I'm afraid we left in a hurry." Appearing comfortable as if she had been doing it for years, Amy moved her daughter to the other breast. She adjusted the blanket and smiled. "It means a lot to have the house so nice."

They shared both the story of Mary Louise's birth and small talk until Lauren noticed Amy stifling a yawn. "Hey, we'll take off and let you two enjoy your home. Remember, I'm close by if you need anything." Lauren rounded up the dishes and cleared them away.

After she and Chance washed the dishes, they left the house. He took her hand and squeezed it. "New life's such a miracle."

She stopped and gazed into his eyes, trying to read his indecipherable expression. "I never thought about it, but— you're right." She leaned closer. "I almost forgot, you're a paramedic as well as a firefighter—have you ever delivered a baby?"

"Well, the women do the work." He chuckled. "But I've attended a couple of births."

"Amazing." It was clear to her that his profession was more than a job. It was a calling. Pride swelled in her.

If only Daddy could understand.

Chapter 47

Dread filled Chance as he entered his suite.

Though it was nearly noon, Wes still snored on the couch and showed no signs of waking. Relieved to avoid the coming conversation with Wyatt's brother, Chance took a deep breath. He poured another mug of coffee and took a gulp. He might put it off for a while, but soon he had to have a serious talk with Wes.

He showered and stepped into clean boxers and jeans. Still hot, with no sign of the weather cooling, he pulled on a white T-shirt with the Sierra Creek Fire Chief logo in red on the front. In the dryer, he found socks, then grabbed his boots.

Back in the living room, he found Wes was still snoring.

Shit. Chance rubbed his chin. He had an idea. Carrying a large mug of strong black coffee, he set it on the side table. "Wes, wake up. We need to talk."

Hard to believe this man is Wyatt's brother. Two people couldn't be more different.

He'd promised Wyatt to have a go at reasoning with Wes about getting help with his drinking. Logically, his friend's brother could tell him to go to hell or to mind his own business. After all, it was not Chance's problem.

True, but for the fact that living rough in the hills, the idiot was likely to start a fire. If Chance had any possibility of helping the man, he had to try.

"Wake up. Drink your coffee."

"Leave me the hell alone!"

"Sit up and drink."

Wes rubbed his eyes, and belched, spewing the odor of putrid beer into the room. "I need a beer."

When Chance handed him the mug of coffee, to his surprise, Wes drank it.

"You need to eat something. He handed him an egg sandwich and a glass of milk.

"Milk? You kidding me, man?"

"Drink. It's high in sugar. You'll feel better."

Wes slammed his empty coffee mug on the table, then wolfed down the food and the milk.

Without being asked, Chance refilled the coffee cup and handed it to Wes. "You ready to talk?"

"About what?"

Chance swallowed an expletive. "Look, you can't go on like you are now. I'll help—if I can. I also need to make it clear, I'm a firefighter and my job is to be sure there aren't any man-made fires in the hills."

"If you're going to lecture me…" Wes jumped up and almost knocked over the coffee table in front of him.

"Hey, calm down. That's not what I meant."

He slumped back onto the sofa and put his head in his hands. "I don't feel so good. I got to have a beer."

Chance searched the kitchen cabinets and found the last one in the suite. He handed it to Wes. "Now, how can I help you?"

"I got a beer, so, you got nothing I need."

Chance grunted at the statement, but offered some ideas anyway, then became silent.

The minutes ticked by. In the end, Wes acknowledged he remembered Chance from their rodeo days on the same circuit. "Back then, you were always fair to me."

After a long conversation and calling to make sure the arrangements Chance had made were still good, he told Wes there was a place for him to dry out.

Wyatt's brother frowned, walked to the window, and stood with slumped shoulders as he stared out.

Now shaky, Wes admitted he'd already decided he couldn't go on living as he had and agreed to go into detox.

Chance called for an ambulance to take him to Sacramento. He'd been lucky to find an opening in a program run by a paramedic who had worked with him in Sonoma County. His friend had told him when a man was ready, it was important to act ASAP. They could take him today, but unfortunately, Wes would have to pay the full freight.

Earlier, Wyatt had agreed he'd cover the cost if his brother could be persuaded to acquiesce. The mill was doing better than expected, so...

"You'll tell Wyatt?" Wes interrupted Chance's thoughts.

"Yeah, will do."

He didn't have to because Wyatt was waiting in the driveway when they left the attic suite.

"I'm proud of you, bro." Wyatt shook Wes' hand.

Chance watched as Wyatt's lips formed a straight line as the rescue vehicle pulled into the driveway and Wes entered.

Only the sound of the hot wind rustling in the evergreen trees continued as the ambulance disappeared. A last, Wyatt looked at him. "Chance, I owe you."

"Hey, you don't owe me anything."

"I do. I've tried for years to support my brother and get him to deal with his problem. He wouldn't listen to me. You did what I couldn't."

"He was ready. I just happened to be there, and was able to locate a place for him."

Wyatt nodded. "Okay." He left and headed toward the farmhouse, stopped and turned back. "But, Chance?"

"Yeah?"

"Thanks anyway."

***

Autumn continued and Lauren could feel the tension as she watched Chance wait for a change in the hot weather. The colorful leaves were gone, and the bare trees cried out for the rain to replenish their roots. Even so, no moisture came from the cloudless sky.

Nonetheless, Lauren spent contented days aided by Chance and their continuing relationship. Though no forever promises were made to each other, it was easy to settle into a routine. She wouldn't mind keeping that for a lifetime, including the long walks and nights together under the stars. Yet, she didn't know if he felt the same.

When he was not staying at the firehouse, they took turns making dinner. Sometimes, they worked side by side; he on his photography hobby and she creating new sketches of the wildflowers from the area. On other evenings, they picked movies to stream and Friday barbecues with their friends continued.

She began to understand the joy of a simple life, no worry about striving to be rich or having the most expensive car, or living in a posh neighborhood. In

Sierra Creek? The corners of her mouth turned up forming a smile. Posh was not a word that came to mind—maybe, comfortable.

Ben would never understand the appeal. Still, she hadn't heard from him in over a week. He probably got the message not to bother her anymore—thank goodness.

It was hard to believe tonight was the concert with the California Cowboys. Vanna, Amy and she worked so hard to put the event together. Between the Fund Me Page and this concert, they hoped the result would be enough money for the needed down payment on the hook and ladder truck.

Forty-five minutes before she and Chance were to attend the concert, Lauren relaxed in a tub of warm water.

Mayor Breen would introduce the band and give the final results, including the ticket sales, and all donations. The total would be given to the Sierra Creek Fire Truck Fund.

After dressing, Lauren's hand tingled with excitement as her fingers slithered down the satin fabric of the pale blue sleeveless cocktail dress she wore. Not since she moved to Sierra Creek had she worn something so elegant.

Should she wear one of her creations? She wrinkled her nose as she looked at her choices. She found the rare orange garnet Chance had given her the first day they went rock hunting.

She had designed silver leaves to surround the jewel as if it had just burst into bloom. She pinned the brooch onto the shoulder of the dress. When the light caught the stone, it appeared to be the color of the sun.

As the gem was valuable and she tried to give the stone back to him. Yet, he had refused to take it. She sighed. The gift was so precious, she would never sell it.

After glancing at the time, she grabbed her clutch bag and rushed to meet Chance.

She opened the front door of the cottage and ran into a man about to knock.

"Ben, what are you doing here?"

Chapter 48

Before Lauren could say anything more, Ben gripped her by the shoulders and kissed her full on the lips. She struggled to break free, dropping her bag on the porch as she did.

"I hope I'm not interrupting," Chance's eyes narrowed as he stared, his deep voice reverberating within her.

She pulled out of Ben's arms. "Chance. I can expla…"

"You don't owe me an explanation," he interrupted. "I've been called to a grass fire near my uncle's home. I was concerned you might need an escort to the concert. I see you're well taken care of." Dressed in full gear, including boots, a hat and holding a respirator, he frowned at her, a look of betrayal on his face.

"I'm Ben from LA." He put his arm around her shoulder and pulled her to him.

"Don't." She shook off his hold.

"Laurie, is everything okay?" Chance glared.

"I think so."

With a grim look on his face, Chance nodded. With long strides, he moved quickly down the driveway of the farmhouse.

"Wait! Chance, please."

He left without a backward glance.

She sniffed and pushed back a tear of frustration. Anger towards Ben swelled in her, but she wouldn't give in to the need to yell at him and make a scene.

She bent down to pick up her clutch bag. "Why *are* you here?" If she thought to control the anger in her voice, she'd failed.

"Whoa, Lauren. Is that any way to greet a friend?"

She stared in disbelief. "You're not my friend, only a guy I dated you a few times... In LA, the last time I saw you, I thought you understood. We are over."

"But your dad said to..."

"My father doesn't make my decisions and I don't like you using him to reach me." So, her father had told Ben to arrive unannounced. Just like Daddy to suggest something like that.

"He knows you and me are good together." He smirked like a salesman trying to unload an unreliable car for a high price.

"Ben, I don't have time for this. I'm going to be late for an appointment."

"I'll go with you."

Lauren slumped into a chair on the porch of the cottage, glared at him, then took a deep breath. He'd come over a thousand miles to see her. Not many men would bother to make the effort. Daddy did like him. To be fair, he would be an excellent catch for some woman—but not for her.

A gust of wind encircled them and she was reminded of the Santa Ana winds of Southern California. But she wasn't in So Cal. She wanted Ben to understand her goals were different now and they didn't include him. "Ben, sit down. We have to talk."

Could she tell him without hurting him?

***

Thirty minutes later, Ben was gone. Instead of being pleased, Lauren's emotions were raw. She had deflated a decent man's ego and Chance, the man she loved, probably no longer trusted her. Yes, she'd explain, but she had the sense this whole episode had changed Chance's opinion of her, and not for the best.

She rubbed her eyes and wondered if Chance was all right. The idea of him fighting a wildfire somewhere in the hills sent anxiety rushing within her. Even in this hot weather, she shook off a chill.

This evening was nothing like the one she'd planned. Lauren had pictured a bash with Chance by her side and their friends celebrating the success of the fundraiser.

She sighed. All dressed up, but now she didn't want to go. The alarm sounded on her smartphone. It was time to attend the concert. How she felt was of no consequence, she'd promised to be there, even if Chance couldn't. She wouldn't let the mayor and the townspeople down. At least Vanna, Sophie and Johnny promised to be there too. Amy would stay home with her new baby girl.

Covering her eyes against the dust swirling around her, Lauren walked down the driveway, entered the car, and started the engine.

Heading toward town, an image of Chance scowling at her came to her mind's eye. What must he think seeing her in another man's arms? She groaned.

***

Mayor Breen was pacing in front of The Barn venue when Lauren drove up and parked in a reserved spot.

Dressed in his usual suit and tie, but wearing hand-tooled leather boots, he rushed to her car. "You're late!

291

Where have you been? Is Chance coming in his vehicle?" He took a quick breath. "Come on. We have to start this ball rolling."

The mayor walked ahead of her, not waiting for an answer to any of his questions. She jumped out of the car and ran after him.

The usual tables and chairs were gone. Now, the huge room was fitted with bleacher seats arranged against the walls, and in the middle of the floor, chairs lined up for the VIPs.

Vanna ran to greet her with a hug. "I heard about the fire. Manny's a volunteer firefighter. So, he's not going to attend tonight either. But the grass fire might help tonight's crowd realize just how important this charity event is."

"Vanna, you're amazing. You always find a way to see the positive side." She attempted to smile. "Thanks. I was feeling pretty low."

"Come girls," Mayor Breen interrupted. "We need to get this show on the road."

Chapter 49

Crowds of people filed into The Barn and took their seats. Some of them Lauren recognized and she waved. But many were not from Sierra Creek and were only there for tonight's concert.

After the mayor greeted the assembly with a short speech, he insisted she and Vanna come on stage. "These are the gals, with their friend Amy Cameron, who started the idea of a fundraiser and put in many hours of work to be sure it was a success. Let's give these women some applause."

The audience clapped and hooted.

When the crowd settled down, Mayor Breen mentioned the total amount raised so far and encouraged any who hadn't given to do so.

The amount surprised and pleased Lauren. They were well on the way to buying the hook and ladder vehicle so needed in Sierra Creek.

When the concert started, the noise level increased and somehow being near the excitement only caused her to miss Chance even more.

A few minutes later, she made her excuses and stepped out of the hot and noisy place in search of fresh air.

Smoke.

When she had arrived in town, the sky had been blue, but now gray smoke swirled in the clouds as the night darkened, the smell of burning grass undeniable. Gazing upward toward the hills, she could see no flames. Chance and his crew could handle this.

Suddenly, threads of lightning flashed, lighting the sky with white slashes to cut the heavens. Fascinated, she watched as another group of flashes lit the sky.

"Lady L, don't stand in the open. You're not safe. Find cover!" Jake waved from the door of the Hitching Post.

Dashing down the street to where Jake stood, she entered the store. "Wow, what a display!"

"Yeah," Jake agreed. "I came in to pick up the feed I forgot." He replied to her unanswered question while he scanned her. "What you doing out on a night like this all dressed up and alone?"

She reminded him of the concert and explained Chance was with his men dealing with a grass fire near his uncle's place. She hoped both Chance and her boss were all right but kept the worry to herself.

Jake glanced out at the gray sky at the same time a flash hit the area. "Damnation." He shook his head, looking a bit sheepish for cursing, but said, "Guess you don't have many lightning storms where you come from—heat lightning I mean."

"Not that I remember."

Together they watched until the storm appeared to let up.

"I better go back to my place and check on the animals." He scratched his head. "You going to be okay?"

"Fine. You go. It won't take me more than a couple of minutes to drive to the farm." She hugged him and waved as he left carrying a bag of chicken feed. She understood his concern for his animals. After the loss of his wife, they'd become his family.

On the way to the cottage, the weather grew hotter and the wind gusts stronger. At times it was difficult to hold the car on the small two-lane road.

She coughed as the car filled with fumes from the blazing hills. The smoke was so thick she almost missed the turn off to the cottage, while ash floated onto the car's hood and windshield. The wipers cleared the window and she drove on. Were Amy, Bobby, and baby, okay? Maybe they had already left the farm.

The stars could no longer be seen, hidden by a layer of soot and smoke. Should she be returning to the cottage?

With a glance at the hills, she saw no flames. The smoke and ash must be traveling on the blustery airstream. She drove faster.

In a short time, the Y in the road would appear. She always took the left up the hill to the farmhouse. She remembered Chance telling her if she went right, it would take her to the poultry farm and onward to Smithy's home.

Was Chance fighting to save his uncle's property? Her hands gripped the steering wheel, forcing the car to go left, when her heart went to the right toward Chance.

The thought of him fighting a blaze at night frightened her. In the forested hills, it would be too easy to fall or lose one's way in the dark. What if the wind changed direction? Would he be trapped by the inferno?

When she reached the farm, she sighed with relief. Everything looked normal. Smoke and ash, but no flames in the hills above the farm.

Wyatt's truck was gone, to be expected, because he was a volunteer firefighter. But the old Volvo Amy often used, was in the driveway.

Amy glanced out of the front door of the farmhouse and waved for her to come in.

Everything was closed to the outdoors, probably to keep out the smoke. An oscillating fan tried to cool the room.

Bobby sat on the floor finishing a puzzle, and the baby slept in a bassinet. All peaceful—normal. Why did Lauren sense nothing was usual?

Amy picked up the baby monitor and motioned for them to go into the kitchen.

"Bobby should be asleep, but it's too warm in his room." Amy handed Lauren a glass of iced tea. "I've never seen weather like this. Did you see the heat lightning a few minutes ago? It was crazy!" She pushed back her red bangs and adjusted the thick-rimmed glasses she wore.

Amy didn't speak about her concern for Wyatt, but it showed in her hazel eyes. Lauren did her best to keep the conversation light, talking about the successful concert and the money raised. Still, she found it hard to stay focused and noticed Amy appeared distracted too.

Later, Lauren stifled a yawn and said goodnight to her friend.

In the cottage, the heat increased and the winds outside continued to howl. Occasional flashes of light slashed the sky, but no rain fell.

Lauren lay on her bed exhausted, but incapable of sleeping. She couldn't rest until Chance returned. Was this the life of a firefighter's girlfriend, always on edge, waiting for the return of her man? Did she possess the strength?

With a sigh, she stood, walked to the window, and peered down the drive. The farmhouse was dim and Wyatt's truck hadn't come back. Poor Amy was in the house with the kids. She'd be on her own should something happen to her husband.

Don't think that way.

She gazed toward the spot where Chance always parked—empty.

In the middle of the night, a blaring truck horn startled her. In the dark, she sat up and blinked.

Over a loudspeaker, a man shouted "Evacuate! Evacuate! Leave everything and get out! Go now!"

Chapter 50

"**Evacuate** now!"

Lauren froze, then shook her head. For a moment, she thought it was a bad dream.

In the kitchen, she stared out the back door of the cottage to the ridge behind the farm.

Flames.

She rushed to the bedroom and stuffed her sketches and gemstones in a backpack, threw in underwear, a change of clothes, and her purse. Grabbing her pack, she ran out the front door and coughed as smoke filled her lungs.

Screeching chickens caught her attention. Bobby, still in his pajamas, was in the coop trying to catch a hen to put in a crate.

"Bobby! We have to go!" Amy, holding her newborn, yelled at her son.

"I want to take Gretchen. She is my favorite."

"We're leaving right now!"

"No! Not without Gretchen."

Lauren had never heard the little boy talk back to his mother. Amy's cheeks turned red, an expression of anger and fear on her attractive face.

With all the tension, Baby Mary Louise began to cry.

"Amy, take the baby to the car. I'll help Bobby."
Lauren ran to the chicken's pen and entered the fenced
yard, pushing down her fear of the hens.

You can do this.

"Which one is Gretchen?" she coughed out the words
as the smoke and ash worsened.

"The Golden Laced Wyandotte."

She had no clue what that meant. Bobby ran around
and the hens became frightened. As they flew in the air
and landed again. Lauren's heart pounded and she
covered her head against their claws. The squawking
chickens ran for shelter in the coop. Just then, Bobby
dashed for a gold and brown hen with a red comb.

The hen ran toward her, she closed her eyes, grabbed
for the bird, and caught it. Pleased, but afraid, she held
down both wings and kept the hen at arm's length.
Somehow, it seemed calmer in her arms and she quickly
shoved it into the cage the little boy held.

The top of the hill was in flames now. She snatched
the crate in one hand and held Bobby's in the other and
they ran.

Amy was securing the baby in her car seat. Bobby
jumped in his booster seat and fastened the belt. With
the hen stowed in the back of the car, Lauren realized
her backpack was still in the coop.

"Amy, I'm going back. I dropped my pack. I don't
have my car keys."

"You can't. You have to go with us!"

"I..."

"Lauren, get in this damned car. I'm not driving until
you do!"

Amy might be right. The fire had turned threatening.
They needed to get the hell out—ASAP.

Even so, she couldn't leave without her stuff. "You go, Amy. I'll be right behind you."

"Lauren, no!"

"Take the kids out of here! I'll be fine." She forced a smile and turned to run toward the pen where she had set the knapsack down.

The Volvo engine revved and she realized Amy and the kids had driven away.

Lauren yanked open the chicken's pen and let out the birds. They might survive on their own.

The bag was just where she thought it would be. With a smooth movement, she tossed it on her back but stopped.

What about Chance? If the fire overcame the farm, all his photo equipment and wonderful pictures would be destroyed. She'd last seen them on the worktable in the attic suite.

Before she could change her mind, she ran to his place and found the key. Coughing, she entered and flipped on the overhead light. As she remembered, everything was on his table. She discovered a camera case, a pile of negatives, photos, and jump drives. With care, she put all of them in a shopping bag found in the kitchen.

Outside on the attic's landing, she surveyed the blazing hills and found the flames had moved closer.

Better hurry.

The roar of the blaze shut out any other noise and her breath became ragged trying to inhale. Running down the stairs with Chance's equipment, she almost tripped but caught hold of the railing.

With the heat and flames increasing, she scrambled toward her car and said a silent goodbye to the cottage she had begun to think of as home. Would it be there when she returned?

For a second, her car's engine didn't respond. Fear rippled through her. What if she couldn't get it started?

On the third try, the engine turned over and she drove from the farm.

It was harder to breathe now, but she ignored that fact and squinted to catch sight of the road through the thick smoke and ash.

Chance was battling this inferno. She gulped back a tear. *Dear God, I can't lose him. Stay safe, sweetheart!*

***

In Sierra Creek, Vanna helped Mayor Breen clear out the last of the tourists from the concert venue, then locked the doors. Hours ago, Chance, Manny, and Wyatt missed the concert to battle the brush fire—no messages from them since. She shouldn't be surprised, they had more important things to do than text her, but...

With the blaze in the hills, the mayor suggested the people from other towns head back to their homes if they could. She understood he felt responsible for their safety and noted the apprehension on the mayor's face.

Vanna worried too, because having grown up in this town, she couldn't remember a fire ever coming this close to Sierra Creek.

Still dark, the occasional heat lightning gave her a full view of the inferno on the ridge line. She watched and coughed as the smoke poured over the surrounding hills toward town.

The wind increased, blowing in the direction of Sierra Creek. If Chance and his men didn't get a handle on the fire, could the town burn down?

Though late at night, vehicles streamed into Sierra Creek. She saw Johnny driving by with Sophie in the passenger seat. He parked in front of the ice cream shop. The back of the car appeared to be loaded with boxes, supplies most likely from their home. She smiled and waved at them.

Relieved, she hugged her mother and helped carry packages into the apartment above the ice cream parlor. Thank goodness it was still empty. At least her mom and her stepdad had a place to stay.

They entered the apartment and set down the packages.

"Have you seen Amy and the kids—or Lauren?" Vanna asked. "I've texted them—no reply." She hesitated. "I'm worried."

"The roads were crowded with people leaving their property. Some of them had trucks filled with cattle and horses. Maybe Amy and Lauren are caught in the traffic jam," Johnny suggested.

Vanna rubbed her forehead. "I hope that's all it is." With no proof one way or the other, she slumped into a chair and fell silent.

Chapter 51

In full gear, Chance surveyed the terrain. No way to drive a truck into the area he needed to control. With the high winds, smoke, and the night sky, any aerial defense was out of the question. He had alerted Cal Fire and they would help, but until the winds calmed down, planes and copters were grounded.

He motioned to his crew and appraised their condition. The coming climb looked steep and only those who were still in good enough condition, after fighting the flames all night, would be able to scurry up the steep incline as the heat increased and the air thinned.

Over the howling roar of the inferno, he shouted, "Listen up, our job is to protect the town we love." He scanned the dirty and exhausted faces of the men and women, then he glanced down the mountain toward Sierra Creek. "People in the valley are depending on us." He took a quick breath and thought of Laurie. "We're not going to fail them! So, let's go!"

***

On the way into town, Lauren sniffed, then coughed. The truck in front of her car spewed exhaust, making oxygen even harder to find.

On the two-lane road, the flatbed loaded with poultry took over much of both lanes. Though she wanted to pass the slow truck, she didn't know what was coming from the other direction. The last thing she needed was to run into a rescue vehicle speeding toward the fire.

Though driving at a sluggish speed, her heart still beat too fast. Out of danger, why did her heart race?

Damn, hurry up. Her frustration with the cars on the road seemed out of place. She realized they were doing the best they could, considering the circumstances. The truth was she was worried about Chance. He rushed toward the fire when she wanted to escape. She struggled with little success to calm down.

Her hand hovered over the horn, ready to honk if the flatbed didn't speed up. At last, the truck's pace increased and she sighed with relief.

Amy and the kids must be in Sierra Creek by now. Thank goodness they left before she did or they'd be in this mess too. She turned left and continued toward town.

About a mile down the road, she slammed on the brakes and screeched to a halt. The old Volvo sat on the shoulder of the road. Amy stood outside waving. Bobby gazed out the window, a scared look in his wide eyes.

Lauren pulled up behind the old wagon and got out. "OMG, Amy, how are you and the kids?"

"Lauren, I've never been so happy to see anyone— we're fine, but the Volvo has two flat tires. I guess I ran over something."

Lauren glanced at Amy's wagon, then the convertible. *Not a lot of room—even so...* "If you put the baby seat in the front, I can carry your stuff to the trunk. You, Bobby and the chicken squeeze in the back seat. We'll be crowded, still…"

"Thanks!" Amy hugged her and swiped a tear. "Bobby, everything is going to be all right. We are going in Lauren's car. Get the chicken and put it in the backseat."

As they drove away, Amy said, "As snug as a bug in a rug."

Presumably, to calm her son, Amy started a round of Old MacDonald Had a Farm, with Bobby deciding the type of animals on the farm.

Impressed by her friend's strength and the ability to keep her children happy in dire circumstances, Lauren joined in the singing. She forced her muscles to relax and pretended it was just another outing.

***

Afterward, Amy texted Vanna. They would all spend the night in Sophie's two-bedroom apartment.

When they arrived, the town appeared quiet. They parked and went to the apartment, bringing the chicken in its crate with them.

After a snack, everyone settled in for a night's sleep.

At two am, Lauren, still dressed in the same clothes she wore when she left the cottage, sat on the loveseat on the deck of Sophie's suite and watched the hills burn.

When would Chance come home?

Chapter 52

"Hot for the middle of the night." Outfitted in a robe and slippers, Sophie came out on the deck of her apartment. "Can't sleep?"

"No." Lauren moved over, so Vanna's mother could sit next to her on the loveseat.

"We're all worried about the men."

"Yeah." Lauren sighed.

"You love Chance."

It was a statement, not a question.

"Does it show?"

"To me, but I'm a mother. Others may not realize." Sophie hesitated. "He's a good man, and they're not easy to find."

"It's just hard to wait, not knowing if he…" Lauren put her head in her hands.

"Yes." Sophie placed an arm around her. "Waiting is one of the hardest things a person can do."

"Thanks for understanding." Lauren leaned on Sophie for support.

***

High winds and smoke continued the next morning, so the water-dropping planes still couldn't fly. Lauren gazed up at the hills surrounding the town and wondered where Chance and his crew were.

She recalled his expression when he saw her with Ben the other night. A look of betrayal had flashed across his handsome face, quickly replaced with a stoic expression and the sense he didn't care what she did.

Ben wasn't important to her and she should have explained right then and there. Still, with Chance on the way to a fire, it wasn't the right time for a conversation. Nevertheless, she should have taken a second to let him understand. *Too late to change anything at this point.*

Mid-morning in the park, tables and benches were set up to provide food for the first responders and any displaced folk who might need a meal.

Some of the men from the Sierra Creek Fire Station came into town. They were exhausted and in need of first aid and food. Disappointment settled in Lauren's chest when she didn't see Chance. She should have realized he wouldn't be one of the early returnees.

Lauren's heart sank. With no sleep all night, Chance had to be worn out. Nonetheless, he would always stay to assist any on his team.

As the day continued, the heat and winds increased. The smoke changed the blue of the sky to a dark gray.

People from the rural areas drove into town, their vehicles packed with everything they cared about or had time to grab on the way to Sierra Creek. Animals were included. The farmers shared harrowing tales of escape from the flames and their sorrow for not listening to Fire Chief Williams' advice to clear a firebreak around their place.

She prayed Amy's farm was all right. And what about the apple orchards?

With the help of the local women, Vanna and Lauren organized food for all and Amy offered the mill's preschool for the children, so they would have toys and a safe place to play.

Strange, but after a day and a half, Lauren felt energized. She was anxious about Chance, but her other worry had been she would be useless and not able to deal with the stress of a fire. Nevertheless, today, she found strength knowing she had something to offer.

Smithy and Jake were fighting the fire, but her boss texted permission to open the store. So, between serving meals in the park, Lauren unlocked the Hitching Post. It allowed people to choose clothes, blankets, equipment, and animal feed for those who were forced to leave their property with little more than a few animals and the clothes on their backs. Though she kept records, payment could be made when life returned to normal.

In the evening, with the local women, she helped cook meals for all who were hungry. Her anxiety for Chance increased, but at least she was doing something to benefit the situation, little though it might be.

At six am the next day, Lauren rubbed her eyes and readied herself for another day that could be without Chance. The realization she'd never told him of her love sent a shard of fear to pierce her heart. What if she never had another opportunity to…

No, she wouldn't finish the thought.

***

Chance viewed the flaming hills. Over the days, they hadn't made as much progress against the forest fire as he'd hoped. With the continuing winds, an air assault was still out of the question.

The fire was succeeding. His heart pounded and breathing became difficult. If he didn't change the trajectory of the blaze, the town would be in real jeopardy. The firefighters had already lost a few outbuildings in the mountains and, considering the situation, the crew had done their best to slow the inferno's course—it just wasn't enough.

Desperate times call for desperate measures.

Wildfires need three things to grow: fuel, heat and oxygen. With no way to manage the heat or oxygen, attacking the fuel became his only choice.

Normally, the flames would be assaulted from the top of the mountain by airplane or helicopter with water and or fire retardant. Given the speed of the blaze, he couldn't wait if he wanted to save the town.

He checked the wind again. *Yes. It changed and now moved toward the inferno.* That locked in the decision he never planned to use—backfire, the only option. *Sometimes you have to fight fire with fire.*

If the blow-back burned the fuel source, it would leave nothing for the flames to devour, and no way for the blaze to move toward Sierra Creek.

He radioed the crew. "We're setting a backfire. We'll move up the hill. Speak up and return to the trucks if you're too tuckered out." He stopped. When no one asked to go back, he said, "All right, it's damned hot up there and hard to breathe—don't panic." He paused. "I'm not having anyone die in this fire. Not on my watch! So, check your gear, stay together and we've got this."

"Hoo-rah!" the firefighters shouted.

Chapter 53

Lauren stared at the morning sky. The smoke had started to lessen somewhat and flames were no longer visible in the hills around Sierra Creek. Nevertheless, the smell of burnt wood lingered and ash floated in the air.

Earlier, fire crews had been seen in the hills, but not now, leaving only the scorched trees and grassland as a reminder they had been in the area.

She took a breath and tried to slow her pounding heart, and then realized her hand was shaking as the anxiety she held at bay began to flow freely within her.

From the deck of Sophie's apartment, she faced the hot wind to watch first responders returning from their time on the front lines of the fire. Appearing drained, local firefighters trickled into town as Cal Fire crews took their place.

She heard one of the returning men say the blaze was nearly fifty percent contained. They seemed pleased. She guessed it was good news. A crew member mentioned Wyatt Cameron had gone to the preschool to find his wife, Amy, and their kids, but no information on Chance was forthcoming.

Where was he?

During dinner preparations that night, Lauren glanced at more returning firefighters.

"Manny!" Vanna screamed. She rushed from the park where she was helping serve dinner and threw herself into the waiting arms of her husband. Lauren smiled as he kissed Vanna and held her to him.

He appeared tired but otherwise looked in fine shape, though Lauren noticed a definite limp as he walked to a picnic table and sat down with some difficulty.

Hours went by and Smithy and Jake appeared, but Chance didn't. She wandered the town like a waif searching, hoping for someone who could tell her anything about the fire chief.

Nothing.

Frustrated, but refusing to think the worst, Lauren walked down the main street toward Sophie's apartment. An image of Chance came to her. She couldn't help grinning, thinking of her love for him.

Chance your team is back home. Where are you?

She folded her arms across her chest and tried to stop shaking.

"Laurie, are you okay?"

Only one person called her that. "Chance!" She ran toward him. "Thank God!" Wanting to hug him, she stopped when he glared at her. As if frozen on the sidewalk, she hesitated, unsure what to do or say.

People stared, then walked around them. Her eyes never left him. Still dressed in his gear with only his hat and respirator missing, she tingled with the need to touch him, but his stern expression prevented her.

"Uh, Chance, is everything all right?" she continued before he could answer, "I want..." she faltered, and then spoke, "I love you, Chance—only you. I realize you don't feel the same, but I wanted you to..."

"Hush, sweetheart." His arms went around her, holding her close as he whispered in her ear. "I do care. I love you more than the air I need to breathe." He gently kissed her. "And more than my words can express. Laurie, you make my life worth living."

She stared into his blue eyes, reflecting the truth of his words. "Chance, you take my breath away."

Epilogue: Christmas Eve

Though the weather continued to be warm for this time of year. The Farmer's Almanac promised rain. Lauren prayed the almanac's report was accurate.

Sierra Creek missed being hit by the blaze thanks to the fire breaks and the hard work of the fire crew led by Fire Chief, Chance Williams.

To Lauren's delight, in December, Daddy and Zoe rented Sophie's vacant apartment in town.

Tonight, Lauren smiled at the small Christmas tree with white lights that twinkled in the living room of the cottage. She touched the ring on her left hand that held a prong-set single-carat Canadian diamond solitaire on a platinum band as it sparkled in the glow.

Thinking of Chance, Lauren held her hand to her heart. She had never worked with the expensive metal before, but Chance had insisted. *Laurie, I love you forever and always and I want you to have it.*

He would be there and they'd celebrate Christmas in the beautifully decorated farmhouse.

An hour later, dinner was served in the dining room of Amy's home. Wyatt added two extra leaves so the table might welcome all for the holiday. Amy set each place with Granny's precious antique China on a red linen tablecloth. White candles and a bouquet of red carnations and green holly decorated the center of the table. The aroma of baking apple pies filled the air. Classic Christmas carols played in the background.

Bobby said grace, and then the traditional dinner of turkey, stuffing, mashed potatoes, gravy and homegrown vegetables were provided. For dessert, the freshly made pie with Sophie's new flavor of apple ice cream would be offered. The local baker had baked Gluten-free cookies in the shapes of Christmas trees and a Santa for Bobby.

Lauren scanned the people sitting around the table as they talked and laughed, enjoying the moment. Amy, Wyatt, Vanna, Manny, Sophie, Johnny, and Jake were all beloved to her, as were Bobby, baby Mary Louise and even Smithy, Mayor Breen, and Grandpa Bill had become dear to her too.

Family, the word came to Lauren. Sitting next to her, Chance squeezed her hand as if he understood.

"Home," he added.

Lauren smiled, stood, and held up her glass, "Dear family—that is what you have become to me. I don't often speak my thoughts out loud, but I wanted to tell you how much you mean to me and how thankful I am that I came to Sierra Creek." She paused. "To be truthful, I arrived wishing I could live anywhere else than this Podunk town."

She heard a small gasp but continued. "Don't get me wrong—I behaved stupidly. Of course, almost running into a truckload of chickens didn't help my first impression, but that's where I met Chance." She grinned. "Anyway, you all welcomed me with open arms as I stumbled, making social mistake after mistake. Nonetheless, because of your patience, I've learned so much. Thanks, you are the best!" Lauren choked back a tear of happiness, "My country heart is full."

"Here, here!" Chance kissed her.

"To family!" everyone shouted and lifted their glasses.

******

Hope you enjoyed this book. Help the writer and other readers by leaving a positive review. Thank you. Amazon.com, Bookbub.com, Goodreads.com. And remember to tell your friends about the book.

Reggi Allder enjoys hearing from readers. Follow her on Amazon, Bookbub.com, Facebook.com.

Find out how the Sierra Creek Series started: **Her Country Heart Sierra Creek Book 1** by Reggi Allder

Excerpt:
"Sierra Creek," the driver shouted as the Greyhound bus came to an abrupt stop on the two-lane highway.

Amy Long pushed her hair behind her ears and grabbed her worn suitcase. Surprised to see her hand tremble, she seized the case with both hands and rushed toward the front of the bus.

A gust of hot wind slapped her face as she stepped outside. Gravel pelted her bare legs when the bus drove away. She squinted and read a faded road sign, *Sierra Creek population five thousand.* There wasn't a building in sight.

After years of living in the city, she'd forgotten how sweltering and desolate it was here. She'd vowed never to return home. Odd it was the first place that came to mind when she and her young son needed a fresh start.

With Granny gone, there was no family left to welcome her. She swallowed a sob. Maybe it was a mistake to come back.

The relentless afternoon sun beat down on her shoulders and her arms began to burn. San Francisco, the air-conditioned city, seemed a million miles away.

Impatient, she cleared her dry throat, wiped the perspiration from her forehead, and let out a groan as the minutes ticked by. What wouldn't she give for some shade and a bottle of ice water?

With a sigh, she pulled out her smartphone and checked the time. Thirty minutes since she'd arrived at the bus stop and not a single car had gone by. Where was the arranged ride into town?

Granny's handyman was supposed to meet her. He obviously wasn't a stickler about being on time. She reminded herself she was in the California foothills not in a busy metropolis where time was money.

The sound of a truck rumbled in the distance. With the back of her hand, she pushed her bangs out of her eyes and squinted. Hopeful, she watched the pick-up come closer. A shiny black Ford F150 with an extended cab pulled up in front of her.

"Amy," a man yelled through the open window as his brown hair fell casually over a high forehead and deep-set blue eyes sparkled in the sunlight. She moved nearer and stared at his wide cheekbones, square jaw, and full lips. *About thirty?*

A flutter of recognition stirred in her as palpable charm radiated from his broad smile—

Wyatt Cameron.

His muscular arms flexed as his huge hands squeezed the steering wheel. "Don't just stand there. Get in."

Surprised by his gruffness, she stepped back.

"I heard you need a ride into town," he said quietly as if he understood her reaction. "It's me, Wyatt."

"Hi, good to see you again." Even now, her cheeks burned with the memory of him. As she gawked, her heartbeat increased and her breathing quickened. "Granny's handyman is going to give me a ride."

"You could say that's me. Toss your suitcase in the back and get in the truck."

She shook the pebbles from her flip-flops and picked up her suitcase. Filled with everything she and her son might need, she grunted and struggled to lift the enormous bag high enough to push it into the raised truck bed.

Wyatt hopped out of the cab and brushed by her. With a sharp intake of breath, she took in his fresh just-out–of–the-shower scent.

Effortlessly, he tossed the bag into the truck.

She quickly hauled herself into the vehicle and slammed the door. "Nice pick-up. Beautiful upholstery," she said trying for casual conversation. She ran her hand over the black and white leather seat.

"It's custom. Had it done in Sacramento by a guy who specializes in tuck and roll car seats."

"Really nice."

Pretty fancy truck for a handyman. The job must pay better than she'd thought. For some reason, she'd believed Granny's handyman would be an old retired guy gnarled from too much sun and hard work, not the hunk sitting next to her.

"Where's your son? Thought he'd be with you."

"He's staying with a friend of mine in San Francisco. Bobby's only four. I thought it'd be better if I took care of things here before he comes to the farm." She paused. "It's only been a few hours since I left and I already miss him."

She sighed, leaned back, and let the air-conditioned breeze wash over her. The purr of the truck's engine was soothing and her breathing slowed.

"Thanks for picking me up. If you drop me at my grandmother's farm, I'll…"

"It's too late for that. We can't keep Judge Wilcox waiting."

*****

Books by Reggi Allder

Sierra Creek Series:
Her Country Heart
His Country Heart
Our Country Heart
My Country Heart

Suspense:
Dangerous Web
Dangerous Denial
Dangerous Money
Dangerous Moves
Shattered Rules

Historical:
With Glowing Hearts

Coming Next:
Dangerous Sisters

317

www.ingramcontent.com/pod-product-compliance
Lightning Source LLC
Chambersburg PA
CBHW072130250626
47159CB00007B/2632